DISCOVERIES THAT CAN CHANGE
THE WORLD—

Timing and knowledge can make all the difference. Down through the time line of our world there have been any number of moments and events that could have changed the whole course of history. The fifteen stories included in *ReVisions* more than live up to the name of this volume, looking at a number of scientific discoveries, and exploring how different history might have been if certain of these discoveries had never occurred, or if they had happened earler, or in another culture.

What if:

—the nature of the Black Plague had been understood centuries earlier?
—our mandate had been to colonize the oceans rather than to reach the Moon?
—the human genome was mapped out in the time of the Mayans?

These are just a few of the fascinating "what ifs" you'll find in *ReVisions*.

ReVISIONS

Edited by
JULIE E. CZERNEDA
and
ISAAC SZPINDEL

DAW BOOKS, INC.
DONALD A. WOLLHEIM, FOUNDER
375 Hudson Street, New York, NY 10014
ELIZABETH R. WOLLHEIM
SHEILA E. GILBERT
PUBLISHERS
www.dawbooks.com

First Printing, August 2004
1 2 3 4 5 6 7 8 9

ACKNOWLEDGMENTS

Introduction © 2004 by Julie E. Czerneda and Isaac Szpindel.

The Resonance of Light © 2004 by Geoffrey Landis.

Out of China © 2004 by Julie Czerneda.

Site Fourteen © 2004 by Laura Anne Gilman.

Silent Leonardo © 2004 by Kage Baker.

A Call from the Wild © 2004 by Doranna Durgin.

Axial Axioms © 2004 by James Alan Gardner.

The Terminal Solution © 2004 by Robin Wayne Bailey.

The Ashbazu Effect © 2004 by John G. McDaid.

A Word for Heathens © 2004 by Peter Watts.

A Ghost Story © 2004 by Jihane Noskateb.

The Executioner's Apprentice © 2004 by Kay Kenyon.

Swimming Upstream in the Wells of the Desert © 2004 by Mike Resnick and Susan R. Matthews.

Unwirer © 2004 by Cory Doctorow and Charles Stross.

When the Morning Stars Sang Together © 2004 by Isaac Szpindel.

Herd Mentality © 2004 by Jay Caselberg.

CONTENTS

INTRODUCTION

by Julie E. Czerneda and Isaac Szpindel

GEORGE Santayana, the Spanish-American philosopher and novelist, is famous for having penned the oft-quoted statement, "Those who cannot remember the past are condemned to repeat it." While this is often interpreted as a warning, it can also be considered an invitation to create a better future by learning from the mistakes of the past. Indeed, Santayana himself may well have borrowed from the past words of the Greek dramatist Euripides, who wrote, "Whoso neglects learning in his youth, loses the past and is dead for the future."

Whatever the case, it is clear both dramatists and philosophers recognize the continuum that is time. Past, present, and future—interdependent and part of each other. Science fiction has been acknowledged as the literature of the future, but that future is built on our past as much as on our present.

The past. Our history is a tapestry of events, social and political. Within the weave is scientific development and technological invention, sometimes as a background, sometimes to the forefront, as during the Industrial Revolution. In turn, these sciences and technologies are influenced intimately by the geography, politics, and timing of their occurrence. Most significantly, they are influenced by human nature.

We glimpse history through its records, interpreted by present-day minds. We acknowledge the impact of that aspect of our past through laws, treaties, customs, and traditions. Yet the science and technology we employ today has a history as well, which should be understood. Our sciences and methods may be objective, but the ways in which we have discovered and applied them are not.

Science and technologies are tied to their discovery times and places, to their inventors and innovators. They are fluid and dynamic, a living process subject to change, influence, and time, as much as the historical actions of empires still impact the political framework of today's world.

Science fiction, while not always predictive of the future, has certainly taken an informed and interested look at its possible direction. It is only fitting, then, that we apply that same speculative tool back on itself and ask *what if* scientific or technological discoveries had happened differently, in different cultures or times. Where would we be now? Where would we be going? The stories you will read in this anthology consider many variables, both historic and scientific, to answer that question. More so, they answer it in ways that, whether subtle or overt, are essentially provocative. Why? Because they force us to examine and accept responsibility for ourselves, for our scientific discoveries, and for the consequences of those discoveries.

For there is one evocative and compelling question raised by an alternate science history anthology such as this: of all the complex variables that have shaped the new and increasingly scientific world around us, does human nature remain the only constant?

THE RESONANCE OF LIGHT

by Geoffrey Landis

"Full many a gem of purest ray serene . . ."
                                    —Thomas Gray, 1750

"We can concentrate any amount of energy upon a minute button . . . which glowed with a most intense light. To illustrate the effect observed with a ruby drop . . . magnificent light effects were noted, of which it would be difficult to give an adequate idea."
                                    —Nikola Tesla, 1897

WHEN I think of Nikola Tesla, I see the pigeons. He was always surrounded by pigeons. I think, sometimes, that the pigeons were his only real love, that he lavished upon his pigeons the romantic affection that we ordinary mortals have for the opposite sex. Certainly he had a way with them. He would whistle, and they would come, from nowhere, surrounding him like an electrical aura, fluttering like the iridescent discharge from an ethereal fire.

"Pigeons," I once told him, "are the scourge of the city, spreading filth and disease. They are no more than rats with wings."

That was, I think, back in 1912 or '13, before the long shadow of coming war stole across the world, and we could gaily talk about pigeons. Nikola Tesla looked at me with eyes of fire, with that intensity of soul that

3

I have seen in no other man, before or since. "Surely you are but teasing, Katharine," he told me, "yet some things should not be taken in jest. Look at them! Ah, they soar on wings of angels." He was silent for a moment, watching, and then continued, "Do you believe, then, that men are so pure? The scourge of cities—would you not say that for every disease that pigeons spread, men spread a plague? The scourge of man is most certainly man, Kate, and not the harmless pigeon. Do doves slaughter doves in vast wars, would you say? Do they starve one another?"

"Men build cities," I said. "Men have art in their souls and aspire to higher things, as mere fowl cannot."

"Some men, perhaps," he said. "But few, few indeed, raise themselves above the mud." He sowed a handful of his peanuts forth, and the air exploded into frantic motion, birds wheeling overhead as others waddled on the ground like winged pigs, shoving each other shamelessly for position to peck for their supper.

Nikola, though, seemed not to notice the greed. "Perhaps the feathery tribe build no cities, but neither have they the need," he said. "As for art, can you say that a pigeon has no art, nor aspirations? What do you know of the feathered heart? Are not they, perhaps, themselves the embodiment of art, the very winged soul of art incarnate? Say no more of pigeons, then, for I tell you that a pigeon can feel, can even love, as a man can."

And, as bidden, I was silent.

Surrounded by his pigeons, Nikola Tesla would forget himself, and be as delighted as a child, and how could I begrudge him that loss of self?

Do you think that I was myself smitten with the prodigal genius? Of course I was, but then, no woman who ever met him was not. Still, I do believe that I was his closest female companion, indeed, his closest companion of either sex, for despite all his personal magnetism, Nikola was not a man who easily allowed himself to open to others.

Robert, of course, could see my infatuation with Nikola; I was ever quite transparent to him. But we had long ago made an agreement that our marriage was to be a loose one. In that bygone gay era when we were both young, we had held to the ideal of a partnership of the soul, and we promised to understand and forgive each other wanderings of the flesh. Over the years it was Robert who most took advantage of that looseness of bonds, and I, holding to our long understanding, never took him to task for the girls he took as mistresses, nor the young men.

Robert quite encouraged my companionship with Mr. Tesla, and even urged us closer. I think that Robert, too, was smitten by Nikola's tremendous personal magnetism, although if that were so, Mr. Tesla seemed oblivious to any overtones.

Tesla had his playful side. He had a tendency to hold his inventions secret, remembering all too well the controversy over the priority for the invention of wireless telegraphy. But to me he showed many of his inventions, judging me, perhaps, too little schooled in the sciences to accidentally reveal his secrets.

One day he admired a pendant that I wore about my neck. This was unusual for Tesla, who usually disdained jewelry of all sorts. "It is a ruby," I said, "a small one, but well colored, and prettily cut. A gift from Robert." I think Robert had intended it as a silent token of gratitude for my forbearance, or mayhap for forgiveness. He had given it to me while he was conducting a liaison with a woman by the name of Miss Kurz (a coarse young woman quite unworthy of his attention, in my opinion, but I made no indication of such belief to Robert who, in any case, became bored with her attention after another week or two).

Tesla smiled a mischievous grin. "If you should like to come up to my laboratory," he said, "I will show to what use I employ such a mineral. I believe that you shall be amazed."

"I should be delighted," I said.

His laboratory was upon the third floor of a building with windows that looked down across Forty-Second Street. It was early evening, and the electric streetlights were just beginning to glow.

As always, his laboratory was cluttered with electrical equipment, from enormous generating dynamos to tiny crystals bedecked with wires thinner than a mouse's whiskers. On the workbench in front of the window he had a ruby of his own, but rather than a jewel, this was a ruby in the shape of a small rod, about the size of a cigarette. In the form of a cylinder a ruby becomes quite ordinary, looking like nothing other than colored glass, for it is the gem-cutter's art that gives a jewel its sparkle. I had never before seen a gemstone cut in such a shape, and commented on it.

"It is not of a gem quality," he said dismissively, "but it is a mineral specimen adequate for my purposes."

He had earlier showed me an invention of his which utilized a high pressure spark in a rarified-gas lamp to produce a sharp blue-white flash, brilliant as lightning. This momentary illumination is quite startling, having the illusion of stopping time in a frozen moment. Now he placed the ruby cylinder into a mirrored box, surrounded with the flashlamps, with more mirrors to concentrate the flash upon the ruby cylinder, and attached the entire apparatus to a system of condensers and coils.

He then darkened the room with black velvet over the windows. "Watch the wall," he said, indicating not the box with the ruby hidden within, but the empty white wall a dozen yards across the laboratory.

With a turn of a rheostat, there was a sudden snapping noise. A flash of white seeped out from the box that held the cylindrical gem, but this was not the light which captivated my attention. Upon the wall opposite the workbench had appeared a sudden glowing spot of a brilliant, pure red. I clapped my hands in startlement, and Tesla smiled in pleasure.

"What is it?" I cried.

He triggered the electrical flash again, and once again the mysterious glowing spot appeared. It was a crimson so intense, of a shade so unalloyed in hue, that I realized that every shade that I had hitherto considered to be red was a muddy, washed-out shade compared to this pigment of unblemished purity. I remarked on the color to Mr. Tesla.

"Your eye is accurate," he said. "If you were to take the finest spectroscope, and analyze the color of the ray I have produced for you, you would find it to be a single shade indeed. All other lamps produce a spread of spectrum, but my new beam is a ray of unalloyed purity."

With that he set the ray to flashing automatically, and the dot appeared as an unmoving, although flickering, spot of brilliance. He passed his hand in front of it, and the spot on the wall disappeared, moving to his hand, which now seemed to cup the glowing spot in his palm. For a moment I had to suppress a gasp of fright, for the spot was so bright I worried that it would burn a hole entirely through his hand. He laughed. "No need to worry. It is mere light."

He lit a cigar, and the smoke from the cigar made the beam visible, a ghostly line of crimson. "The secret," he said, "is resonance. I have contrived to trap light between two parallel mirrors, so that it must resonate against itself as a standing wave, and so intensify until it escapes."

His explanation made no sense to me, for as I have said, I have no training in the sciences, but I nodded my assent, as if he had clarified everything. After a bit of coaxing, I was persuaded to put my own hand in front of the beam and, although it seemed too bright to look at directly, it was completely intangible—the beam had no force to it at all. I bent to look directly at it, but before I could put my eye to the ray, Tesla seized me and jerked me away.

"The eye is a delicate instrument," he said somberly, "and my ray is a thousand times, no, ten thousand times brighter than the sun. You would not look into it a second time."

Although we had known each other for many years, we had never before touched. His arms had quite surprising strength, considering that he was slender and almost womanish of figure; I could still feel the heat where his hand had been upon my arms.

I placed my hand upon the spot where his hand had been, and tried to feel again how he had touched me. Mistaking my gesture, he looked down, and said, "I apologize most humbly for my ungentlemanly conduct, Mademoiselle Kate. I acted only by instinct, I assure you, worried about your safety."

"I take no offense," I said. "Indeed, I thank you for your protection."

He stared down at the floor for a moment, and then, apparently forgetting the incident entirely, said to me, "Look! Let me show you what my ray can do!" With that he drew aside the velvet drapes and raised the dusty window wide open. The windowsill was stained with bird droppings like a thick spill of white paint.

Outside, the city was now cloaked in night. In the distance, the silhouette of the Woolworth Building was visible, the newly-erected colossus of the skyline.

"Do you carry a mirror with you?"

I produced a gilt-backed hand mirror from my handbag, and Tesla secured it upon the workbench in front of the ruby apparatus with a clamp. He adjusted the mirror until it was angled to his satisfaction, and then once again set the ruby to flashing.

The tiny dot of light suddenly appeared on the facade of the building across the street. What must the passersby be thinking of it, I wondered, a mysterious dot of light above their heads? I thrust my head out to look down, but of the few pedestrians below, none thought to look up. Tesla adjusted the direction slightly, and then angled the mirror to point over the rooftops.

To my astonishment, the crimson spot appeared on the Woolworth Tower itself, although it must have been half a mile or more distant. "The beam does not disperse," he said proudly. "I could bounce it off of the moon; I could send it to Mars."

"Can anyone see it?" I asked.

"Certainly," he said. "They will see it, and be puzzled indeed." He laughed, pleased with the thought. "I believe that none of them will guess at the origin of the miracle in a humble laboratory distant across the town."

Following that, he disappeared into his laboratories, and although Robert and I both attempted to entice him out with invitations to dinners and garden parties, he was hard on one of his ideas, and would not be seen again for several weeks, save only as a furtive figure, walking through Bryant Park in the early morning with a handful of peanuts to feed his beloved pigeons.

On an afternoon some months later—the weather that July of 1914 had turned suddenly sweltering—Robert and I were prepared to insist that Mr. Tesla must join us in our excursion to see the fireworks at Coney Island. "We will bring him with us by force if necessary," Robert said, "but come with us he must, for he will ruin his health with excessive work."

I came to his apartments at the Waldorf-Astoria to deliver our invitation, but found him already seeing a visitor in the anteroom of his suite. The door was open, and without turning he gestured me to enter. His visitor was perhaps sixty or seventy years of age, and despite the great heat she was dressed in long skirts and a laced-up white linen blouse covered with several shawls, and had a scarf over her head in the style that I have heard called a "babushka." She was pleading with Tesla in her own language, and Tesla was answering her with a calm, soothing voice in the same language. I took this speech to be Serbian, Nikola's native tongue, for I speak a few phrases of Russian, and understood enough words to recognize it a kindred tongue.

After some talking, Tesla stood to his full height, and in a voice of momentous tone, made her a great pledge. Such was his personal magnetism that even I, unable to understand a word, understood completely that whatever it was he had promised her, not heaven nor Earth should prevent him from accomplishing. At this pledge, his visitor fell to her knees and attempted to kiss his feet; although Tesla moved back slightly, just enough to avoid her touching him. Something had transpired, although I did not know what.

Later, when I talked with Tesla alone, he explained that this was a Serbian woman, with whom his family was acquainted, for she was native to the same small village as he. She had come to plead for the lives of her thirteen grandchildren.

"For war is coming, Katherine, a great and awful war, and it will sweep over Serbia like a tide of destruction, leaving only death behind."

"Surely it will not be so bad. We are civilized now, Nikola—"

Tesla's eyes were cold fire. "You understand nothing, my darling Katherine, nothing at all. We know what war is like, we Serbs, as you innocents do not. For five hundred years we have lived in the paths of armies, and when the rest of Europe looked away, we stood down the Turks, and died for it. The armies have washed over Serbia for years, like tidal waves, like plagues of rats, diseased and crazed with aggression, ravenous and destructive, leaving only corpses behind. Before, at least some survived, but in these days of Gatling machine guns and poisoned war gases, war will be total—there will be no survivors, I fear, in little Serbia."

"It will not be so bad, Nikola, I am sure of it. What did she ask of you, that woman?"

"She asked if I could help her sons, and their wives, and their children, to come to America to avoid the war. She asked me for money to pay the passage, and promised that she would herself work day and night to pay me back."

I winced inside, for I knew of the inventor's straitened circumstances. A genius he most undoubtedly was, but for all his inventions, his genius had not made him rich. "And you said?"

"I told her I could not do that, but I would do something else for her."

"How can you help her? What will you do?"

"I told her that I would stop the war."

"What?"

"I gave her my pledge, my word of honor. I, Nikola Tesla of Smiljan, will stop the coming war."

I was amazed. Tesla was a prodigy, the greatest genius of our age—possibly of any age—but this was more amazing than anything I had yet seen. "But how will you accomplish that?"

"I don't know," he answered. "It will require, I believe, some study."

We sailed to Europe on the Cunard liner *Lusitania*. She was perhaps somewhat less elegant than the late, doomed *Titanic*, but still quite richly appointed, her interiors lavish with columns, works of art and tapestries, mahogany paneling and gilded furniture. More importantly, she was fast; the greyhound of the seas. Tesla said that making the passage quickly was of the essence, and worried that even the six-day passage to Liverpool would be a crucial delay. *Lusitania* also had capacious holds, enough to carry the crates of mysterious electrical equipment that Tesla paid to have shipped across with him.

Tesla had brought with him piles of newspapers, in a dozen languages, proposing to use the time of the passage to study the situation. The headlines spoke of the coming war. The first day of the voyage he spent inspecting the ship's steam turbines, and the radio shack; following that, he divided his time between reading, and pacing along the promenade deck, staring across the water and watching the gulls, who apparently lived on the ship and soared in updrafts of the ship's passage.

All during the passage I dreamed of icebergs, although Tesla laughed, and said that in July it would be unlikely for us to be lucky enough to even see one.

"I should like to see an iceberg," Tesla told me. He

was standing on the main deck, at the very bow of the ship, gazing into the horizon. "I am told that they are a most startling shade of blue, and I would like to see this myself." The day was warm, but the wind of passage ruffled Tesla's ascot and blew strands of his hair across his face, despite the tonic he had combed into it to avoid just that. He tossed his head to free the errant strand from his eyes, just like a young girl, probably not even noticing he did it.

"I have been designing an invention that will remove the threat of icebergs forever," he said. "A ship will broadcast high-frequency electrical waves, and from reading the reflections of the waves, will instantaneously know the location of all of icebergs to a distance of hundreds of miles."

"And so chart a course to avoid them," I said.

"Yes, avoid them. Or, when I am done, if they prefer not to deviate from their path, they will simply melt the iceberg out of their path."

"You can do this?" I said. "Oh, with your new ray! Can it be made powerful enough?"

"The ruby? No. It is a toy, nothing more." He shook his head, the errant strand once again swinging like a pendulum. "But the principle of light amplification by resonance—ah, that is something very wonderful indeed." Tesla smiled. "I have produced some improvements, and combined it with certain features of my earlier work, to make something quite—interesting."

I shuddered involuntarily. Was this, then, how he proposed to stop the war, with a new death ray? If so, his quest was doomed, for I knew that, once started, armies were not so easily stopped. Tesla's ray might level battlefields and set aflame all of the capitals of Europe, but the war would go on.

But when I mentioned this to Tesla, he merely

shook his head. "In war, I think, as in physics, the key
to effect must be to choose the right place to apply a
force. It is not the magnitude of the force, but its
precision, that is most critical. Resonance, Katherine,
resonance is always the key—if an action is placed in
the correct spot, it will be amplified by circumstances
into a great effect. If we but knew enough, I have not
a doubt that a single flap of a pigeon's wing would be
enough to change all the course of history."

"And your many boxes of equipment? Are they
filled, then, with pigeons?"

Tesla laughed in delight. "Ah, Katherine, wouldn't
that be rather cruel, to so confine such noble birds?
No, I would that I had the subtlety of knowledge to
be able to apply so gentle a force, but I must make do
with lesser knowledge, and so apply a greater force."

An electrical ray, then, I thought. A death ray.

The *Lusitania* arrived in Liverpool, and we then
shipped immediately to Paris. From France I had expected Tesla to book passage on the Orient Express
toward the Balkans, but instead he surprised me by
taking rooms for us on the Seine. He spent his days
reading newspapers, and the afternoons and evenings
simply sitting in cafés, and talking earnestly to people
he met long into the night.

I have always loved Paris, but that July the weather
was beastly hot. I had expected the mood of the city
to be somber, anticipating the looming war, but instead there was almost a visible eagerness for battle,
with all the young men of the city excitedly discussing
plans for the coming conquest of Germany. Not a single one had even a casual thought that perhaps the
Germans had other plans. "It will be over in a
month," one of them told Tesla. "We will bring the
Kaiser to heel, and wipe out the arrogance of the Prus-

sians. The occupied territories of Alsace and Lorraine will again be French, and Germany will be made to pay dearly for their arrogance."

"Vive la France!" was the cry, and no one talked about death. Or if they did, it was a romantic image of death they pictured, all heroic poses, with no actual pain or dying involved.

Tesla's questioning was about the diplomats, and by what means they were endeavoring to stop the war. It gave me great cheer that he still had hope for diplomacy, although the young men he talked to seemed visibly disappointed at the prospect that diplomacy might thwart their desired war. "Austria will declare war upon Serbia; the honor of the Hapsburg emperor allows no other course," one of them said. "And so Russia will come to defend their ally, and then Germany must certainly attack Russia in defense of their ally, and when they do, as Russia is our ally, we will defend them—and thus we will invade Germany! *Vive la France!*"

"Serbia," Tesla said. "Austria, then Russia, then Germany, then France. And then Britain, I am sure, and then America will be unable to stay out of it."

"Yes," I said. The coming sequence reminded me of the chains of dominoes with which we had often played, in happier times, at parties. Each country falling into war would bring in the next one in the sequence, until the whole world was at war.

"Indeed," said Tesla, when I told him of the dominoes. "And that is the key. If we can remove one domino . . ."

"Then the chain will still stand, and another day, the slight touch of a wind will set off the reaction," I said.

"Perhaps," Tesla said. "Or, if I calculate correctly, perhaps not. The engines of commerce are slowly but inevitably drawing Europe together, and if the war can just be postponed, I think that soon Europe will be so well entangled in commerce that there will be no France, no Germany, no Austro-Hungarian Empire, only a prosperous and peaceful Europe." At my evident skepticism, he said "Observe the table you sit at."

He picked up the glass sitting in front of me. "Sparkling water, from France," he said. "It is in a goblet of Czech crystal, sitting next to a plate of Dresden ceramic, with English silverware, and a napkin of Italian lace. On the table is a Chinese vase, holding a tulip grown in Holland. And so, as you see, even the least café in France is international."

A table setting seemed to me to be a rather weak guarantee of peace, but I did not say so, and in a day we left Paris, and set forth for Russia.

To embark by train across Germany would have entailed too many uncertainties, so from Paris we went by ship first to Rotterdam, then from Rotterdam to Riga, and from Riga we arrived in Saint Petersburg. Tesla's crates of equipment followed half a step behind us.

Saint Petersburg was a surprise to me. I had always pictured Russia as gray and cold and uncultured, but the city was bright and gay, the summer climate pleasingly cool compared to the brutal heat of Paris, and the lazy evening twilight was long and delicious, with the sky still aglow well into the night. The city seemed filled with treasures of art and sculpture, with golden-domed cathedrals and palaces of marble. The people were quite cultured, and although my Russian is so poor as to be nearly useless toward being understood, I discovered to my delight that a great number of the

Russian citizens spoke quite good French, and reveled in the possibility of conversation with foreigners.

Tesla found us apartments near the Troitzky Bridge, with windows that looked out across the Neva toward the Tsar's summer palace and the Field of Mars. Petersburg was not as well electrified as New York, or even Paris; the streetlights here were gas lamps, and not electrical. With the long evenings, though, streetlights were little needed. The lack of electricity drew disapproval from Tesla, but he set up in his rooms an electrical generator of his own, using a small but powerful turbine he had designed, and soon he had a miniature electrical laboratory in his rooms.

He was still reading piles of newspapers, turning the pages so quickly that I wondered how he could absorb any information at all. His questions, now, had turned to a single purpose, to learn the movements and activities of the Tsar. I cautioned him that the incessant questioning would most certainly tag him as a foreign spy, and that he would be arrested, or worse, but it turned out that all the Russians loved nothing more than to gossip about the affairs of the Tsar (and more particularly of the Tsarina), and we were soon swamped in rumors, speculation, and most scurrilous innuendo about the movements and motives and intentions of the imperial family.

The conflagration we were all dreading was coming fast. On the afternoon of July 23, Austria delivered an ultimatum to the Serbian embassy. Confident in the support of Russia, Serbia rejected it.

I put down the paper, where I had been puzzling out the Cyrillic characters to read the headlines. "The war has begun," I said. "The Austrian armies are on the move. We are too late."

"Not quite yet," Tesla said.

Tesla, at last, had the information he had sought. He knew precisely the movements of the Tsar.

"At one-fifteen tomorrow afternoon, Tsar Nicholas the Second will declare the support of the Russian Empire for their ally state Serbia, and instruct his generals to mobilize all of Russia for war," Tesla told me. He pointed to his crumpled map of the city. "He will stand here. The Tsar has a great fear of assassination, and so he will appear on a balcony, out of the range of a thrown bomb, and no one will be present who has not been searched, to make sure no one has a gun."

"I fail to see your point," I told him. "Unless you intend to assassinate the Tsar?"

"As he stands, he will grasp this brass railing," Tesla continued, ignoring my comment, "which I have ascertained is electrically grounded."

"And?" I said.

"I have made reservations for us to leave Saint Petersburg at noon on a ship bound to Helsinki. I expect all of Russia to be in chaos by then, but I believe that the ports will not yet be closed."

"You do intend an assassination," I stated.

Tesla lowered his head, and did not respond.

"And so," I said, "for all your exalted talk about removing a single domino from the chain, I find now that you intend no more than a common assassination. Surely you know that this entire situation is the result of a political assassination? Has any assassination, at any time, ever produced any positive result? Nothing good can come from such a deed, I believe, not a thing."

Tesla turned his back. Without looking at me, he said, "Ah, Katherine, your idealism is as great as your beauty, and I cannot deny the depravity of my intended deed, but I simply have no more time. This once, we must hope that good can come out of evil. Russia is the critical link; once the Tsar mobilizes the

Russian army, no force in the world could stop the war. How many people are in the armies of Europe, do you think? Five million? Ten?"

"Perhaps twenty million, as I count it," I replied slowly, for I was averse to following his reasoning.

"And what fraction of those will die, if the coming war is allowed to take place? Half?"

"Ten percent," I said, and then reluctantly added, "in the war. But disease and starvation follow war, and those will kill twice that number."

"Six million, then," he said. "Tell me, then, is the life of one man worth so much?"

His plan was simple. He had affixed a mirror near the field. With his ruby beam, he adjusted the inclination of the mirror until, by bouncing the beam from our apartments onto the mirror, the crimson spot appeared exactly where the Tsar would stand. Then he had cemented the mirror to fix it in its position.

The ruby beam, however, was too low in power to have any useful effect. For his needs, he had made a much larger apparatus, working upon the same principle of concentrating light by resonance, but this one using an electrical discharge in a blown-glass tube of rarified gas. The more powerful beam would, he told me, actually break down the air itself, turning it from an insulator into a conductor.

"And so?"

He pointed behind him. I had seen high-voltage generators before, of course, in his laboratory in New York, but had not paid attention to the fact that he had set one up in his chambers here. "Ten million volts," he said. "It will discharge along the path of the beam."

And at this, I had nothing at all to say.

It dawned a clear, cloudless day.

Tesla had spent the night and the morning working

on his apparatus, adjusting and tuning every piece. I had hoped against hope that something would go wrong, that the day would be gray with fog shrouding the city, or the Tsar would change his mind, but exactly on schedule, the Tsar, in a blue military uniform bespeckled with gilt and medallions, appeared on his balcony to address his generals.

The generators whined like dogs eager to be unleashed, and the air was filled with the bite of ozone from the high-voltage generator and the smell of the heated oil from the transformers. My hands were trembling so much I could barely hold a pencil, and I sought desperately for something to say.

But Tesla was ice steady. He watched the spectacle across the river for a minute, judging exactly where the Tsar stood. Tsar Nicholas moved forward to grasp the brass railing and my heart went still, but Tesla did not move. Why, why didn't he fire his machine? Had he had a sudden change of heart?

Then a pigeon sitting on the brass railing spread its wings and flew off. As if this were his signal, Tesla said, very softly, "Now."

He fired the beam. An instant later, the high voltage triggered, and a horizontal lightning stroke reached out across the river in a dazzling blue-white flash, followed instantly by a clap of thunder.

Rather than following the straight path of the beam, the lightning stroke at the last furlong diverged, curving upward in a jagged arc, reaching over the green copper sheeting of the summer palace roof to strike a gold cupola above. A golden eagle on the point of the cupola exploded into a shower of sparks, spraying molten droplets of gold, and then the copper roof began to burn.

The Tsar looked around for a moment, puzzled, but then turned back to continue addressing the generals.

My ears were ringing from the thunderclap. "Failure!" Tesla cried. "Again!"

It took nearly a minute for the generator to recharge the condensers, and in that long minute we agonized. The crowd was clearly distraught, half of them still watching the Tsar, who continued to talk, oblivious, while the other half had craned their necks upward to watch as the flames on the rooftop of the summer palace slowly died out. Tesla frantically adjusted the apparatus.

"Now," Tesla shouted, and again the beam of light shot out, and a moment later the electrical arc, a blue-white lightning and a clap of thunder. The lightning bolt curved across the river, flashing down a dozen secondary strokes into the river, each of which puffed up in a small cloud of steam. The lightning crackled up and down, dancing now toward the bridge, now playing over a huge statue of some ancient Tsar mounted on a horse.

The living Tsar, untouched, stopped speaking to stare at the spectacle.

Behind us, with a great snap, the overloaded condensers burst into flames, and the lightning faded to nothing. Tesla, cursing in his own language, turned to beat the flames out with a blanket before they set us on fire.

I turned back to gaze at the spectacle across the river. The beam and its ten-million-volt generator were dead. He should have tested it first, I thought. But it was too late to offer him that advice now.

The air was stinking of vaporized copper wire and burned wax insulation.

Sitting on the workbench beside me I saw the small ruby beam apparatus, which Tesla had long ago demonstrated for me. There was no trick to operating it, once it had been set up, and Tesla had set it up earlier to check the alignment of his mirrors. I turned the rheostat to set the ruby to flashing. The beam went out across the room, and I took my hand mirror out of my pocketbook, and carefully angled it, as I had seen Tesla do, to direct the beam across the river, and to the Tsar.

The beam was harmless, as I well knew from having put my hand in it. A toy, Tesla had called it.

The glowing crimson spot appeared on the Tsar. The beam jittered up and down, looking almost alive, for I was unable to hold the hand mirror perfectly steady, and flashes of impossibly bright light from the medals that bedecked the Tsar's chest threw dancing glints in all directions. Even from across the river, I could hear the awed voices of the crowd. The Tsar moved left, and then right, but I followed him with minute motions of the mirror, and the crimson spot stayed fixed to his chest.

And then the Tsar knelt down, and stared directly into the beam.

Tesla destroyed his gas-discharge tubes, pounding the glasswork into sand until he was convinced that there would be no possibility of anyone ever reconstructing his work. The electrical generator and its equipment he donated to the Academy of Sciences, for he believed that they would have no visible connection to the events of July, and the Russian engineers, he judged, would benefit from the equipment.

The Tsar was blinded. The monk Rasputin proclaimed that the events of the day had clearly been a sign of God's wrath. A horizontal lightning bolt from a clear sky, a fire of no known origin in the palace, a glowing blood spot upon the Tsar's chest: these miracles could signify nothing other than the anger of God with the Tsar's warlike nature, and the fact that the

Tsar had merely been blinded, and not killed, was an indication of God's mercy.

The Tsar postponed his plans to mobilize his army. And then, remarkably, over the next few days his eyesight returned, although for the rest of his life he would complain of a missing spot in his vision. The monk Rasputin declared the return of his vision to be a sign of God's pleasure at the Tsar turning from war.

Tesla took out his pocket notebook and wrote a note: "Flash blindness: temporary in effect. Apparently clears up in two days." Then he looked at the note, ripped the page out of his notebook, and burned it.

Faced with the undivided might of the Austro-Hungarian empire, and with no allies, Serbia acceded to the ultimatum, and eventually allowed itself to be peacefully absorbed into the empire. As Tesla had predicted, once war had been averted, the forces of commerce eventually overrode the dissections of Europe, and a new union of all of Europe emerged, rivaling the United States in its size and power, a great force for world peace. Even Germans and Frenchmen, once the greatest of enemies, now sit together at a common table in perfect peaceful conversation, and together make business plans for the greater prosperity of all mankind.

Would peace have come if, as we had planned, we had killed the Tsar of all the Russias? I have turned this thought over and over in my head, pondering every aspect of the question, and come to no certain conclusion. But on the whole, I think not. I think that a murder, no matter by what good intentions motivated, would have led the world into an even greater war than the one that had been impending. I now believe that the monk Rasputin, although he did not know it, had been right, and it was the hand of Providence directly that prevented us from murder, and saved Europe from war.

Before he smashed it, Tesla removed the tiny ruby cylinder from his apparatus and presented it to me. "You are fond of jewels," he said. "Perhaps this mineral specimen could be cut into gems. I have no further use for it."

I did not cut it up, however, but kept it to remind me forever of the day. I had it strung on a silver chain, so I could hang it from my neck to replace the ruby pendant.

I have it still.

Revision Point

Nikola Tesla, the mad Serbian inventor (and genius rival to Thomas Edison) could very well have invented the laser. By the end of the nineteenth century, he was experimenting with flashlamp stimulation of ruby crystals and with electrical discharges in rarified gases, researches that could, if aimed in the right direction, have resulted in production of a laser. Perhaps he even did (in his later years, Tesla talked ceaselessly about his researches in creating "needle-point beams of energy"), but if he ever made a working model, he never revealed it in public nor left a detailed description of a laser in his writings.

The origins of the first World War, and the question of whether the war could have been prevented, have been a matter of great debate among historians. The war seemed both inevitable, a huge and powerful machinery of destruction that was waiting only for a trigger that must invariably occur—and yet at the same time it seemed a result of a haphazard chance, the product of a handful of rash actions and ill-considered choices that fanned a spark in Bosnia into a worldwide conflagration. Some historians claim that with even one or two days more time, the diplomats might have managed to salvage the situation, and prevent the war, if only Russia had not mobilized its forces, setting into motion the chain of action and preemption.

Could the war have been prevented? Could Tesla, with his crude laser, have had any effect? Or, absent one cause, would the inevitable cataclysm have been started by another? These questions are beyond the realm of historical study: the stuff of speculation, and alternate history.

In our world, the first ruby laser was demonstrated in 1960 by Theodore Maiman, and the gas discharge by Ali Javan later the same year.

                                                              G.L.

OUT OF CHINA

by Julie E. Czerneda

A village in Yunnan, China, 1301 A.D.

"THEY say the surface of a clear lake is an aperture into another world, another time, an other reality."

The rat, unimpressed, lapped at the aperture under consideration, ripples from its tiny tongue distorting the reflection of leaf, bamboo, and stone. The scholar smiled and shook his head. "You show as much respect for philosophy as our present chancellor." He scooped the rodent back into its place within his coat. "Or perhaps yours is more in tune with the times." His heavy sigh was met with a squeak of protest and the scrabble of claws. "My apologies, Little Blossom."

He watched the last ripple reach the pond edge, then reflect back through the first, and so on, each fading with every encounter until the pond was still once more. His garden was full of metaphors this afternoon, Xuai Chi decided, fighting an inclination toward bitterness. He was too young for the life of a recluse, too proud of his learning and sure of his purpose to isolate himself from the world. But the Mongols and their *semuran* lackeys had rejected older and more educated men. Confucian scholars were presently unwelcome in public service and Chi's tactful absence from Kunming City served his family best.

"Our time will come again," Chi assured his garden. "When the canals clog and no one remembers how to count taxes. Barbarians."

It would help if his garden needed work, but it was perfect. Nothing missing, nothing superfluous. Without the presence of an insolent rat for scale, Chi could believe he gazed down at the "Pearl on the Plateau" of his home, missing only the rose-tinged clouds of sunset.

Chi was loath to lose what tranquillity he'd gained in some household squabble, but the youngest servant girl had been standing between the red-lacquered pillars of his garden gate for some time. She appeared anxious. Probably nothing. Still. *A summons from his family, at last?* Chi acknowledged her presence. "What is it?"

He might have opened floodgates. The servant sprang forward, bowing, hands wringing the muted gray cloth of her coat, words spilling out almost as quickly as the tears down her cheeks. "Master Chi! The rats—the rats are dying in the streets. It is as you warned. The villagers have left for the Stone Forest. We must go, too. We must run for our lives! Haste, Master Chi!"

Chi rested one hand over the warm lump inside his coat as he stood, glancing down to be sure his favorite trousers hadn't collected stray leaves. "Which streets? Be thoughtful in your answer, girl. I need to know exactly where these rats have appeared."

"Yes, Master." A hiccup, but her face lost its rictus of fear. Not one of the brighter lights among his small household if a stern voice and question stemmed her tears. Anyone who'd survived the recurring plagues in this region knew the only hope was to outrun the death that emptied so many homes and filled so many graves. Anarchy and famine were lesser evils than the Disease of the Rats.

"The magistrate's house," she gulped. "More, by the temple gates and through the market." Her voice rose. "They'll be here next, Master!"

He hoped so, with all the fervor of a man kept from his calling until this moment—but kept the wish to himself. If this was truly the last of his servants, he'd need her calm, not fearing for his sanity as well as her life. "You are true to your duty," Chi complimented. "What is your name?"

Her eyes turned downward and she gave a deep bow. "Xiao Li, Master Chi."

"Xiao Li. Go to my chamber and fetch me the small baskets you will find there. They are covered in red silk—you will not mistake them. Quickly now."

She ran to the house and disappeared within. Chi knew she believed he'd come to his senses and the baskets were for his belongings.

They were not.

The village streets carried silence. People, carts, and pigs might never have rung music from their tiles or drummed across their wooden bridges. The red-roofed buildings sheltered emptiness. They might never have been the site of commerce, personal and business, for generations. And corruption, the curse of more modern times.

"Hurry, girl."

Chi could have sped her pace by taking one or both of the baskets, but only her burdens kept her following. As it was, she stumbled often, her eyes wide and staring, flinching at the touch of a breeze as if it was the outstretched finger of death coming to claim her.

Chi kept his hands within his sleeves and walked at his accustomed pace. The possibility of success made him as nervous inside as his servant was outside. He licked dry lips and checked the landscape around them.

A ball of frenzied movement burst from beneath an ornate gateway. It appeared made of tails, fur, and blood. Even as Chi froze in place, the ball broke apart to reveal itself rats, biting at one another and themselves, writhing as if they were miniature demons.

He shouted: "Quickly! A basket—" only to have both land at his feet, their silk covers drifting to the road as his servant took to her heels.

Chi wasted no breath calling her back. Instead, he swallowed the gorge rising in his throat, glanced around to be sure there were no witnesses, and picked up the nearest basket.

The rats looked exhausted. A few bit and clawed at one another, but the rest lay limp on the tiles, their fur blood-streaked and covered in filth. Some of the filth moved, like crawling pepper.

Fleas.

Disgusted, Chi put the basket down and picked up one of the squares of silk his servant had dropped. He tore it in two, wrapping a piece around each hand. It was soiled from the street, but, like the fabric of his trousers and coat, had been steeped in essence of chrysanthemum. Any flea that touched the silk would be stunned or killed.

Would he could so easily protect himself from the Disease of the Rats.

True to the writings Chi had studied, the afflicted animals were insensitive to his presence. He had raised his own rats for three years and his experienced eye could see these were more than starved. Their fur was

coming loose, revealing sores and boils upon the skin.
Their abdomens were bloated and a crust had formed
around eyes and nostrils.

They were sickness personified. Chi shuddered as
he scooped up three with his basket, covering the top
with the remaining square of silk.

He turned and hurried back to his home, hunched
over the basket and its miserable contents. The ball
of rats might have been a signal. Everywhere he
looked, limp brown bodies clogged the drains and
filled the shadows of open doors. Hundreds. Probably
thousands. The hedge lining the road rustled with the
dying. Their desperate squeaks seemed to echo sobs
from the distant hills. Chi concentrated on his task.
This wasn't his home; it wasn't his family fleeing for
their lives through the labyrinth of limestone pillars
that gave name to the Stone Forest.

It could be soon. Just because the Disease of the
Rats had struck this rural village didn't mean it spared
cities, no matter how civilized or distant. He could
only refuse to believe it had already reached Kunming City.

The basket might have been empty, except for its
weight. Perhaps the rats inside were already dead. By
contrast, Little Blossom shifted restlessly within his
coat, tickling his ribs. *Could she smell what he carried?*
He'd observed the sensitivity of her tiny nose, watched
it twitch ever so delicately to discover which of his
hands held her evening treat. "Hush. Hold still," he
told her.

Xuai Chi had planned for this day. Within his courtyard, safe from passersby, within his garden, safe from
even servants, he had fitted his pavilion with cages
of the finest workmanship, originally crafted to house
nightingales. As he entered, each cage rocked on its

hanger as its occupant rushed to peer down at him with dark bright eyes, tiny paws tapping softly at the bars as if asking to play or for a treat. The sweetness of apple bark and fresh grass filled the air.

Although descended from wild stock, his rats were healthy and sleek, their fur as soft and rich as any ermine's. Even Chi found it hard to credit these were the same beasts the servants chased from the kitchens with their brooms.

The same beasts that lay quiescent within his basket. Chi checked the silk was still covering the top before going to where a pair of cages, as fine as the rest, stood empty and waiting. He put the basket down gently, then lifted his hands, watching them tremble in their wrapping like leaves in the wind.

Dead rats in the streets meant human death to follow. Agonizing, painful death. That was no myth.

There had to be a connection. He was a man of observation, of learning. Surely the secret of how this disease spread could be seen, if one was brave enough to watch. Surely knowing that secret could provide a means to protect his people.

Xuai Chi had hung his rat cages to keep their occupants from any contact with their wild kin. His servants had been instructed to tolerate no wild animals on his property. Now, Chi took a bamboo pole and used the hook at its end to bring two cages to the table.

There was a rat in each. The animals should have been running around with excitement. The lowering of their cages meant food, or a bath, or time to explore Chi's lap and fingers. Each crouched quietly, staring at him. It was as if they knew something was wrong.

For an instant, the scholar hesitated. It wasn't usual for him to think about his captives as anything but a means to an end, a welcome reminder he had a purpose even in exile. Little Blossom had been the exception, her personality as shining as her white fur and pink eyes. Yet he paused to offer the rats the hint of a bow.

From that moment, Chi worked quickly. He lifted the silk from the basket with a pair of tongs. Two of the afflicted rats lived; the third was curled in death. Their fleas seemed intent on desertion, springing to the arms of his coat. They fell to the floor before Chi had to brush them off. *Foul things.* He promised himself to be careful of them. It was well known that fleas would lie in wait. That was another reason Chi had hung his cages. To keep his animals free of such vermin.

He used the tongs to lift a living rat from the basket. It squirmed feebly as he placed it in one of the empty cages, then buried its head in the soft grass and lay still.

The second rat went into a cage containing a healthy rat. The afflicted animal also buried its head and lay still. The cage's original occupant retreated to the far side and, to Chi's surprise, stayed there. When he'd introduced a new individual before, the rats immediately engaged in mutual inspection, grooming, or dispute.

Could the animals sense—and fear—the disease? He had read accounts of birds sounding an alarm before an earthquake. A study of animal senses might prove worthy.

In a distant future. Chi set their cage to one side. He then took the cage with the second healthy rat and placed it beside the one with the sick animal, their bars almost touching.

After checking food and water, he left the rest of the cages hanging from the rafters as before. The basket, and its foul contents, he took outside and burned, first pouring oil over the entire mass. He removed the silks he'd wrapped over his hands, tossing them in the fire to blacken, curl, and disappear.

And after that, Chi checked to make sure the courtyard gates were closed, then made himself and Little Blossom tea.

Xuai Chi dipped his brush in ink, then began the final sheet of his record. With each press and lift, the sentences took life before his eyes. His arm wanted to shake with fatigue; his triumph defied it. "I have found the means by which the Disease of the Rats is transmitted from one living creature to another," he wrote. "It is a means we can defend ourselves against. . . ."

Chi laid the brush on its jade rest and steepled his fingers, considering his next words. If he was wrong, if he'd misunderstood or missed something, he could be offering a false promise of safety. Would he trust his family to his idea?

"Yes," he said aloud, looking through the screen at the smoldering pyre that had been his pavilion. From her perch on his desk, Little Blossom paused in her fastidious grooming ritual as if she thought he spoke to her. Chi offered his ink-stained fingers for her to sniff. "You were the final clue, my tiny friend," he said.

Starting the day after capturing the sick rats, Chi had visited the pavilion each dawn and dusk, careful to wear clothing whose fabrics he knew had been soaked in essence of chrysanthemum. He wrapped his hands in silk treated the same way. It might be an idiosyncrasy, to loathe the rats' fleas so, but he succumbed to it. There was no one to judge him vain or a fool.

The two afflicted rats had died almost at once. He left their bodies alone and watched the healthy animals. Three more days passed and all else seemed normal. As normal as life could be without servants. Chi dug undersized turnips and onions from the garden to add to his boiled rice. He buried the peels for fear of attracting the village rats, should any survive.

The morning of the fifth day, running through a downpour, the scholar entered the pavilion and knew something had changed. The animals were silent.

The rats in cages on the table were lying on their sides, mouths bloodstained. They'd bitten through their own fur and skin, as if in terrible pain. As he approached, they squeaked piteously as if he, their faithful caregiver, could help.

Both? Chi frowned. He'd expected the rat sharing its cage with the dead animal to become ill, not the one separated by bars. He looked up. The rest appeared unaffected, paws tapping at the bars for his attention.

He went closer to examine the sick animals, then started back. Their fur was swarming with fleas. The creatures must have survived the death of their hosts, the sick rats. He should have killed the dreadful things by bathing the sick animals before bringing them into his pavilion.

Xuai Chi's first impulse was to take the cages and burn their infested contents, before the fleas could spread further. Later, he couldn't explain what prompted him to instead unhook a cage with a still-healthy rat and bring it near the cage of a sick one.

Before he could put the cage on the table, he saw a flea leap into it from the sick rat's cage.

Moving very carefully, Chi put the cage on the floor, then covered it with the nearest cloth to hand, a plain muslin sack. He could hear the rat sniffing the cloth, then scampering about as if entertained.

Four days later, Chi was filthy, weak, and almost out of food. It didn't matter. The rat under the muslin sack was dying. The rest, out of reach of the fleas, were healthy.

Little Blossom, who had stayed within the protection of his treated coat, was healthy, too.

Chi had dreamed of an accomplishment to restore his place as a scholar. He'd found far more. Kunming City, his home, was a hub of trade. From its wharves, ships carrying silk and other goods traveled via canal and river to the ocean, then to India, Africa, and as far as the newly opened markets of Venice.

Ships that swarmed with rats. Rats that carried fleas.

Chi dipped his pen and stroked the words that would change the world:

"The Disease of the Rats is transmitted from the sick to the healthy by the bite of fleas who have fed on the first then attack the second. Actions that prevent fleas from biting, such as essence of chrysanthemum and removal of flea-carrying animals from dwellings, will protect people from the ravages of this disease. I have seen this with my own eyes and swear it is true. . . ."

Venice, 1302 AD
"They say the surface of a clear lake is an aperture into another world, another time, an other reality." The tall figure leaned out over the balcony rail, then turned away in disgust. "You'll find no clear lakes near Venice these days, Merchant. Silt, sewage, and poison. There's good reason we drink wine. Come inside. Sit with me. I would hear this urgent news of yours."

"I appreciate your granting me audience, Doge . . ."

Fingers crusted with emeralds and gold wrapped themselves around a goblet, lifting it to thin, unsmiling lips. The eyes above the rim reflected both gems' fire and something of the blood-red tint of the wine. "Grant?"

The merchant inclined his head immediately, his hands twisting together. "Please accept my apology. I failed to follow the appropriate channels." He peered up, his look bolder than his words. "But my information can't wait on protocol—or worse, be lost."

"Sit."

He started to obey, then froze above the lush tapestry seat. "I'm fresh from the docks, Your—" as if the most powerful man in Venice couldn't see and smell that for himself.

His host waved him down. "Chairs can be replaced. I'm told you have news out of China, news of such marvelous nature that your ship's captain refused to dock until assured you'd be escorted to me by my guardsmen, snarling a number of barges in the process. There have been calls for his head. And yours."

The merchant paled. "As the Lord is my Witness, Doge, that's your right. Let me speak first, for the sake of Venice."

"Speak, then."

Long past midnight, the doge sat at his desk, candles unlit. He didn't need them to know what lined his walls. Latin alchemical manuscripts lay stacked on shelves, translations from the original Arabic and Egyptian. There were accounts from travelers, curled maps and fanciful drawings. To his left, behind glass to show their inestimable value, some of the new encyclopedias. Knowledge was his passion.

And now he possessed more.

But what to do with it?

The merchant and everyone who might have spoken to him were in custody, guarded by those loyal to the doge. Safe from rebels who would overthrow the republic and replace it with princes. Safe from a papacy that claimed dominion over all.

Safe. *For now.*

Sheets of parchment lay cool and bare beneath his restless fingertips. He had urgent letters to write, beginning with one to each of his ministers. This knowledge would ensure Venice's supremacy as well as the safety of her people.

Or would it? The doge stared at the darkness beyond the glass, as if seeing the face of Europe. He knew firsthand how politics filtered knowledge, hoarding its potential, dispensing what was expedient, distorting source and content. What if he couldn't control it? Worse, what if his enemies controlled it first?

He lit a single candle and studied its flame. The risk was too great. A nod. He would write to them all, every learned man he could find, starting with the medical school in Salerno and its upstart cousin in Montpellier. He would charge his network of informants to disperse this new knowledge out of China as far and as quickly as possible.

To stop the Black Death. Yes. He wanted that. Any sane man would.

To stem the rising power of the Church and its meddling in governance and trade?

He wanted that even more.

London, England, 1497 AD

"They say the surface of a clear lake is an aperture into another world, another time, an other reality."

"I think I'll use that in my 'Ode to Seasons,' William. You don't mind, do you?"

"It's not my saying, Byron. I believe it is out of China—as is so much else these days." William bent into the oars, easing them through the water so hardly a ripple spread to disturb the lilies. Or the eligible young ladies seated along the shore. They were supposedly preoccupied with ink and brush, but their display of bright silk gowns and parasols was likely more artistic than any sketch produced by a group so consumed by giggles. They weren't unguarded. Sentinel cats dozed in the sunlight at their feet and servants waved pyrethrum fans to fend away insects.

"I'd love to study there. You could come."

"What, China?" William shook his head. "Too far from home, my friend. I plan to attend the London College of Physicians, or mayhap the Collège Royal in Paris. Lenses. The mechanics of the body. Medicine is where to make a mark, Byron. And fortune."

"I've sufficient fortune, William. Medicine doesn't interest me. Public office, now. There's a future."

"Ambitious, aren't you?" William stopped rowing, his round face troubled. Lily pads kissed the hull. "You'd have to pass the civil service exams. Not to mention you have to qualify to take the bloody things. Scant few who do come from England. By the time you make Lord Mayor of London, you'll be gray, and they—" a nod to the shore lined with dewy-eyed maidens, "—won't be waiting."

Byron dipped his hand into the water, then brought his fingers to his lips and licked them. "The Thames, William, safe to drink within our parents' lifetime. Their lifetimes, a third longer than our grandparents'. Trade routes to Zimbabwe, Ghana, and Songhai, protected from the threat of malaria, typhus, or sleeping sickness. Our world is changing for the better because it is served by those educated in the arts, philosophies, and sciences. I know I must study. Public office must be filled by those who understand the past and can build for the future."

"I'm all for clean water," William replied, "and I won't deny the inventions of our time are marvels, Byron. But have you tried getting an audience with one of those old men? Before every city wanted nothing but esteemed scholars, you could at least bribe a permit from a bored young clerk with a pint." He dug in the oars again, as if straining against fate. "You heard they refused John Cabot permission to cross the Atlantic?"

"What did you expect? The inspectors found a rat in his hold."

"And I say it was probably put there—" William paused. "I know what you'll say. There are no rats left in England and Cabot deserves time in the Tower for being so careless, no matter how it came on his ship. But there's a difference between care and obsession, Byron. You have noticed, I'm sure, the wealth of our northern neighbors, the Danes. They traffic with the New World and have managed to avoid contamination."

"They claim."

"Who's to call them false? We're being closed off from the rest of the world, Byron, while scholars from the East build us better toilets."

"It's not a perfect system," Byron said. "Yet, imagine what things might have been like if China hadn't shared the knowledge of how diseases spread from beast to man?" He gave a theatrical shudder. "Thousands dying, without understanding how or why. At best, they'd seek answers from religion, fearing divine punishment. At worse, they'd hunt for those to blame. It might have been people, not vermin, who were slaughtered." Another shudder, less contrived. "It would have been a black time, William. The scholars spared us that."

"Ay. Well, if you must become a dusty old thinker, where will you go?"

"I've applied to Maimonides, in Tudela, Spain. Some of the most famous Jewish, Arab, and Chinese scholars have attended."

"Then you'll come home."

Byron leaned back, arms behind his head. "I'm more ambitious than that, fair William. Maybe I'll find a way to set foot in the New World."

"And maybe," William laughed, "you'll start by acknowledging the frantic waving of that dainty treat before she falls into the river and you must explain your woeful neglect to her father."

An estate in Yunnan Province, Central Asian Bios, 2003 AD

"They say the surface of a clear lake is an aperture into another world, another time, an other reality."

Song Xai squinted at the tiny pond, ablaze with reflected sunlight. "If that's so, Grandfather," she ventured, "it must be warmer there." She'd already pulled her sleeves over her fingers; now she tucked her hands under her arms.

Her grandfather's face creased into a hundred tiny smiles. "You don't have to stay out here with me, Little Blossom. Your mother values your visits also."

She didn't move from her seat on the stone bench. Any chance she had of convincing him and, through him, others meant persistence. The chill of late autumn was a small price to pay for the future. "I've something to discuss with you, Grandfather, that is best said out here, in your garden, where there will be no interruptions."

Dr. Song Li's smile faded. "Perhaps it is something best not said at all." For an instant, Song Xai glimpsed the will her grandfather must have shown in the Council of Civils, when he was one of the Thirteen who governed this bios.

"I must. I need your wisdom." She paused to marshal the arguments that had seemed so irrefutable on the speedtrain, then changed her mind. His familiar presence comforted her into the simple truth. "Grandfather, there is a man—" His expression cheered until Song Xai shook her head. "A colleague. A visionary. He leads a team of researchers. His work—our work— could change the shape of the world."

"Why would you wish to do that, Granddaughter?" The wording might have come from a civil inquisitor. Song Xai refused to hear any threat in her grandfather's soft voice. She needed him. Even in retirement, Song Li wielded immense influence over the reigning civils, his age and experience treasures beyond price.

In his own way, he had been a visionary. And he loved her. With his support, her dream could happen. *Would happen*, she told herself.

Like a lucky omen, a flock of cranes appeared in the sky, their huge wings beating in synchrony. Gathering her courage, Song Xai pointed at the birds. "That is our dream, Grandfather."

"To visit the Sub-Saharan Bios?" He tilted his head like one of the tiny birds flitting through the branches of his garden—migrants lucky to avoid the harvesters in the befogged mountain pass. "It can be arranged, Little Blossom, but even I can't shorten the months in quarantine you must endure in both directions. Surely such a trip would disrupt your research."

Despite what depended on this conversation, she couldn't help but smile. "To fly, Grandfather."

He rose to his feet, startling the cats dozing around his ankles. "What?"

She stood also, bowing ever so slightly. "We have completed model prototypes stable in the four required dimensions. The new waterjet engine proved ideal for controlled propulsion through air. We are ready to build an experimental atmosphere ship to test with a human operator. To fly like the birds, Grandfather." Song Xai heard the longing in her own voice.

Her grandfather frowned. "The waterjet was developed in one of the American bios. How did you—?" His eyes narrowed as he looked at her. "Your 'visionary' colleague is one of *them*."

She blinked at the venom in his voice. "Most of our team is based outside this bios, Grandfather. There's nothing unusual in such collaboration."

"There was when I took my oath of service."

"The war has been over for a hundred years . . ." A war, Song Xai realized with a sudden chill, her grandfather had witnessed.

As had most of the world. The combined might of the western continents had sought to conquer the east, to overthrow six hundred years of growing, deliberate physical isolation, to reshape countries, bios, formed on the basis of naturally-occurring biomes. Their warships never reached shore and the western continents paid the price for misunderstanding their enemy. A knowledge of living things must include the knowledge of death.

When the diseases had run their course, toppling governments and economies, thousands of civils had volunteered to be exiled in the west, taking with them both cure and future.

Today, those born after the conflict saw only the result: a jigsaw pattern of bios, united by similarities in governance and mutual goals, completing a world where change was planned, scrutinized, and usually deferred.

Song Xai, like many of her generation, wasn't interested in waiting. "I need your help, Grandfather," she insisted. "We need to come together for the next phase of experimentation. I suggested here. Well, more specifically down the watershed, on the flood plains—" His upraised hand stopped the words in her throat.

The old man returned to his place on the bench, and patted the seat beside him. "Sit, Little Blossom." The words were heavy and slow.

"We will work with the civils at all stages, Grandfather," she assured him, even as she obeyed. "There will be every safety precaution."

"And what of the Shipping Guild? Have you spoken to them?"

"We will, once we succeed. The Guild will be in charge of implementing the technology—"

"The Guild will destroy it," her grandfather said softly and with utter certainty.

"But—but why?" She wanted to take his frail shoulders in her hands and shake him. Instead, she used words. "Flight will do so much for us, Grandfather. Imagine being able to travel anywhere, quickly, without the need for canals or tracks. Some of our group postulate similar machines could reach high into the atmosphere, possibly to space itself. What wonders await us there?"

"Nothing worth the risk," he told her. "The Shipping Guild protects us. They know their duty: no living thing may move from one bios into another unless it is free of disease and historically occurs in both."

"Our atmosphere ships won't change that," she protested. "The Guild would arrange sterilization and verification, just as it does for every ship and train now."

"And how long before someone young, someone foolish, someone malicious decides to build their own atmosphere ship? They will. We've seen it on the oceans and rivers. How can the Guild control the sky as well?" It was he who took hold of her, wrapping one chilled hand in his bent and dry ones. "Do you remember Zheng He?"

Song Xai couldn't keep the sullen note from her voice. "No."

"I'm not surprised. His grave was hidden, lest others become so—adventuresome—again." He gazed at her. "In the 1400s, he led the largest armada the world had yet seen—over 300 ships, some over 300 meters long—taking them to Africa, and what was then Europe and the New World."

"Then why isn't he famous?"

"Because on his return, China, his home, judged Zheng He misguided. He had found nothing of sufficient value to justify the risk of contamination from unknown diseases. The Shipping Guild records its first act as the destruction of Zheng He's fleet; their next the enforcing of new laws governing the maximum size of ships, so no others would be tempted."

"This is no longer China," Song Xai said, snatching back her hand.

"Yet this," her grandfather lifted his arms to the world, "came out of China. If you wish to fly, Little Blossom," he shook his head once in caution as she sat straighter, "if you ever wish to fly, you must remember how today came to be. You and your visionary colleagues must strive to become members of the Council of Civils. If and when you succeed, you will know for yourselves if your passion is truly wise for this world. If it is, you will build your atmosphere ships."

Song Xai gazed into the pond for a moment, then looked up at her grandfather. "Done that way, it will take my entire life."

Song Li's face creased into a hundred tiny smiles.
"Little Blossom. Is that not what dreams are for?"

Revision Point

Plague. The Black Death. *Yersinia pestis*, the
bacterium responsible, killed untold millions in
Asia, Europe, and Africa. It passed like a storm
of death over a world without the knowledge
of life and disease we possess today. Perhaps
the most infamous epidemic began in the early
1300s, when a ship carrying infected rats, and
their fleas, is purported to have landed in Venice with goods from China, already ravaged by
the disease. From there, the plague spread
until it helped plunge Europe into the Dark
Ages, causing unspeakable hardship.

The plague bacillus was discovered in Hong
Kong, in 1894, by Swiss scientist Alexandre
Yersin (and by Japanese bacteriologist Shiba-
saburo Kitasato). Shortly afterward, Professor
M. Ogata, of the Hygiene Institute in Tokyo,
found this bacillus in rat fleas. But the experiment to prove that the flea was the vector,
carrying the plague from rat to human waited
for a Belgian, Paul-Louis Simond. In 1897, after
noticing flea bites on infected humans, Simond
found that if he let fleas from a plague-killed
rat reach a healthy rat, that animal would be
infected by the plague. Eradicating rat fleas is
now a fundamental weapon against the plague.

At the time of my story, the Chinese already
made and used pyrethrum—essence of
chrysanthemum—to repel fleas. They called
the plague the "Disease of the Rats" because
they'd observed a mass death of the rodents

always preceded an outbreak in humans. They had a civil service staffed with scholars, who had to study and pass exams before being accepted.

If only one of these scholars had done Simond's simple experiment before that ship left for Venice, what else might have come out of China?

J.E.C.

SITE FOURTEEN

by Laura Anne Gilman

"**N**EREUS Shuttle Four to Gateway Station, you have control."

Robinechec nods confirmation as though the pilot could see him. "Roger that. Bringing you in." I watch as, palming the flat-topped lever, he moves it gently back toward him, pulling the bullet-shaped transport into the shed, an external framework of metal beams just large enough to hold two minisubs, or one shuttle.

Robinechec has nightmares sometimes about something going wrong here. Forget the fact that it's the safest maneuver in the entire procedure; he still talks about waking up in a cold sweat because he screwed up.

You'd never know it to watch him work.

When you're six hundred feet down—well below the twilight zone, in the bathypelagic or "deep water" zone—your perception shifts. Nothing as arcane as the chemical balance in your brain changing, although there's some of that, too. No, it's more the realization, slowly sinking into your brain, that there's not damn-all between you and dying but a duraplas shield and some canned oxy-blend.

You realize that, really process the concept, and you're okay. If you can't, you get the screamin' mee-mies and they cart you Topside where you spend the rest of your life on solid dirt, carefully looking any-where but oceanward.

Not everyone's cut out to be an aquanaut. No shame to it. Even now, only about a third of the appli-cants make it into training, and more than half of them dry out before graduation.

The shuttle docks outside with the faint bump-suck noise of a solid seal. Lights on my board match the one on the wall as they cycle from amber to green and the door slides open with an oily hiss.

I don't have to be here for this, but I always am. Call it a benefit of rank, to take the fun stuff with the boring. "Welcome home, boys and girls. Please show your tickets, next station stop Site Fourteen."

Fourteen, for the thirteen tries before it. First through third were qualified successes: nobody died when the hardware failed. Fourth left bodies floating in a pressurized can: irretrievable. Five and seven were mothballed after the regions became unexpectedly un-stable. Nine was a chemical misfire: four more memo-rials floating out at sea. You can see them on sat photos: orange markers rising and falling with the waves, never moving from the graves they mark.

Robinechec checks ID through the scanner, like there's some way unauthorized bodies could make it this far, while the arrivals step through a full body scanner one at a time. He nods. Everyone's clean.

Clean's a good word for it. The Gate room is sparse, the sole console fitted with a clear plastic cover for emergencies. In case we have to hose down the room for some reason, or—God forbid—there's a lock breach. Despite regulations, we try to keep it homey, anyway. There's a ficus tree in one corner, under a battery-powered grow light, and a welcome mat on the floor when you come through the scanner and another one that says "come again" in bright pink letters when you leave by the Slide.

You take your humor where you can, I suppose.

"Hey, Martin. You coming down with us?"

I shake my head in regret. "Not this time, Kim. Chosen People and higher, only."

She laughs like it was a joke. Until now, nobody without Secret clearances got past us. Even the construction geeks running the prefab plas shields into place got screened like they were having tea and footsie with the President. I'm just the guardian at the gate. But what a gate! What an unbelievable dream of a gate.

Forty years ago, Kennedy promised that we'd reclaim the seas. It's taken longer than we thought, but Fourteen's the next giant step toward making that promise come true. It still awes me that I'm part of it.

The five newcomers enter the chute and strap themselves in with a minimum of fuss, low-voiced conversations continuing without a break. Kim's got fourteen slides down to Site Fourteen, the others no fewer than six. It's like taking the subway to work for them, I think. Means to an end.

Used to be a submersible would take you into the depths on its own power. That ended with Site Eleven, and the first Slide, back in the '80s, putting the Goddard engine to uses its creator never dreamed of. Safer this way—even if something goes wrong, we can pull them back from up here. Safe as houses. Hell, one of the dive-boys went down on a dura sled a year or two ago, testing out one of the Navy's new equalizer headsets that are supposed to protect your eardrums in a high-speed drop. Headset didn't work all that great, but our dive-boy was grinning even while the medics fussed around him after retrieval. Said it was like taking the wildest, longest pool-slide in the world.

We haven't been able to do anything about the slow climb back up, though. Yet. Rumor has it the brain-kids at NEREUS' think tank are working on a way to pull the nitrogen buildup out faster. Cutting the decompression day out of shift rotation will make a lot of people happy, for damn sure. We get more fights break out in deco than we do anywhere else.

"Yo, you with us?" Gordon, who usually runs the board when I'm not poking my nose in, is impatient to reclaim his post. Standing aside gives him the right to yank my chain. "Let's get this show on the road, boss."

I nod and flip the toggle that connects me to the massive plas-and-metal growth half a mile below us. "Site Fourteen, this is Gateway Control. Sending you guys down a care package."

There's a delay, then the echo-soundbyte of Site Base responding. "Roger that, Gateway." They used to just ping us, but the brass got a bug up their butt and put a stop to it. Something about having voice check-in at all times. Like someone's going to sneak down there and take over? They've been reading too much Jules Verne. Nobody else has the capabilities, especially after the fiasco with the Chinese program a few years ago. When Jordon Mott snatched up the plans to that underwater breathing apparatus of Henry Fleuss' back in 1878, he knew what he was doing. So did the government, when they bought the patent from Mott's heirs during World War I. But the tech didn't really pay off until the 1950s, when the Cold War kicked into gear and control of the oceans became as much a public relations coup as a military one. Other countries can try and play catch-up, but

NEREUS—National Energy Research Endeavor: Underwater Services—made us the kings of the sea.

The door slides open, and Sanderson comes in, beady-eyed and mock-disapproving. Must be shift-end already, if Sandy's come to collect me. I swear, skip a few meals and some people don't know when to stop mothering. She claims it's just her duty as shift psychologist to make sure that the commander's taking care of himself.

Kim gives me a thumbs-up through the plas window, indicating they're ready to go, and I amend my earlier thought. *Royalty* of the sea. Despite her lack of height, she is queen of all she surveys. First draft pick right out of MIT, she's smarter than any four other geek-brains put together, and everyone knows it. Being in her rotation team is considered an honor.

She and I got staggering drunk in a Key West dive one night, Christ, almost a decade ago. Dry-eyed and emotional, she told me she'd never a moment regretted all the things she'd given up—spouse, kids, any kind of so-called normal life. "The ocean's the dream, Martin. And we spend all our days praying we'll never wake from it, y'know?"

We crawled out of the ocean primeval four hundred and fifty million years ago. There are folk who say it's a waste of money better spent elsewhere, that we should look forward rather than back. I look at the sat photos showing a blue planet, and wonder, where the hell else could we go?

"Site Fourteen, they're on their way." I tap the toggle that opens the Slide. Water rushes up into the tube, gray-green in the Gate room's lighting, and the capsule slips down before I can finish waving good-bye. Two weeks on the ocean floor, then another three days with us. Rotation up here's a month, plus twenty-four in deco.

The last time I was topside, I spent the first two days just staring at the waves. It all looks so different on the surface. Unreal, almost. The reality is all here, in rippling shadows of green and blue and black.

Robinechec resets the hatches, and I scan the boards. Green all the way across. In the aftermath of the Tube's whoosh, the chamber is almost painfully silent.

"You going to stare at that thing all day, or we going to get lunch?"

"Bite me."

Sanderson bares her teeth, and I offer her my elbow, as though daring her to try. The jumpsuit they make everyone down here wear is bright orange, like the markers. It doesn't look good on anyone, least of all a Scandy blonde like her.

Then again, color coordination's never been our strength. Bright orange safety fabric, the NEREUS trident logo in dark blue, and the Mariner Tech Program patch in foam-green and gold. It's one of the most god-ugly combinations ever invoked. Our names are sewn onto the left lapel, obvious in black, like we don't all know each other too many ways from Sunday. You don't get to work the Gate unless you've done time in the Mariner program, and you don't get picked for Mariner until you've been cleared to work for NEREUS, so there isn't a whole lot of turnover.

In fact, this project's had the same crews almost since the beginning: five years since they sank the pylons for the halfway station. Two years since the first materials went down to lay the foundations. Six months since Site Fourteen was pumped with oxyblend and opened for business.

Next Wednesday, they're taking her live. Site Fourteen will become NEREUS Station One, corporatefunded scientists and the academics will scramble for their place in the brine, and we'll have taken the next huge step to reclaiming humanity's birthright.

Christ, I get butterflies in my stomach just thinking about it, like the day before Christmas and your birthday and first day of school all rolled into one shivering ball of anticipation. I don't believe in any particular god, but if I did, I'd have to believe she/he/it would be smiling in pride.

"You good?" I ask Robinechec.

"Get the hell out of here, boss."

"I'll take that as a yes." Gordon steps forward as unobtrusively as he can, willing me gone already. I get the feeling they're handing control of me over to Sandy: one uptight commander, roger that and good riddance. "All right, you have the Gate. Try not to let any merfolk storm us, okay?" It's an old joke and they don't do it any favors by pretending to laugh.

Unlike the Gate room, the rest of the station's surprisingly comfortable. The walls are cream colored, and there's carpeting underfoot, a soothing brown-and-cream pattern that reminds us of soil, not sea. Or so the psych specs claim. There are more potted plants, and everyone's got something green and growing in their quarters; letting a plant die on your rotation is considered a pretty nasty insult to the person on the next shift, so we've developed intense green thumbs.

The dining room is midway on the station, with work space on one end of the elongated oval, and living quarters on the other. Down below, there's Control, where the techs spend their days poring over data coming in, sending data out. The Gate room and Slide are part of the working area, looking from the outside like strange growths on the otherwise sleek construction. Pundits who pointed out that the plans looked a lot like a flying saucer were missing the point—it wasn't science fiction becoming science; science fiction had stolen the basics from us.

The dining room is a cave, there's no other way to put it. But it's a cave with a view: half the room has a clear wall to the outside, and half is taken up with monitors on a 24/7 feed to the outside world. Everyone's watching the monitors, most of which are currently tuned to one news feed. We've got 148 channels and we still end up watching CNN more often than not. Even people who won't crack open a newspaper when they're Topside devour the news down here. So much for Casel's theory of learned inertia.

A moderate-sized giant squid floats by the dura window, briefly illuminated in the floodlights they installed to give us an actual external view: only the newbies bother to look.

The noise in here is astonishing. Seventy-two bodies serve on the Gate, and all of them seem to be having lunch at the same time. Whoever said the sea was silent never spent time here.

"Yo, Martin!" Leggo calls my name as he sees us, but whatever else he says is lost in the din. He tries to yell again, but his tablemates, still listening to the talking head reporting the latest movements from the African front, take offense. Leggo rolls his eyes, makes a silent come-hither motion with his arm. I shake my head, point toward the salad bar, then tap my watch.

"You still pissed at him?"

"Nah." And I wasn't. Much. So what if he'd managed to snag a date with Gretchen, who was only the most delectable hotshot to ever come down the Slide? He was too good a tech manager to begrudge a little nookie. When Leggo was happy, my techs were happy. When my techs were happy, Gateway hummed. Anyway, she dumped him a week later, and got tapped for a Topside position in Houston a couple of months after that. "There are some calculations on the OTEC expansion they want finished before next shift comes on."

"You're not the only brain down here, pal. Let someone else carry some of the workload." She's said it before, as friend and as psychologist. I just shrug. So I obsess. Every Mariner worth their patch does the same. This is our baby. Our dream.

"I promise I'll chew five times for every bite," I tell her seriously, and am rewarded with a long-suffering sigh.

"I should put you on report," she says, also not for the first time. "It's the only way I can make sure you'll get downtime."

I make a rude gesture, and escape before she has time to reply.

The taco salad is crisp, crunchy, and colorful. It also tastes like different flavors of desalinated water, but you can't have everything. I put the empty dish on the tray on the floor, shove it with my foot until it's out of the way. I'll drop it off in the recycling bin later, when I get up.

We don't have real offices here, just prefabricated half-wall cubicles you have to back out of, but the illusion of privacy is everything. The carpeting is thicker here than in the hallways, so our chairs slide over it without squeaking, and it absorbs conversations that are held at a low pitch. If you yell, everyone on-shift hears you.

As shift commander, I rate something double the size, which means I can turn around and pick something up off the floor without hitting my head, if I want to, and I don't have to share with my swing-shift equivalents. There are three of us—Marcie, Seth, and myself—and we each have a slice of office that's all our own.

I pull the keypad back out toward me, letting it hang for a moment while I consider the figures scrolling down on my screen. A tap of the space bar, and the numbers freeze in place until the thought clicks in my brain, then I start the flow up again with another tap of the keyboard. I don't have the answer yet, but I'm hunting it down. Something in the OTEC configuration isn't working at peak efficiency, and that bothers me almost as much as it bothers the folk Topside. But for them, it's a matter of professional pride. For me, it's a question of comfort. Be damned if I'm going to let them build any extraneous slack into the system.

"If not perfect, Lord, let me be both fast and accurate." The Mariner tech prayer, hammered into you from hour one. OTEC powers everything we do at Gateway, from the lights to the computers to the pressure in our showers. Only our toilets and our air pressure are outside the system—we have chemicals for the former, and a nice, secure, double-blind system directed from Topside for the latter.

A ping sounds from the console built into my desk, interrupting my mental progress. "Ping yourself. What's up?"

Gary's voice comes through clear as a bell, his usual academic precision softened by the hint of laughter. In the background I hear a weird wa-waaaing noise that means there are other people in the room, talking just beyond the pickup range. "Kimmie says you were frothing at the bit this afternoon."

"I was a perfect gentleman."

The site director snorts at that. "Yeah well, such behavior is rewarded. Just heard from the disjointed chiefs," our name for the combined brass of Mariner and NEREUS. "They drew names from a pointy cap. You get to lead the parade."

I don't think I choked, but something must have escaped because Gary just laughs. "You can thank me by bringing a bottle of the good stuff, not that rotgut they give us in Houston."

"Deal. Absolutely." There's a grin on my face you couldn't sandblast off. I'd just leapfrogged over a long list of dignitaries and political foofahs to be the first down the Tube when NEREUS Station went live.

Who says brown-nosing and sucking up never worked?

"Of course, all this presupposes our go-live date doesn't get pushed aside in favor of our brethren in the Armed Services getting some." Gary's voice is grim suddenly. "Tension's climbing again."

Way to ruin my mood, pal. "Saw that." Before he can make a crack I add, "Yes, I do catch the news on occasion. Personally, I think we should just go in there and shoot anyone holding a weapon, no matter what side they're on."

I can visualize Gary shaking his head, gray eyes rolling up in mock exasperation. "There's a reason they kept you in the civilian services."

"Damn straight." The ocean has her boundaries, but they're gentler ones of current and tide. And you rarely get shot for holding the wrong opinion on the wrong side. Unless that wrong opinion has to do with pressure per square inch.

"Kim says they almost didn't let her people come down, that they're talking about yanking everyone off the floor. For security reasons, they say." His voice reveals what he thinks of that. A sound in the background, higher-pitched waaa-waaaaaa, is probably Kim adding her own comments.

"So long as they're talking, we're working."

"From your mouth to the president's ears," Gary says. "Leave us alone and we'll get them their damned food sources." One of the few projects they have going down there that Gary can talk about is sea-harvest: finding a way to use the geothermal vents to force-grow protein. What else they're doing around the vents, I don't ask. We may not be—officially—a military organization, but the government's got its fingers in every pie, and I sleep better at night having lower clearances.

"Anyway, just wanted to make the news official, before you heard it through the gossip train. Congratulations again. We'll start warming up the welcome band now."

"You do that. Gateway out."

I save the file I had been working on before his call interrupted and push the chair back as far as it will go, just enough room for me to put my feet up on the desktop and stretch my arms behind my head; the timeless pose of a soul in contemplative relaxation. But my brain's going a mile a minute in a completely different direction than before. This kind of acknowledgment might mean I'm in line for a new assignment, something with higher visibility, better retirement levels. Problem is, most of those jobs are Topside, pushing papers and talking to the Press. Christ. I'm a Mariner, I'll dry out and die if they ground me.

On the other hand, it might also be a sop—sorry we can't do more, but here's your moment of fame and glory.

There are pluses and minuses to both, and it's going to take some weighing to figure out which option I'm hoping for. Still—

"Zweeeeet!"

I'm out of my chair and on my feet before my mind recognizes what's wrong.

"Zweeeet!" A klaxon bleating in the air, and amber lights flashing along the wall. The floor shakes once underfoot, and the desiccated giant red mysid perched on the top of my monitor falls to the carpet and breaks in two.

A decade's worth of drills takes over, and my heartbeat settles into something that's only panic-level. A lifetime of swearwords fight to get out of my throat.

"All hands, all hands. This is not a drill. This is not a drill."

A failure at Gateway would be intense red lights and a ringing of bells. This is a Site failure. *Please, God, let it be something small, let it be something repairable. . . .*

"Krrrreeeeee! Kreeeeeeeee!"

A second alarm, this one harsher, starts in counterpoint to the first. A particularly pungent curse escapes, and I break into a run. *NO! No no no no no. . . .*

Gateway seems small when you're trying to avoid someone, but want to be at point B when you're at point A, and it can seem like miles of hallways and hatches. I swing over the railing and drop the three steps that separate the living quarters from command. The alarm is muted here, but the amber lights flash as quickly, pulsing with my heartbeat. Worthy—the best-named kid on board—comes around a corner and matches my stride perfectly within two steps.

"We've dispatched Sub Three, as it was cruising in that vicinity."

"They didn't report anything beforehand?"

"Not a damn thing, sir." His ruddy skin is blotchy with stress.

"Fuck."

There's a sick feeling in my gut like too much sea-water swallowed too fast, an elevator in free-fall, cold sweat shriveling my skin and chilling my bones. I'd been a kid when Site Four went to hell. I still remember watching the coverage on television: serious-faced men in suits talking about instantaneous decompression and shock waves and acceptable losses.

There's no such thing as acceptable loss. Not then, not now. It may be unavoidable, it may be inevitable, but it's never acceptable.

Control Center is lit in an overdose of marine-greens and -blues, the kind of encompassing darkness that feels good at first, but makes you yearn for the sunroom at the end of your shift. There are too many people already crowded in there, a mass of orange faintly glowing in the darklight like a patch of fluorescent tube worms; I put a shoulder forward and plow through. They move aside like sheep, none of them taking their eyes off the action below. Someone hands me a headset and I clip it to my ear as I step down into the Pit. Seven stations, each one of them manned by some of the best, brightest, and most dedicated minds available to Mariner.

"Talk to me, people, one at a time." They are the best, but as commander on shift, the fan the shit is hitting is me.

"You on-line, McCarthy?"

"Yessir." Admiral Gregor Frants, scourge of the underclassmen when he was at the Academy. Mariner Project's Big Grouper, we call him. The conduit directly to the White House.

"What the hell is going on, Martin?"

"We're finding that out for you, sir." He knows that, damn it. He knows and is talking to hear the comfort of his own voice. I tune him out and concentrate on my own people.

There's a chair the OiC is supposed to sit in, more often used by someone's jacket, or once, for almost two months, a giant blue stuffed bunny someone had smuggled down for Easter. I pace back and forth instead, touching shoulders, glancing at screens where information flows in a steady stream.

"No reported seismic activity anywhere in the area, the blast was purely localized. Reading came from below and to the left side, traveling outbound."

"Roger that," a voice says in my earpiece. "Sats show no geologic movement in your area preceding the blast."

The satellite program had been a godsend to oceanography, but it wasn't perfect. No technology could compensate for human intuition and observation. Still, if they didn't see it, odds were it hadn't happened.

"Electrical systems are off-line. OTEC's still pumping, but nothing's being drawn down. Geothermal likewise."

Could mean anything. We do failure drills on a regular basis, nobody's going to panic just because it's dark. Hell, they sometimes turn off all the lights, interior and exterior, for a day or three, just to see what will go bump against their windows. Fucking scientists.

"Life support still registering, sir. Went to backup the moment of impact."

I breathe in; hold; out. Slow. Keep it cool. Hope kills, if you let it ride your decisions. That meant only that the backup is still working, not that there's anyone at the receiving end of it.

"No subs reported to be in your waters." Another voice from Topside, a cool, competent female voice. Thanks, babe. If there had been anyone prowling our zone, we would have known about it before Topside. Useless, they were all useless up there.

That second klaxon was the one indicating hull

breach. Worst case scenario. Hope kills. But hope is all we've got right now.

By the time console five chimes in, I'm at the master board, checking the displays in real time. Not that I don't trust what my people have to say, but they might have missed something, might have overlooked or misread.

"Reports coming in from other research stations." That female voice again. "Chatter's jumped, everyone wants to know what's happened." She reels off names; scientific outposts and military installations halfway around the world have felt it. The only thing that travels faster than gossip is gossip underwater. The ocean's a superconductor of disaster.

I can almost feel my brain split into two halves: listening to the clamor from Houston coming into the wire in my ear, sorting out what's needful and important and discarding the panic—panic filter turned way up high—the other half moving my hands, coaxing instrumentation in a desperate, already—damn it— hopeless effort to raise someone, some way.

"Site Fourteen. Site Fourteen, this is Gateway Control. Site Fourteen, respond. Gary, talk to me." My jumpsuit sticks to my back when I reach across the board, sweat thickening and stiffening the fabric. The two halves of my brain chatter at each other, trading information, making connections. So damn cold in here, shivers consuming my skin. No time for that now. Don't waste brain on it. "Fuck. Michaels, what's your ETA?"

"Three minutes." The voice from the minisub is hollow, fluted, metallic.

"Too much time." An impatient voice from Topside: worried, older, male. Not Frants.

"I know that," I snap. "Let me do my damned job,

will you?" Just cut off a general, probably. Screw it. I'll suck up to him later.

"Come on, people, give me something." Please. Please, God.

"Sir . . . site pressure's dropping, fast. Down to— Sir. We've lost all readings, sir."

"Life-support backup has failed." The red display on the left corner of my screen has already told me that.

"That's it, then." Topside, graveled voice of authority dropping and leaving silence in its wake.

"No!" Voices rise around me in protest against that silence. We still believe. We still *have* to believe. Those are our people down there. Our responsibility.

"Gateway this is Mariner Three. I'm almost on site. Too much silt down here, can't see for a damn. . . . Oh hell!"

"Michaels?" His voice had been panicked, beyond fright into an awareness of something dire and un-avoidable. And then an awful, quiet whoosh in my headset, followed by wet crackling static.

"Michaels!"

Something inside me breaks; very quiet, very gentle. I don't have time for this, not now.

I hold hope in my lungs for half a second, then: "Allen, send out a warning along the trajectory of the blast. Code it for widest vector—every language of the nations known to be seaworthy. Declare this area off-limits until further notice. All subs, back to dock. I repeat, all subs back to dock. Mission Control, we hereby request an AUSS system be dispatched." Advanced Unmanned Search System—the janitor of the seas, sent in to clean up where humans no longer go.

I feel the dull-edged stares in my back, and fight

the urge to defend myself against them. Hope kills. Whatever's going on down there—we have no idea what's happened. It might have been a freak accident. It might have been system failure. In this imperfect, knife's-edge world, it could also have been human action. It might have been deliberate. It might have been murder. I won't lose anyone else to find out.

I pace the halls, the sweat of my jumpsuit dried to residue. I probably stink. I can't bring myself to care. The sounds around me are muted, the lights dimmed or shut off.

It's past midnight Topside, in the halls of Mission Control. I can visualize it, if I try. Lamps still burning over coffee-strewn desks; quiet voices and self-doubt and if-onlies, those who aren't beating off the press or justifying themselves to the president and God and everyone else with a sudden interest in the fate of NEREUS. The only ones asleep are those who have medicated themselves out of the pain.

I don't have that option, not yet. Sleep is impossible.

Gateway station is empty: of the seventy-two warm bodies that used to fill the space, only seven remain. They're the cleanup crew, clearing and scrambling the servers so nobody can take anything from here but memories. Everyone else has gone already, hustled off within hours. Just enough time to stuff a kit bag, knowing you won't be back.

The last sub comes for us in the morning. Four hours, maybe five. I'll be the last one to leave. Turn out the last light. My responsibility. My right.

The wheels of investigation are already turning, but there's only so much you can do. The site is off-limits, my order confirmed by NEREUS Command. You can't send bomb-sniffing dogs in, or lay the pieces out on a hangar floor, backtracking until you come to the moment it all went wrong. All we have are records, and readouts, and the hope that someday we'll know what happened.

But that will have to wait. The country's drifting on other currents now, moving into war. It fights us for space on the news feeds, making reporters' heads spin with the glorious glut of news.

But all wars end, eventually. They'll come for Gateway itself then: there's too much here that can be reused, or worse, used by someone else. No squatters are allowed on our failures. The machinery of progress, the massive claws and levers of industry, will dismantle what can be reused, leave the hull sitting here, the Slide a rooted stem without petals, without a head. Rebuild farther down the ocean floor. Somewhere the orange markers won't mock us.

I'm broken and bleeding inside. I know that, the way you know impossible things that are nonetheless true. I'm bleeding inside, and it's flooding me until I can't breathe anymore. I don't know what I'm supposed to feel. I don't remember what I used to feel.

They tried to retrieve me first, bring me Topside for debriefing, but I wouldn't go. Not yet. There will be time for all that. There will be nothing but time, soon enough. The shrinks will pull it all from me, the anger and the pain and the fear. They'll drain me and patch me and if I'm not as good as new; well, nobody who knows will tell. And then they'll reassign me to a very important desk job, somewhere miles from the brine.

I can almost accept it. I'll lie to myself, all for the sake of the dream, that there will be a Site Fifteen. That Kim and Gary and Seth and Michaels and all the others didn't sacrifice everything for nothing.

Tomorrow, I'll believe that.

* * *

I've been walking all this time. It seems inevitable, somehow, that I end up outside the Gate Room.

Red across the board. Out of habit, I flick the toggle. "Site Fourteen, this is Gateway Control."

Somewhere inside the broken silence within me, I hear the echo of a single ping.

Revision Point

There were several turning points I played with in "Site Fourteen." Foremost among them is the invention of the first practical self-contained dive apparatus by Henry Fleuss in 1878. For the first time, divers were freed from lines connecting them to the surface, able to move freely (if only for very short periods of time, and at relatively shallow depths). At the time, traveling into the depths of the ocean was more the matter for novelists (Verne's *20,000 Leagues Under the Sea* was published in 1873) than serious scientific consideration, and certainly not a matter for, say, businessmen.

But what, I wondered, if some foresightful businessman had read about Fleuss' invention and seen the long-term, practical applications? Say, Jordon Mott, an American millionaire who had both the quirky turn of mind and the money to invest in such a thing?

Certainly, the invention of the first diving suit (actually in 1837) would have been sped up, with a wealthy investor funding undersea research. And once the money was there, the first underwater camera (Louis Boutan, 1893 in our time line) and the oxygen rebreather (Draeger, 1911) could conceivably have followed in close order, as natural human scientific curiosity developed the need for them.

And if the government got involved in the possibilities of the deep sea (as they did in our time line during the early years of submarine warfare) it seemed entirely possible that we would have NEREUS rather than NASA. . . .

L.A.G.

SILENT LEONARDO

by *Kage Baker*

1505 AD

THE inn is dark, low, and uninviting. Its ale is not good, nor are its rooms cozy. The locals give it a wide berth. Even travelers benighted in English rain generally prefer to ride on to the next village, rather than stop at such an unpromising spot.

This is precisely why it stays in business.

The inn, as it happens, is subsidized by certain shadowy men. They made themselves so useful to the late king that their services have been retained by his usurper. Royal paranoia keeps them on the move, listening, spying, collecting evidence; and this remote country tavern has proved a great place to meet unseen, to interview witnesses, exchange information. Or to sequester those whose status is somewhere between political prisoner and guest. . . .

The man entering the inn has no name, at least none that will ever make it into history books. He hangs his cloak of night on its accustomed peg. He climbs the stair without a word to the innkeeper. He has no need to give orders.

Two men are seated at a table in an upper room. He sits down across from them, studying their faces by the light of one candle.

They are both men of middle age, in travel-worn garments. The one leans forward, elbows on the table, staring into the eyes of his visitor. He has a shrewd, coarse, sensual countenance, like an intelligent satyr. The other sags back against the wall, gazing sadly into space. He has the majesty of a Biblical prophet, with his noble brow and milk-white beard, but also an inexpressible air of defeat. The visitor notes that his left arm, tucked into a fold of cloak, is withered.

Preliminary courtesies are exchanged. The satyr speaks easily, with ingratiating gestures and smiles, congratulating the visitor on his precise Italian. Ale is brought; the satyr seizes up his tankard, drinks a toast to their enterprise, and wipes his mouth with the back of his hand. He begins to speak. Unseen behind a panel, a clerk takes down every word.

No, he don't talk. That's what I'm for!

Is he my master? No, no, Signore, we're more sort of partners. Almost like brothers, you see? His mama and mine, they lived on the same farm. But Leo's a gentleman, yes. Father was from a good old family. Much too good to marry his poor mama, but Ser Piero couldn't get no sons by any other girl, so he kept his boy and brought him up, with a tutor and everything.

And was the boy smart? Why, Leo was writing with his left hand (and, you know, that's hard to do) by the time he was four! But then, one fine day, we boys were playing out in the orchard, and there was this big apple out on a high branch. Leo climbed out after it. And the branch fell! Boom, down he came and broke his left arm. Broke it so bad, the bones stuck out and the doctor thought it might have to come off.

Even when he saved the arm, it didn't work so good anymore. It'd been shattered. Never grew right, after.

So then, Leo had to learn to do everything with his right hand. And I guess maybe it threw his humors out of balance, because he started to stutter. Stammered so bad nobody understood one word he was saying. Except me! I *listened* to him, you see, Signore? And I could, uh, interpret for him. He got so he wouldn't say nothing to nobody, except when I was around. We got such a, what's the word, such a rapport, Leo and me, that I know what he wants to say before he says it.

And his papa said, "Say, Giovanni, you're such a smart boy, my Leo needs you around to do his talking for him. You come live with us. I'll pay you a nice salary." Which was a big opportunity for me, I don't mind telling you. When Leo was studying in books, I got to play in the street and learn a little something of the ways of the world, you understand? And I learned how to fight, which was good, because nobody dared call Leo a dummy or steal from him, while I was around.

I said, "Don't feel bad, Leo, you're plenty smart! One of these days we'll get rich off your cleverness, wait and see!" And we did, Signore. Plenty of times, we've been rolling in scudi. We just had bad luck. It could happen to anybody.

Ah! Well, let me tell you about Florence. Leo's papa sent us to Andrea del Verrocchio, that was a big rich painter there. I said: "How are you today, Signore? I'm Giovanni Barelli and this is Leonardo da Vinci, and he's the greatest painter you're ever going to teach, and I'm his manager."

Signore Andrea didn't take that too well. He must have been thinking, "Who are these kids?' But he looked over Leo's little pictures that he done, like this rotten monster head he painted on a shield, with dead snakes and flies so real you could practically smell it, and he agreed to take Leo as an apprentice.

It probably didn't hurt that Leo was good-looking as the Angel Gabriel himself, in those days. Those artistic types, they like the boys, eh? Saving your grace's presence, but that's how it is in the Art World.

So we settled into that studio, with all those other boys there, and Leo painted better than any of them. He painted so good, pretty soon he was better than Signore Andrea. Signore Andrea painted this big picture of Jesus getting baptized, but Leo helped him some. And, I'm telling you, there were these two holy angels standing side by side in the picture, and the one Signore Andrea painted looked grubby and sneaky as a pickpocket, but the angel Leo painted was just beautiful, shining so bright you'd think he had a candle stuck up his, uh, hidden under his robe or something.

I watched Signore Andrea, and I could tell he wasn't so happy about this. The little boys were crazy jealous, and I knew sooner or later somebody would slip poison into Leo's dinner. So I went to Signore Andrea, I said, "Thanks a lot for the training, Signore, but it's time my Leo opened his own studio someplace else, don't you agree?"

But he didn't agree. He said Leo had to work for him a certain number of years and a day, or he wouldn't get into San Luca's Guild, blah blah blah. I saw Signore Andrea didn't want no competition. So I knew it was time to get us some leverage.

Any rich man has secrets, eh, Signore? You know what I mean, I can tell. And I could climb drainpipes real good, and open windows, too, and get locked cabinets open with one of Leo's palette knives. Pretty soon, I knew some things about Signore Andrea I'm sure he wouldn't want the Pope to hear about. You'd

be amazed how fast he changed his mind about Leo
getting his own studio, after I put a little word in his
ear! Even threw in a nice parting gift of money.

And, Signore, the commissions poured in! Big mu-
rals for churches. Painted shields and armor. Portraits
of little rich girls. Half those little girls fell in love
with Leo, good-looking as he was. Of course, to talk
to him, they had to go through *me*, and I wasn't so
bad-looking either, in those days. Life was sweet,
Signore.

The only problem we had, and I'm only telling you
this because it turned out to be a blessing in disguise,
was, if I left Leo alone in his studio while I was out
with Ginevra or Isabella or Catarina, I'd come back
and find he'd been, uh, distracted by his little drawings. Just filling up page after page with pictures of
his hands, or water, or clouds or dead mice or anything. "Leo," I said, "think of that nice bishop, waiting
for his painting of the three wizards adoring Baby
Jesus! You got to concentrate, Leo!" I told him.

I thought if I took his pens and paper away and
locked him in, he'd have to paint. And it worked. But
then one night I came in late, and I was a little,
maybe, upset, because I was having troubles with Isabella, and I went to let Leo out so he could eat. There
was this big canvas he was supposed to have been
working on, still white as Isabella's—well—he hadn't
painted one brushstroke on it, Signore. What he done
was *drawn all over the walls*. I was so mad I socked
him, boom, and he went flying. The candle fell and
set fire to his straw mattress. What I saw, with the
room all lit up, was that these were all drawings of
machines.

Which was something new for him, see? Instead of
useless things, here were pictures of gears and blades
and ratchets, with soldiers and horses getting cut to

little pieces by them. "Giovanni," I said to myself, "You're looking at a fortune here!"

So I beat out the fire, and I gave Leo all the pens and paper he wanted. I went off to the kitchen and made him a nice dish of fried cheese. And while I cooked I figured, figured, all the time figured the angles.

Well. You heard of Galeazzo Sforza, eh? Duke of Milan, Lord of Genoa, the one they call *il Orrendo*? Yes, him.

He was crazy mean. The kind of little boy that liked to pull wings off flies, and worse when he grew up. No beauty, either; eyes too close together and a weak chin. But he respected artists, Signore.

The duke had only been on the throne a couple of years then, but people already knew the way his tastes ran, which is why I thought of him when I saw Leo's pictures. So Leo wrote this beautiful letter to him, about what he could design for his dungeons and armies. I told him what to write. Such a letter we sent, Signore! Such a lot of promises we made. I knew it was our necks in the halter if we couldn't deliver, but I had faith in Leo.

Pretty soon the duke sent a letter back, too, mostly saying "Why don't you boys come to my palace in Milan so we can have a nice little talk?" It came at a good time, because Isabella's papa was about to send over a couple of *his* boys for a little talk with me, you follow, Signore? So I bundled up Leo and his books and his papers on one fast horse, and me on another, and away we went.

Now, one book Leo had with him was by this old Greek named Hieron, full of clockwork and infernal machines. Leo studied the whole time we traveled. First, he copied the pictures. Then he made new drawings, taking all the old machines apart on paper and mixing up the pieces. Every inn we stopped at, he'd sit there at a table, drawing, while I got the drinks and talked to girls. We had to buy another horse to carry all the ideas Leo had.

We went to see the duke, in Milan. You know what he was doing, when we were shown in? He was gambling with a pretty girl. He'd bet her, she couldn't keep an egg in her open mouth from the stroke of noon until midnight. Her father's life was the stake. She was standing there the whole time with tears in her sweet eyes, her mouth stretched wide around this goose egg, and I knew her jaws must have been aching bad. He was just ignoring her. If I didn't know what kind of man he was before, I knew then.

But I acted big, I told him about the great machines Leo invented, that would make him powerful as Caesar, Alexander, Charlemagne! And, maybe I'm a little crude when I express myself, and I was only a country boy then and didn't know much about impressing people. I could see the duke smiling, like he was going to enjoy sending us to the dungeon for wasting his time.

Lucky for us both, Leo had his papers with the drawings all ready, and his beautiful clear handwriting that anybody could read. Leo bowed before him and offered the sketchbook. The duke looked at the pages, and he couldn't take his eyes away after he'd seen the picture on top. He started reading, saying nothing, turning pages. After a while he called for some wine. He didn't give us any. We stood there, and the girl stood there, too, with the egg still in her mouth, staring at us. The sun slanted across the tiles on the floor and the fountain outside splashed the whole time.

Finally, the duke closed the sketchbook. He asked Leo if he could really build all these devices, and I told him of course we could! Only, we'd need some of his best armorers and blacksmiths, not to mention money. "Well," said the duke, "Smart boys like you, you'll have everything you want!"

I thought to myself, "Giovanni, your fortune's made!"

So you can imagine, Signore, how I nearly wet myself when Leo walked over to the girl and took the egg out of her mouth. Who were we, to criticize a rich man's fun? But the duke, he took it all right. He just laughed and said we could have the girl, too.

Her name was Fiammetta. She was crazy in love with Leo from that moment. Waited on him hand and foot, in the nice rooms the duke gave us. Cooked and cleaned and brushed his clothes, which was nice for me, because I was too busy for that now.

But, Signore, you should know that Leo is chaste. Eh? No, no, not like that at all. It's all *up here* with him, see? So you can be sure there wasn't nothing sinful going on. Which I'm telling you in case your king has any question about his morals.

So, I got busy. We had a whole kind of blacksmith-studio to build, and workers to hire. I got a clerk to copy Leo's drawings and pass them out to the workers, so everybody understood what we were making. There was iron and coal to buy. Getting it all up and running was like making a big machine, too, but I'm good at that. I can run around, yell at people to get going. I push things, you see? And I pushed Leo on the job, so his mind didn't wander. He kept wanting to change the design once he'd finished, kept having new ideas. "Leo," I told him, "Get *organized!* One thing at a time!"

But once all the workmen understood Leo's designs, he could afford to draw his little pictures. The big machine started rolling. The master smith, smart man named Tognazzini, such a pity he's dead now, he really caught fire with the idea of Leo's steam engine.

He even pointed out one or two ways it could work better. Pretty soon the forges were going day and night. The workers were coming in all hours and forgetting to eat, they were so excited.

The duke himself came in to watch. I showed him all the models, and the work going on. He had the brains to appreciate good ideas. He was happy with our work, I tell you. There was a look in his nasty little eyes that was almost pure. You know what I mean? Bad men don't love God or other men, but sometimes they love *things,* and that's the closest they ever get to being human.

So what happened? The duke got himself armed for war and, sure enough, one started. The Ligurians sent in condottieri to take Pavia.

Yes, Pavia, you know the name? Famous siege. Changed the way wars were going to be fought forever after, and I should know, because I was there. You want to hear what really happened?

Pavia was defended pretty good. *Il Orrendo* had built new walls only a little while before. The condottieri got there and saw they had one tough nut to crack. Then up came this Pavian traitor named Lazzaro Doria, and he said to them: "Say, there's this big place called the Mirabello over there. It's the duke's own hunting estate with walls and a castle, and he ain't home. If you camp there, you can starve out the Pavians from a nice defensible position."

"Good," said the condottieri. Pretty soon they were living high, eating venison from the duke's own park while the Pavians were rationing food, marching out in the morning to make big threats and fire off a gun or two. At night they slept in the duke's feather beds. One soft campaign!

Until the duke heard about it. I was there when he

got the news and I saw him smile. *Uh-oh,* I said to myself, *I sure wouldn't want to be those condottieri.*

"Barelli," he said, "I think we'll give our new toys a test. Load the engines; we're going to Mirabello."

Well, *that* was easier said than done, because of what-you-callems, logistics. But I'm good at pulling things together, see? All we had ready was the Horse, but I pulled Leo from playing with his models and got him to make a few changes. We finished a few other little surprises, too. And on the day the wagons rolled for Mirabello, Fiammetta begged to come along. Just like a woman, eh? Crazy in love. We took her with us, in the baggage train.

You should have seen us marching along, Signore. Soldiers with their steel armor shining in the sun. The duke with his pretty armor and the Sforza banner streaming, such bright colors! What a day that was, the sky so blue and the hills so green! Leo rode next to me on a white horse and half the soldiers thought he was an angel, with his golden hair, sent from God to work miracles for us. The war-wagons were all loaded, so heavy their axles creaked, with bad news for Mirabello. . . .

You a soldier, Signore? No, that's none of my business, you're right. But anybody, soldier or not, would have admired the duke's strategy.

When we got to Pavia, the duke ordered his men in without any of the special stuff we brought. Just like they were an ordinary army come to relieve Pavia, see? The condottieri were caught with their pants down, saving your presence, but they beat his men back and ran to Mirabello.

So there they were, safe behind the wall of the park. The game was turned on its head, a siege to break a siege. The duke brought his army up and occupied the land north and east of the park. He sent his herald to the Porta Pescarina to say, "Hey! You! Genovesi big shots! Come out here right now, or I'll send your heads home to your mamas in a bunch of fruit baskets!"

The condottieri didn't know *il Orrendo* like we did, or they'd never have said what they did in reply, which was something real rude, saving your presence. He got their answer and he smiled, and spit out a fig he was eating and said: "Barelli, let's have some fun with them."

So I grabbed Leo and we ran back to the wagons. I ordered the Horse to be unloaded.

The duke sent troops in a feint attack, as though they were going to breach the wall at the Porta Pescarina. He did it so slow, and so obvious, the condottieri laughed and whooped from their places on the wall. But in a few minutes they stopped and got real quiet, looking east, where our wagons were.

What they saw, Signore, was teams of men pulling on ropes, raising with pulleys and tackle a big monster, an iron Horse. We'd brought it lying on its side, lashed to three flat wagon beds. It rose up slow. When it stood at last, tall as a church tower, it looked like Sin and Death.

It stood there maybe a half hour, while we made it ready. All the time the condottieri were staring at it, trying to figure it out. We could hear their officers telling them it was just a Trojan Horse. "That's the oldest trick in the book!" they said. "Dumb Sforzas!"

But then it began to roll forward, all by itself, belching steam. The rumbling and clattering it made was the only sound for miles. The condottieri were frozen like rabbits. We hardly drew breath ourselves, watching it. The duke looked like he was in church, seeing something holy. Leo was biting his lips to blood, praying I guess that everything would work. Fiammetta was crying, but that's what women do, eh?

And the condottieri were so busy looking east, they didn't think to look north, which they should have done.

Because, there was the duke's cavalry, racing along like they were at full charge. But they weren't charging the walls, Signore. They were pulling the flying machines. Yes, that was the first place they were ever used. You didn't know? Leo's invention! Oh, he sweated blood over those, his little clockwork bird models, no use to anybody until I slapped him and said: "Not flapping, gliding! Look at how vultures fly, dummy!"

Fast and faster the horses ran, and men ran behind holding up the big machines with their spread canvas, bouncing, looking foolish until they lifted off—one, two, three, ten angels of death rising up on black wings! And such big shadows they cast, crossing the bright face of the sun that day. You had to look hard to see the tiny man in each one, clinging tight to the framework, but I could make them out, and, I'll tell you, Signore, every one of them had wet himself.

Some crashed right away, ran into trees or only got across a few fields before coming down, but there were three that remembered to work the controls. They circled and soared. Only one or two archers on the wall noticed them—nobody else could tear their eyes away from the Horse, that was coming on faster now, but it didn't matter. By the time they got a few shots off, the Flying Machines were high up out of range. Still they circled, just like vultures. Then—ha, ha!—they laid their eggs, Signore.

Yes, they dropped balls of Greek Fire, on the army camped in the park behind the wall. Dropped from so high, how far it splattered! What screams we could hear! Smoke began to rise, and you could see the men on the wall thinking: "We've been tricked! They sent this stupid Trojan Horse to make us look the other way while they attacked from the sky!"

But they were wrong, Signore.

Because, while half of them were running from their positions on the wall to try to put the fires out, the Horse just kept rolling closer. The ones who were smart enough to stay at their posts, you could see them wondering: "What's it doing? Do they think we'll let it through the Porta Pescarina?" Because, see, they expected a Trojan Horse to be full of soldiers. That's called, ah, what's that big word, Leo? *Misdirection.*

Only when it got right to the base of the wall did they figure out it must be some kind of siege engine. They started peppering it with crossbow bolts, which only tinkled off like rain. The Horse just stood there a minute, smoke coming from its nostrils like a real horse breathing out steam on a cold morning.

Then it began to rise up, rearing from its wheeled platform, and the gears ratcheting echoed loud over the field. I was keeping my fingers crossed because I didn't know if we'd made it able to extend high enough. But up it went, and pretty soon it brought its big iron forefeet down, *clang,* on the battlements. Men on the wall were hitting the feet with axes; no good. Up above, the Horse turned its head slow, like it was looking at them. Smoke twined out of its nostrils, past the flames dancing there, from the little oil lamps we'd built in.

Now, in the head there was a little room, with one gunner in there. He worked a pump. Nasty stuff—worse than Greek Fire, Leo's own invention—came spraying out of the head, igniting as it passed the flames in the nostrils, splashing all over the men on the wall. *Then* we heard screams! Some of them died right there, cooked like lobsters in their own armor. Some jumped down and ran, trying to get to the little Vernavola stream that ran through the park, but it was already full of men trying to wash off the Greek Fire.

And so they left the wall undefended.

Now, Signore, the Horse's head opened right up, like one of Leo's pictures of cadavers opened out, and from his platform the gunner opened fire over the wall, but not with a cannon! No, this was a machine with rotating chambers, fired hundreds of little shells, looked like bright confetti flying, but where they came down there wasn't no carnival, you see? *Boom boom boom,* black smoke and red flame, men flying to pieces, little pieces, arms and legs blown everywhere! We found them for days afterward, all over the park.

But that ain't the best part.

The Horse's behind had a room in it, too, and three men in there got busy, cranking the reciprocating gears, and the Horse's prick—is that the word in English, not too rude? Well, saving your presence, but that's what came out of the Horse, an iron prick turning as it came, with a burin on the end, all sharp points. It bit into the wall. Oh, we laughed like hell! Round and round it went, boring at the wall, one big screw!

When the screw had gone in deep, the men set the Horse in motion, thrusting and pounding at the wall like it was a mare. I thought the duke was going to rupture himself; he laughed so hard the tears were streaming down his face.

But when the wall broke, when it fell in with a crash like thunder, he was all business: he gave the order and his men charged the breach, shrieking. They poured through, looking like silver ants below the

Horse. Not that there was much work for them to do, when they got inside. You never saw such a sight in your life, Signore. Most of the condottieri burned black, or blown to bits, or both. It was fantastic. Magnificent. You wouldn't believe ordinary men could do it, but we did.

What happened afterward?

Well, ingratitude is a terrible sin. The duke got to thinking, I guess, that he could conquer the world, as long as he was the only one with these machines. He figured the only way to be sure nobody else got them was to see Leo and me didn't go nowhere, and the only way to be sure of that was a nice unmarked grave for us. Tognazzini put a word in my ear. Me and Leo were out of Pavia on fast horses the same night, you can bet.

. . . The girl? Oh, Fiammetta. Funny thing about that . . . she hanged herself, after the battle. Women! Eh?

But we went other places, made stupendous things. We never made another Horse, but *il Orrendo* got what was coming to him when it blew up the next time he tried to use it. That's how God punishes bad men. Plenty of other great princes were happy to see us! War ain't like the old days, Signore, oh, no. You don't need hundreds of peasants to send in waves against your enemy's walls; all you need is a few smart guys with a good machine or two.

And you don't need hundreds of peasants to work your fields, either, if you got the steam-powered plows and mowers Leo invented.

But that didn't go so good, with the riots and all; maybe you heard about that? Well, it's all quiet over there now. After we helped Cesare Borgia take over France, Machiavelli called us in. He said, so nice and polite: "What do we do with all these useless, disobedient peasants? Nobody needs them anymore. Please, Ser Leonardo, with your brilliance in solving logistical problems, with your unparalleled talent for orderly arrangement and innovative thinking—could you not propose a final solution to this problem?"

And, you bet, I kept Leo's nose to the grindstone until we had one.

But, can you believe it? Even with us being big shots with defense contracts, there's always some rich man after Leo's valuable time, trying to get Leo to paint his wife's portrait or some other foolishness. And that's the reason—well, that and a few other things, like Cesare Borgia getting murdered—that Leo and me thought we needed a nice vacation someplace besides Europe. So, we try our luck here in England, eh?

The satyr falls silent, gazing intently at his host. The melancholy man for whom he speaks appears disinterested in the conversation; he has watched the shadows on the wall the whole time.

The nameless man smiles, sips his ale, refills the satyr's tankard. With a slightly apologetic air, he explains that all this is most impressive; it is certainly an honor to converse with the men who fathered modern warfare. His master found the flying machines, in particular, of great use in the late civil strife. And it is a shame, before God, that such artistry of invention has not been suitably rewarded. However—

England has no need of the redundancy camps nor the crematoria. Two generations of dynastic war have left it with a shortage of peasantry, if anything; and in any case, it is a country of smallholdings. Steam plows, able to subdue vast acreage in Europe, might prove impractical in a country of lanes and hedgerows. Even if that were not the case, it has of late been rumored abroad that in Europe corn is so plentiful now, as a result of the new devices, there is even a glut on the market. His master is a thrifty man; it would scarcely be in his interest, therefore, to invest in steam-farming.

Perhaps his guests have another proposition?

The satyr narrows his eyes. He is silent a long moment, pulling thoughtfully on his lower lip. He glances at his silent friend, who does not respond. At last he smacks the table with the flat of his hand, laughing heartily.

Well, sure, we have lots of ideas!

And it's a good thing for your master we're here, and I'll tell you why.

You had those Roses Wars over here, right? First the Red Rose up, then the White, then Red, then White. Now your Henry Tudor's on top, but for how long?

England's confused. That makes the crown slippery on the head. I heard about those two little princes in your Tower, eh? Pretty convenient for you that they just disappeared like that. Who done it? Nobody knows what to think. What you need, Signore, is to *tell them what to think*.

Leo and me, we're old men, now, and we know something about human nature. You got to tell your story like it was the truth. Make it such an exciting story everybody wants to hear it, and make sure your version is the only one they get to hear. Then everybody will believe it. So, what do you do?

You get some smart poet to write a play, and you send actors to every village in England. Not just one troupe of actors, but a hundred, a thousand, and Leo will build steam-coaches to get them everywhere fast. Not in threadbare old costumes but in scarlet and purple silks, cloth of gold! Leo will make it so gorgeous the people have to look. He'll make it a spectacle, with fireworks, music, dancing! All to show how Henry Tudor is the best thing that ever happened to England.

You got to get your message out, Signore. That's how you'll win wars, in the future.

Revision Point

A Life Well Wasted: Leonardo da Vinci is the secular saint of science, the ultimate Renaissance man. His notes and sketches on such diverse subjects as optics, hydrology, painting, engineering, and anatomy remain impressive to the present day. The paradox, of course, is that he actually accomplished almost nothing. Da Vinci's career is a long catalog of unfinished projects. He seemed content to keep his discoveries to himself, encrypted in his mirror-image script, and all his marvelous inventions remained sketches, theories, experiments.

Still, so many of the "marvelous" inventions were singularly horrible engines of war. As it happened, the Battle of Pavia did change the face of warfare—but a generation later, and only in the sense of changing balances of power in Europe. Yet if da Vinci's genius had been harnessed and made productive, all the horrors of modern warfare might have descended to snuff out the Renaissance. Steam power was in existence as far back as the ancient Greeks, and might have been used to great effect for agricultural purposes—but how would unemployment have affected already-rising anger in the peasant classes? We can be grateful that princes who believed they ruled by divine right never had access to efficient modern methods of destruction.

K.B.

A CALL FROM THE WILD

by Doranna Durgin

No one ever has to know.
I'll take care of this here and now.
No one ever has to know . . .

WINTER followed him down from Utah's Markagunt Plateau.

Neil's breath came in clouds of white as the temperature dipped down for the night, ending a sunny day of painfully blue sky for the crisp middle-desert night of brilliant stars and familiar constellations.

The chill itself he didn't mind. The unseasonable clouds moving in from the west . . . those could pose a problem. Cold rain to chill his bones, sicken his animals, and rile the already furious river. Cold rain to trap them east of the crossing, vulnerable to wolves, to coyotes . . . to the pieds.

All of them, bound together in modern times by an age-old pastoral system. Neil, his two sturdy little tolting ponies, his gelding guard llama, and most of all, the five hundred sensible Churras under his charge.

As sensible as sheep ever got, anyway. Even personable, some of them. Neil had his favorites; all the *partido* herders did. With nearly five hundred ewes and another fifteen rams to service them, any herder picked out a few individuals for special attention. The uniquely spotted ones, with striking splotches of black and white among the brown, black, and graying animals who made up the herd. Those with odd horns—the rare polled ewe, entirely hornless among a flock of ewes with stumpy scur horns and rams with three to four horns apiece. Or the ram he'd named Screw not only for his enthusiastic performance but the curly twist of his upper horns.

They were commodities of wool and meat and breeding stock, left to his care and entirely isolated from modern society and conveniences. Throughout the summer he moved them around the high plateau's natural pasturage, receiving supplies from the roving camp boss and keeping the Churras close by dint of the tolters, bells on a few tethered sheep, and pure determination. Keeping them well-fed while protecting the range from overgrazing, keeping them safe from the thriving wolves, the bears, and mountain lions that called these rugged highlands home even in the late twentieth century.

But the Churras would die if they were trapped here.

Not from the cold. That would come upon them regardless, if more slowly in the winter lowland pastures that spilled out south of the Mukuntuweap Canyon and just north of the Arizona line. And not from the lack of forage, for they wouldn't last that long—none of them. Not the sheep, the guard llamas who so fiercely protected their herd and territory, or the swift, tireless tolting ponies.

A thin ululating cry startled the air, swiftly joined by others. A gleeful cry.

A hunting cry.

Neil lifted Zip's reins, halting the tolting pony along the eastern Mukuntaweap rim to listen carefully, pretending he could ignore the goose bumps the sound raised along his spine. The white dun's short, fat ears swiveled within a thick brush of pale mane and forelock, also listening. Unalarmed.

Neil took his cue from the tolter. Short, stout enough to carry any man, the tolters came in every shade of dun from near-white to near-black, red to sand. Bred for thriftiness, herding drive, and their amazingly smooth tolting gait, they made it possible for one herder to manage so many sheep in this high, craggy country. And now Zip as much as told him that the pied wolves were on the other side of the river, separated from them by the roiling North Fork and several thousand feet of canyon walls. Safe. For now.

But down at the river's edge and the south entrance of the canyon, the Churras would be smack in the middle of pied wolf territory. Caught there by unseasonable rain and rising water, they'd have to wait for the river to drop—and not even Neil's wickedly accurate shooting eye would keep them alive.

For the moment, he hesitated, the dark bulk of Watchman Peak looming before him and the flat expanse of the east rim behind him. He'd meant to push on tonight. Now he wondered if the smarter course would be to return to the station he'd just passed, spending several days there to wait out the rain and the river.

The pieds might find them there, too. But they preferred the lower elevations.

All except the one.

On cue, a lonely yip from well outside the herd perimeter gave tentative reply to the call of the pack. The loner. The exception.

Tenaciously pack-oriented were the pieds, notoriously so. Modern scientists said man had once tried to domesticate them, fifteen thousand years ago. *Give*

or take a year, Neil thought, and snorted softly. He
didn't believe it, himself—in spite of DNA evidence.
The creatures worked together in an eerie fashion, so
tightly knit as to read each other's very glance or the
flick of a huge, upright ear on the run, shifting formation, surrounding and harrying their prey with deadly
skill. The only thing Neil believed of the scientists'
claims was their interpretations of the archaeological
digs where ancient pied and man had died together.
Where man had let the pieds too close, and paid the
price. Massacre. Betrayal, if one could call it such from
a species so self-serving as to be traitors by nature.

Unlike the llamas, who understood their place in
the herd and embraced it with fierce intent. Unlike
the many domesticated creatures who served man—
the miniature horses who guided the blind, the compact scenting pigs who inspected vehicles for drugs
and explosives alike, the loud-mouthed, sharp-clawed
Siamese cats guarding hearth and home, highly territorial after thousands of years of specialized breeding.
Unlike the tolters, who trusted him so deeply they
had defied instinct to save him from landslide, from
predator . . . and now, he hoped, from flood.

No, the pieds knew only how to cleave to themselves, forming the large packs who harried every rural
farmer, herder, and unfortunate hiker across the low-
lands of Utah and the southwest, into the midwestern
states and even against the edges of the more populated southeast. They effortlessly shared territory with
the larger predators in the hard-to-tame western
states, avoiding conflict with anything bigger and
toothier than themselves. They evaded even the latest
predator detection devices, already in widespread use
in populated areas—where headlines constantly blared
of yet another clash between bear or big cat or wolves
and mankind. Indeed, the pieds looked after their own

with a wily skill that permeated folklore and news broadcasts alike.

Except . . .

That lonely yip again. The yearling pied who'd joined up with them at the spring crossing to summer turf, clinging to them all the way up to the Markagunt Plateau and circling just close enough to keep Ben the llama on constant guard, stomping and blowing and occasionally charging. Neil hadn't worried about the lone pied. No one even knew why, but every now and then the packs evicted a loner male . . . who inevitably perished. Alone, they weren't effective hunters of anything bigger than a ground squirrel, and they pined for the company of their own. That this one had survived to make the return journey with the herd surprised him, but unless the pack received him—and they wouldn't—the pied would die over the winter. He wasn't even worth wasting a bullet.

Not that he'd ever given Neil a chance.

Neil looked over the herd, thinking of his apartment in Rockville, small but snug and full of the conveniences he lacked on his summer rounds. Things everyone else took for granted, like plumbing and electricity and the computer games his nephew Cort had given him during the last winter holidays. Half the year Neil spent his time like a herder from the previous century, exposed to the danger of the wilds, living a simple life based on eating, protecting Churras, and surviving. The other half he rejoined contemporary life—fast-paced, full of disposable things and disposable people, making his last paycheck last until first the spring shearing, and then next *partido* contract.

When he made camp boss, he'd have work all year round.

Except he'd never make camp boss if he lost this

herd, never mind the college diploma hanging on his wall that declared him academically fit to run a ranch. He'd never make it if he lost even a tenth of the flock to either the river or the pieds.

Ben swiveled his head atop a long neck to look at Neil, his silhouette distinctive and evocative of the llama's characteristic pursed-lipped annoyance. Ben the alert, wisely uneasy at the increasing separation between Neil and the still ambling herd. Neil's second tolter had enough sheep sense to keep the herd moving evenly; Bessa tackled her job with a glint in her eye that Neil could only call wicked, whether she was under saddle or free of it. But Ben cared not about chivying from a chunk-bodied pony. If he looked to anyone other than himself, it was to Neil.

Neil again glanced up at the sky. Above the dark blot of darkness at the western skyline, Orion the hunter chased his prey, clearing the sky of predators. On his heels shone the bright star of Ovis, the sheep following safely in wake of the great hunt. *Be an omen*, he told Orion and Ovis, though he was more worried about the clouds than the great predators on this particular night. He touched his legs to Zip's sides. The pony leaped forward in his smooth, swift tolting gait, the sheepskin-padded saddle rolling evenly under Neil's seat.

They'd try to make the next station, where at the least Neil could replace the batteries in his tired hand radio and send out a trouble call. They'd try to beat the rain. And maybe, just maybe, the rain wouldn't even make it into this region. It didn't belong here, not in the strong, beating storms they'd been getting these past few days. Making a shambles of Neil's pasture schedule and turning a routine journey into nothing but trouble.

But they'd beat the rain. They'd reach the river.

They'd punch through pied territory in the daytime, and make the safety of the mesh-fenced range perimeter.

Because they had to.

Loneliness forced a whine, flattened the pied's generous ears. His long, lanky legs picked up a loose-limbed walk, pacing the sheep. A trot now and then, circling in the darkness when he got too far ahead. Watching the long-necked one for signs of trouble.

They were not of his kind. None of them. But they were all he had. He'd learned to lick splattered bacon grease off fire circle rocks once they'd gone cold and abandoned, he'd learned how close he could get before he was noticed by man, pony, or llama. He'd learned that the traveling herd often flushed small ground creatures for a quick satisfying crunch-and-swallow. Squirrel, shrew, even jackrabbit.

He did not go hungry. But he went lonely. This night he went lonely with the fresh cold biting the inside of his nose and the scent of rain waxing by the moment, all of which made him uneasy.

But not half so uneasy as the scent of unfamiliar human on the rising breeze.

A long-eared owl swooped from the hardwoods to the east, bringing its wings together in a clap of territorial sound. Zip snorted and shook his head, tangling a mane damp with the first drops of rain. The moon hung sullenly over the eastern treetops, as though it was trying to rise and the weight of the descending clouds kept it prisoner.

But Neil knew this spot, where the trees crept closer to the canyon's edge—beech, maple, and hard, thorned locust. The next station waited only moments from here—and the ponies, the llama, and half the sheep knew it. There'd be fences—mesh reinforced fencing, this close to pied territory—and shelter and the kind of food a man could throw into dinner within moments.

Even better, light already winked through the window, glaring in the increasing rain. Solar-powered light, battery-stored—it meant the boss was already there, changing his own plans to help Neil manage the herd in the unusual weather. No surprise. It's what a good boss did. It also meant the hot water heater would be fired up, the troughs already filled . . . Neil's wet late-night arrival suddenly became a lot simpler.

Within the trees, the lone pied wolf gave a sharp alarm bark. Ridiculous creature, the young pied—all lanky leg, with its bold calico-cat coloring and plumy brush of a tail trailing behind it. A pointed nose spent most of its time to the ground, and those *ears* . . . big, upright, scooped in shape and alert in nature. They flattened anytime the creature saw Neil looking its way, but that didn't surprise Neil. The pieds had an uncanny ability to read human expression and body language. Those scientists claimed the skill came as a result of failed domestication, of man's short association with the ancient pieds. Neil didn't much care, as long as the pied understood Neil's contempt for it, his desire to kill it. He thought it did. It never appeared when Neil's rifle was to hand.

It barked again, challenging something. Unusually bold. Within the Churras, Ben's neck lifted, stretching tall; he gave a blasting snort into the wet night and took a few steps against the tide of movement, toward the trees.

Not because of the pied. Ben knew the pied, ignored it as the pale threat it wasn't.

"Hold on, girls," Neil murmured to the sheep as their movements became more sporadic, signs of anxiety rippling through the bunched, rounded shapes. A shift of his weight sent Zip toward the spot where a bulge threatened to turn into sheep bursting away from the herd. "Another minute and we'll have you safely away. . . ."

Ben hesitated, looking from the station cabin to the woods rising from the tall grasses of the plateau, brushy hackberries making way for the taller trees. Thin at first but then . . . plenty of cover for anything from bobcat to bear. With economical motion, Neil jerked his rifle from the scabbard. Well-trained, Zip stopped, steady beneath him so Neil could aim and shoot.

If he'd known what to shoot at. Or where. For now Ben had settled his protective gaze on the station itself, taking a few swift and threatening steps in that direction.

But Ben knew the camp boss—had known him longer than Neil. Would never alert to him.

But he'd alert to human strangers.

Humans in the woods, humans at the station—

Bad news.

"Hold, Bessa!" he cried to the pony mare, urging Zip forward to help. It wouldn't be easy now, stopping the sheep when they had their mind set on the station. Not only stopping them, but turning them.

No man belongs here.

No man but one who's looking for trouble. Or to take a few convenient sheep along with them—or even the sheep fleece. He'd heard of such rustling operations, and the Churras grew fleece so fast that shearing them now, months early, would still provide an easily marketable fiber.

Losing fleece was better than losing sheep . . . but either would be the end of his chances for promotion. For this year, and maybe the next. For the chance at steady work, at building more than just a job. At building a life.

He'd take no chances with the occupied station. Exhaustion dropped over him with the realization that he had but two choices—back to the last station or forward to the swelling river, all in a drumming rain that chilled him deeply in spite of his canvas and goretex riding duster under the broad-rimmed hat that caught and channeled the rain away from him. Neither choice was a good one, and the animals were as tired as he.

Zip lunged beneath him, leaping forward to cut off a breakaway. The sheep thought to make a contest of it; the stout little tolter tucked his haunches and anticipated every move the woolly made until the sheep sullenly retreated into the herd. Neil, riding out the abrupt changes of direction with practiced ease, rifle still to hand, gave the tolter a pat of appreciation. Then he waved a broad direction to Bessa. "Turn 'em around!" he yelled. "We're going back."

The pied understood. The man wanted his sheep turned. *His* sheep. For the man was the alpha here, and the pied was the lowest of them all. The pied knew to leave alone that which the alpha claimed. He knew to cling to his edges, his barely acceptable perimeter. And he knew danger when he scented it. Unfamiliar humans, tainted with the acrid smell of gunpowder and gun oil and the sweat of those in fear and stress.

Those unfamiliar humans moved as the man moved the herd, chivvying it with the tired ponies. The unfamiliar humans circled, quick and quiet, following the woods to a spot where they could break into the open ahead of the herd.

The pied knew that hunting maneuver. Had used it.

Clinging to the shadows, he gave another warning bark. That was his job, though the man had not yet realized it. The youngest, the most submissive . . . the out guards. Warning the more valuable members of the pack when danger neared.

This time, the man heeded him. Noted his change of position and his persistence—along with the increasing agitation of the long-necked one. Lifted his shaped, noise-making wood-and-metal staff.

Not soon enough.

Neil understood immediately. Ben told him, the damned pied told him. Those in the woods were moving in response to his retreat. They'd try to cut him off. *Damn them.* And though he couldn't see them, not yet, he lifted his rifle—

He felt the impact before he heard the shot, rocking in the saddle as his upper arm took a bone-breaking bullet. He barely managed to keep hold of his rifle— barely managed to snatch Zip's pale mane and keep himself mounted. In the next instant Zip leaped forward, nearly unseating Neil all over again. *The Churras!* Rain pelted his face, escalating waves of agony clenched his arm at each new movement; he could not hold it close to his body and still grip the wet mass of mane that had become his lifeline. The night swept by in streaky images of shadow and shape, in the sound of running horses and the softer, endless ticking of cloven sheep hooves, in the smell of wet wool and steaming horses and his own fear and the sharp tang of his own blood, spilling freely down his arm and onto his thigh, streaming off the duster in a mix of water and life.

After a whirl of random movement they straightened and went downhill. Down, with only one thing at the end of their run, that which grew loud in his ears, a roaring that battled with and overcame the personal roar in his ears.

The angry river.

As suddenly as the run began it stopped, with Zip bouncing to a stop to avoid slewing them both into the river, his smooth tolting turned into a crow hop of desperation. Cold air bit at Neil's bottom as he lost the saddle; his mane-trapped fingers weren't enough to keep him there and he cried out an angry, betrayed curse as he lost his stirrups and still fought to stay mounted, knowing even as he greeted air that beneath him lay only the—

Rocks.

Panting at the edge of the herd.

Exhausted, as all of them. Rubbery legs, hot hot tongue. But the cold of the rain pelted against his wet fur. Not yet penetrating the soft, thick undercoat of his body, but soaking his legs, his ears . . . and soon enough, the whole of him.

The unfamiliars were behind them. One, attacked by the llama, smelling of blood. Another, lost in a sea of horned sheep and no longer moving. Others from the cabin, not yet following.

Not yet.

But the pied knew predators when he saw them.

Daring much, he slunk between the man's sheep to find the man himself. The alpha. He fully expected to be struck down, to find teeth at his throat. But he found the man motionless, bleeding on the rocks with his hands clutching the reins of the pony beside him. The pony, too, lay on the rocks, too used-up to stand any longer. Its breath still came panting from flared nostrils; it did not bother to notice the pied.

The pied licked a bloody rock. It licked the man's head where fresh blood still welled, and then pawed slightly at the arm that stank of being wounded, raw flesh and blood combined.

The man groaned; the pied startled away.

But it came back. Uncertain of its role, waiting for direction, even waiting to be driven off, it curled up beside the man to lick its sore paws and soak up what little warmth rose between them.

In the midst of darkness, the man shifted. He groaned, the kind of noise that comes from creatures not truly aware of themselves. By then the pied was a safe distance away, shivering in fear and cold and the startling *want* to return to that warm spot by the man's side . . . his first companionable contact since the spring. The loss of it made a huge spot into which his loneliness rushed.

Not far, a sheep lay cooling, stiffening in the night. Not the pied's doing . . . but he looked on it with hungry longing.

His own pack rules kept him from it. It belonged to the man. The pack leader. The pied licked his lips, drooling . . . and waited. The pack leader would not let him go hungry, not once the pied's submissive restraint became clear.

The man groaned again, and this time struggled to sit, reaching for the horse beside him in dreamy, fumbling movement. One-handed, he found the bulging leather case at the horse's flank and pulled an object free, a rustling, flapping thing that drove the pied even farther away.

When the pied ventured back, full only of weak and tentative courage, he discovered the man covered by a tarp, and rain beading to roll off the sides. Uncertain, he nosed the stiff material . . . and heard the others arriving. The unfamiliar, and those whose scents had started this miserable course of events in the rain. Those who had shed blood. His rain-soaked hackles rose, and he stalked the edges of the herd, Churras growing uneasy with the new intrusion. The pony mare called a greeting, was answered. Fake man's-light reflected off the wet backs of the sheep, the glistening blades of grass and the small bushy willows scattered through the area.

The pied glanced back. The man hadn't moved beneath his tarp. The man had no idea his territory had been invaded.

But the pied knew.

The pied crouched, whimpering. Shy and frightened and keenly aware of his role here. *Protect the territory.* The sheep were territory; the ponies were territory.

The unfamiliar humans on their unfamiliar ponies, easing in from the east . . . they did not belong in this territory.

The llama knew it; he gave an outraged snort, rose to his feet from the center of the herd, and charged the interlopers. A noose flashed through the darkness, looping over the llama's neck; pony and llama set against one another while men closed in on the long-necked one. The llama gave a sudden bleating cry, one the pied had never heard from its kind before. Moments later, it settled heavily into the grasses. The smell of blood came thick and rank.

In a sudden spurt of action, the pied sprinted from his hidden crouch, bolting through the rocky grasses in a streak of patchy color. All but invisible in the overcast night, he employed the only offense a single lightweight pied had at his command. He struck like calico lightning, slashing an equine hindquarter, a human leg, a soft whiskered muzzle. A horse grunted in pain; a man cried out in surprise. Someone lost control of his panicked mount and crashed away into the night, cursing until the crash of a branch silenced him.

The pied circled tightly for another run, darting and biting and slashing. What he saw clearly, the men seemed unable to perceive in the darkness; their fake lights strobed wildly through the night, hunting him. The ponies were another thing; a hind hoof flashed and the pied dodged—not fast enough. The impact knocked the wind from him and sent him flying to the side.

But it was enough. The men spoke sharply to one another, listened momentarily to the surging cry of the pieds closing across the river, and wheeled their ponies around, leaving in a hasty clatter of even-stepping hooves.

Panting with nerves, cold with the rain, the pied could not move right away. His breath steamed the air, offering up precious body heat. Moments passed; the men did not return. They were not night creatures . . . the daylight would bring them back. But the pied had done his job. *Protect the territory.* Eventually he dragged his bruised body upright. The disturbed sheep slowly huddled back together again, seeking the familiar, but they left a gap around the body of the long-necked one.

The pied went to it, snuffling and inspecting and finding it truly dead. With a furtive glance toward the man, the pied lapped at the blood of the llama's woolly neck, drinking stolen sustenance.

Then, mustering all its courage, it crept back to the man and nosed its way under the tarp to share the shelter and the warmth of their battered bodies.

Sunshine. Steamy warmth. The most excruciating pain.

At first Neil wasn't sure just what hurt. His whole body reverberated with it, making his world tilt and swoop. Or was it just that he had to—

Neil managed to roll over on the rocks before he retched up the meager contents of his stomach. For a long while after that he just lay there, head reeling, stomach roiling, his arm making it perfectly clear just what hurt the most. After a time, he recalled a sense of danger, regained a vague impression of the night's stampede. Remembered the stark biting shock of being shot, but not how he'd ended up on the ground. Not how he'd come to be under the tarp.

With an awkward curl of his good arm, he flipped the tarp away, looking down at himself. Formerly wet, now drying. Except for a patch along his belly and side, where his duster had come open and the layers between had all dried. And the ground beside him . . . a small warm hollow of dried grass, directly adjoining that spot he himself had kept dry. A tuft of white and black hair.

He frowned, didn't try to make sense of it. Spent a few precious moments ripping tarp with his hunting knife, binding his arm to his side in the most awkward of ways. Sweat poured off his face and sprang up on his chest; he took a timely lurch to the side and heaved over the rocks. Finally, carefully, he sat up.

Zip grazed to the south, saddle slightly askew, reins looped just behind his ears and under one hoof. As Neil watched, the pony deliberately lifted that foot, moved his head aside, and grazed on. Wise creature. No doubt the tolter had saved his life several times over during the night.

The other tolter, her light packs in place, grazed at the other side of the spreading herd. Ben was nowhere to be seen. Not far from Neil's uncomfortable resting spot, the river roared, full of rain and fury. They wouldn't cross it today. Maybe not tomorrow. A full-sized horse could make it, but not the sheep. Not the tolters.

He couldn't go back. The station was compromised. And he needed help, before this arm became infected and he lost it—or it killed him. He was lucky enough he hadn't bled out.

In his packs, the radio sat useless. Drained.

Abandon the sheep? Take a tolter back upstream along the canyon, where a footbridge over the narrows let a man cross?

Say good-bye to his career with that. The ranchers might nod, might understand and might offer sympathy for his plight, but they wouldn't hire him. Never mind the college degree, the two years of proving himself as a *partido* herder. He'd spend his time as an itinerant shearer who did catch-work the rest of the year.

Neil ran a hand over his face, rubbing gritty eyes and bringing his hand away bloody. He stared, puzzled, and began to understand that somewhere along the way—most likely right in this spot—he'd fallen from the pony and hit his head.

From staring at his hand, dirty and scratched and now bloody in all its work-worn creases, he focused outward. For the first time he found the dead Churra not far from him, its legs stiff in a parody of death, a grimace lifting its muzzle so its teeth showed, its dull eyes only half closed. No blood. Just driven to exhaustion in the pouring cold rain and stressed beyond its endurance.

Neil knew just how it felt.

Over the tumbling sound of water against rock, a high, sharp whistle hit Neil's ears. He turned—not too fast, but with the creaky bones of a man much older than his twenty-seven years—and caught the broad wave of a man on horseback, standing on the other side of the river.

The camp boss.

Relief washed over Neil, relief so great it caught his breath and came out in a short, sharp sob. He waved back, glad there was no opportunity for shouted conversation over the river noise. He couldn't have trusted his voice.

The man rode a tall, rawboned bay. He'd make it over the river and then back; he'd have food and he'd be able to radio for help. And most of all, the sheep were here. Not all of them; even in his blurry state Neil could see he'd lost more than a few. But it was the boss's job to keep the stations secure. As long as Neil hadn't abandoned the flock. . . .

He'd come out of this okay.

He took stock of things. There was his rifle; he caught it up, checked it. A round waited, chambered sometime during the night. He tried to remember; couldn't. Dammit.

Movement caught his eye: the pied. Gangly yearling pied with its sweep of a tail held low, its absurdly large ears canted back. Not laughing, as so many of them seemed to be. Worried. Focused on Neil, as if waiting to see what happened next. As if it mattered.

Neil looked again to the dry hollow beside his own resting spot, reached out to catch the clump of hair and rub it between his fingers. Soft. Undercoat. Surely not . . .

No matter. The pied would run when Neil climbed, so painfully, to his feet.

It didn't.

From his new vantage point Neil could see the ravages of the night. Three more sheep down, stiff and dead. The others scattered enough to make half a day's work in gathering them up again, some even straying uncharacteristically into the lowland willows, cottonwoods and hackberries that sprang up fifty yards back from the water's edge.

In the middle of it all he found Ben, a lump of llama fur somehow too small to have fit the animal's bold personality. Dried dark blood smeared Ben's throat, splashing down his chest with the powerful spurt of a cut throat.

He gave the pied a sharp, narrow-eyed look, seeing for the first time the way blood smeared across its face and, diluted by rain, pinked across the white fur of its chest. But no single pied could bring down a llama. No pied could even get close without taking damage.

The pied took a hesitant step. Limping. Stiff and sore, and newly bolted from the warmth of his place by the man's side. But he couldn't read the man's body words, so mixed up as they were with injuries and unsteady posture. Even as he watched, the man sank slowly down to his knees next to the dead sheep.

The pied gave a tentative wag of his tail, low between his hocks. Flattened his ears, tipped his lowered head slightly.

The man sank down lower behind the sheep. An invitation.

The pied took another step. He thought of companionship and warmth and the sheep this man might offer, feeding his pack members as he should. He thought of the strange satisfaction of a night at this man's side.

Another step.

No pied could bring down a llama . . .

But Ben hadn't been wary of this one. And here it came, covered in blood, limping and hurt. Kicked, as likely as not. *But no pied could . . .* He closed his eyes, trying to connect the unusually scattered sheep, the dead llama, and the wounded pied into some logical summation of this tortured night.

Behind Neil came the splash of the rawboned bay entering the water, its repeated snorts of disgust and protest. He shoved away the whisper of a thought that something wasn't quite right. That something *more* had happened than the seemingly obvious.

Because no boss would understand how Neil had let the pied live this long, never mind that it had been no threat. No boss would see the blood, look at the llama, and fail to mark Neil down as the most remarkably foolish *partido* herder ever to handle a flock of sheep.

No boss would give him a second chance.

Neil's rifle rested on the back of the dead sheep, the glint of its barrel hidden in wool, the muzzle aimed at the pied. Oh, God, it was all sly, all submissive, slinking up to him with blood on its lips. He glanced back at his former resting spot. Where there'd been two of them.

No one ever has to know . . .

His finger squeezed the trigger.

Revision Point

People have domesticated many animals, from companion species to the great variety of food- and fiber-producing creatures to working animals. None of these is more beloved—or bred to cover a greater spectrum of humanity's needs—than the dog. According to recent research, domesticated dogs came on the scene about 15,000 years ago, aided by deliberate breeding efforts in East Asia. But . . . what if our ancestors thought they had reason to reject rather than embrace an animal we now take for granted (and some of us can't imagine living without)?

D.D

AXIAL AXIOMS

by James Alan Gardner

The Axial Age (approx. 600 to 400 BCE):

PERIOD of intense intellectual innovation in Europe and Asia, including the births of Taoism, Confucianism, Zoroastrianism, Buddhism, Jainism, and modern Hinduism, as well as work by the great Greek philosophers and the later Jewish prophets; a renaissance two thousand years before the Renaissance, wherein older, more staid modes of thought were questioned and replaced.

Thus Spake Zarathustra (music by Richard Strauss[1])

Light. Dark. Light. Then fire . . .
(Light is the Wise Lord, Ahura Mazda. Dark is the Enemy, Ahriman. All persons, whether they know it or not, choose one or the other: life or not life.)
Light. Dark. Light. And fire . . .
(Those who choose light—they add to the world. Those who choose dark—they subtract. All people are

---

[1]*Also sprach Zarathustra* (Thus Spake Zarathustra) is a symphonic work by Richard Strauss. It is best know for its opening bars, the famous theme from *2001: A Space Odyssey.*

marked by the lord they have chosen: a sign invisible to earthly eyes, yet shining forth after death when all must pass over the Bridge of Judgment.)

Light. Dark. Light. Ahh, fire!

(The true signs of light and dark cannot be written by human hands. Yet, my followers, if you wish to carve symbols, use these: a simple cross for good, a horizontal stroke for evil. The cross points in all four directions, showing how the Wise Lord reaches over all the lands. The horizontal stroke suggests a corpse lying dead on the ground. The signs are unambiguous . . . are they not?)

Fire is light. And fire, it burns. Burns the dark.

Fan the flames!

The Zero'th Turning of the Wheel of Dharma

(Thus have I heard from the Buddha, the Enlightened One.)

My disciples, all is emptiness! All that lives, all that dies, the stones of the field, the waters of the stream, all, all is emptiness.

What is emptiness? Emptiness is the quality of a thing being nothing in and of itself, but being composed of smaller parts and having no existence except in relation to other things.

What is an example of emptiness? A cart. It is made of components: the wheels, the axle, the box, the hitch. Point to a cart, then look where your finger is truly directed. Behold, you are not pointing to something you would call a cart; your finger points only to a wheel or the box or the hitch. You cannot point to the cart itself—there is no cart, there are only pieces. The cart is a mental concept we impose upon an aggregation of components. At most, it is a sum of fractions.

Yet the fractions, too, are emptiness. The hitch, for

example, is made of wood pieces and leather bindings. The wood (when viewed closely) is made of smaller strands we might call slivers. Slivers can be split into smaller slivers . . . and who is to say how small one can go, components breaking into components, fractions breaking into fractions, emptiness into emptiness? An infinite regress of smaller and smaller fragments.

What does it mean, to have no existence except in relation to other things? A cart is useless unless it is drawn by an ox or by some other being; and a cart has no purpose except insofar as it may carry loads in its box. A cart makes no sense without an ox and a load. A cart also makes no sense except when a people's way of life requires heavy burdens to be borne from one place to another. Yet again, the cart makes no sense unless there are roads that connect starting points to destinations. Is there not a dependence between the cart's existence and the existence of many other things? Indeed, is a cart's function not a dependency on many variable aspects of the world?

So, my disciples, meditate on these truths: aggregation, fractions, functional dependencies. All these things are what is meant by "emptiness."

And what is the symbol of emptiness? Visualize a hole . . . an unfilled circle . . . a mark one can use instead of blankness, but a mark that means blankness.

That mark, the empty circle, is the beginning of all wisdom.

The Book of the Way and its Powers

The road that looks like a road is not the true road.
The truth put into words is not true enough.
The numbers known to be numbers are not the fullness of numbers.

For though the sage of Persia taught of positive and negative . . . though the sage of the Dharma taught the Noble Truth of Zero and of fractions beyond fractions, even unto degrees deemed irrational . . . despite such wisdom, their teachings fell short of completion. They had no answers for the greatest mystery of all: what number multiplied by itself yields -1?

That number is the Tao.

And from the Tao has sprung the ten thousand things.

The arrogant man says the Tao is imaginary.
Scholars say the Tao is complex.

I say the Tao exists and is simple. Like water, it flows where it wills. It also commutes.

The ten thousand things of this world . . . what are they?

Each has a worldly part—call it A.

Each has a part that is Tao—call it B Tao.

So each of the ten thousand things is A + B Tao.

When summed, the worldly adds to the worldly, the Tao to the Tao. Therefore A + B Tao plus C + D Tao equals (A+C) + (B+D) Tao. Again, there is a worldly part and a part that is Tao. As the worldly adds, so does the Tao. The one is not without the other.

So, too, with the ten thousand things as they couple together and multiply:

$$(A + B \text{ Tao})(C + D \text{ Tao}) = (AC-BD) + (AD+BC) \text{ Tao}$$

A worldly part and a part that is Tao. Thus will it be for all ten thousand things.

Subtraction and division are left as exercises for the acolyte.

*   *   *

How can one picture the Tao?

As a grassy field. As an open plain. As an arrow that points to the truth beyond words. As a map that is into and onto.

You can't hold the Tao in your hand.
You can't close it up in a jar.
Yet the Tao encompasses all the roots of unity.
Those who know don't talk.
Those who talk don't know.

The Pitcher and the Stones

A crow nearly dying with thirst saw a pitcher. But the pitcher contained so little water, the crow couldn't get at it. He tried everything he could think of to reach the water, but all in vain. At last he collected as many stones as he could and dropped them one by one into the pitcher, until he brought the water within his reach and thus saved his life.

Moral: Necessity is the mother of invention.

A crane watched the crow fill the pitcher with stones. She noticed that some of the stones were black while others were white. The crane had three children who liked pretty things, so she decided to bring them each a stone. To avoid quarrels, the crane knew all three children should get the same color of stone, though it didn't matter whether the three stones were black or white. When the crane stuck her beak into the pitcher, she could not see what color of stone she was picking up . . . so how many stones did she have to remove to ensure she got three of the same color?

Moral: In order to be certain, one must plan for all contingencies.

A stork watched the crane and decided his three

children would also like stones. However, because storks are white, the stork-children would want white stones. The stork asked the crane how many stones he would have to remove from the pitcher to ensure the procurement of three white stones. The crane replied that if the stork was unlucky, he might have to remove all the black stones first before getting any white stones. The stork decided that would be too much work and flew away without trying . . . but the crane knew the stork was foolish. If the stork had been clever, he would have looked into the pitcher and determined the proportions of white to black to see how likely it was to pick three white stones at random in a small number of tries.

**Moral: Do not give up before you have
assessed the facts.**

When the stork got home, his children wept because their father had brought no gifts. The stork was forced to go back to the pitcher, where he found a monkey at play. The monkey had agile hands and excellent vision; she could easily pluck three white stones from the pitcher. But the monkey was also mischievous. She got two white stones and gave them to the stork, but when she seized a third white stone, she said she would not give it away unless the stork played a game. The monkey would hide the stone under one of three walnut shells, and the stork would have to guess where the stone was hidden. If the stork guessed correctly, he would get the stone; but if the stork guessed wrong, he must fly to the forest and bring back a ripe banana for the monkey to eat. The foolish stork agreed to this wager . . . . and ended up flying to the forest many times until the monkey had eaten her fill.

Moral: Do not play games with a cad.

As the stork was flying yet again to the forest, he

passed a lion. The lion said, "Friend stork, you seem tired. Perhaps you should land beside me and rest." "I am not that foolish," the crane replied, "but I am tired. The monkey is playing tricks on me, and will not give me what I wish unless I bring her bananas." "Where is this monkey?" the lion asked. The stork gave the lion detailed directions. This time, when the stork returned from the forest, he found the monkey gone, the lion walking away well-fed, and a white stone lying among the walnut shells.

> **Moral: O children of Greece, gambling may seem like a glamorous path to easy rewards, but it's a cesspool of crime and betrayal, even if you know the odds.**

When the stork finally returned to his unattended children, they'd all been eaten by ferrets.

The end!

The Angle of the Lord

Now it came to pass in the second year of the reign of Nebuchadnezzar that the king dreamed dreams, wherewith his spirit was troubled and his sleep broke from him. Then the king commanded to call the court mathematicians for to show the king his dreams.

When they came, they asked the nature of the dreams, but the king could not say for the memory had gone from him. Yet still he demanded they give their interpretations, on pain of death. The mathematicians answered him, saying, No man upon the earth can show the king's matter; none can but the gods, whose dwelling is not with the flesh.

Yet in the king's household lived Daniel, a son of Judah and a righteous man whom God had given understanding of dreams. He came before Nebuchadnezzar and said, "The Lord God of Israel has revealed thy dream's secrets unto me—not for mine own sake, but that thou shouldst know the wisdom of the Ancient of Days.

"Thou, O king, sawest, and beheld a great image. This image's head was of fine gold, his breast and his arms of silver, his belly and his thighs of brass, his legs of iron, his feet part of iron and part of clay. Four great chains ran up from the ground to the head, that the fiercest gale should not topple the image. And thou stood beneath the southernmost chain in such manner that thine own head but touched a single link. Each link of the chain was a cubit in length, and the link at thy head was the tenth from the ground.

"As thou watched, a stone was cut out without hands, which smote the image upon his feet that were of iron and clay, and broke them to pieces. Then was the iron, the clay, the brass, the silver, and the gold, broken to pieces together, and became like the chaff of the summer threshing floors; and the wind carried them away, that no place was found for them. Only the chains remained; and thou sawest the southernmost chain had four hundred links, which had run from the ground to the image's top, but now lay flat on the plain.

"This was the dream; and I will tell the interpretation thereof before the king.

"Thou stood at the tenth link of the chain, which was like unto a hypotenuse of a right-angle triangle whereof the farthest leg was the graven image itself (if we but ignore the sag in the chain, which was drawn very tight, thereby making the variance negligible). The chain was four hundred links long, which is two score tens. Therefore, O king, since thy head just touched the chain, by divine similarity of ratios, the image was two score times thine own height. Though the image and its feet of clay were sore destroyed, the wisdom of the Lord yet enables thee to take the image's measure."

Then Nebuchadnezzar said unto Daniel, "I care not the image's height, but rather its portent. Is there some meaning to these ratios? The height of the image to the length of the chain?"

"Verily," said Daniel, "that ratio foretells what is to come, for surely it is a sine. . . ."

The Confucian Analytics
The Master said:

Piety toward one's ancestors and submission to one's prince: are these not the origin of all benevolent actions?

The superior man measures himself with respect to this origin. He charts his piety and submission on two perpendicular axes.

Positive piety and positive submission lead upward to the rising sun, while negative piety and negative submission lead downward to hell.

Positive piety without submission rises straight toward heaven, but does not spread outward to the people.

Positive submission without piety lies flat and does not rise.

When piety equals submission, the superior man's life passes through the origin and rises with balanced harmony.

(Those who would rise more quickly must appeal to a higher power.)

The people may be made to follow a path of action, but they may not be made to understand it.

However, the superior man studies diligently, that

he may comprehend all paths—even those of exponential difficulty.

He also learns to factor polynomials.

By nature, men are nearly alike; by practice, they get to be wide apart.

The degree of divergence at any point depends on the slope of the tangent.

What the superior man seeks is in himself. What the inferior man seeks is in others.

The difference between the two is the square root of $(\Delta p)^2 + (\Delta s)^2$.

Many of the Master's sayings generalize to higher dimensions.

Without recognizing the geometry of Heaven, it is impossible to be a superior man.

Without knowing the rules of algebra, it is impossible for character to be established.

Without logarithmic scales, it is impossible to conserve paper.

Achilles and the Tortoise: The Second Heat

SOCRATES: I went down yesterday to the Piraeus with Glaucon the son of Ariston, that I might offer up my prayers to the goddess; and also because I wanted to see how the city would celebrate the festival. I was delighted with many of the events, particularly the sports competitions. But then that old madman Zeno showed up and began to rant loudly to his neighbors during the races.

POLEMARCHUS: No doubt he declaimed his paradox?

S: Can he speak of anything else?

THRASYMACHUS: What paradox is this?

P: Zeno pictures a race between the swift Achilles and a tortoise, in which the tortoise is given a head start of perhaps ten paces.

T: Unless the race length is ten paces and the width of a fingernail, Achilles would surely win.

P: Zeno contends otherwise. For before Achilles can close the ten-pace gap, he must run the first five paces. And before he can close the remaining five-pace gap, he must run the first half of that: two and a half paces. And before he can close the remaining two and a half paces, he must run the first half of that distance, too. You see the pattern?

T: Yes, certainly.

P: Therefore Zeno says Achilles must run an infinite number of these half-distance races; and although each such race is half the distance of the previous, yet there are still an uncountable number of them. How can a man run an infinite number of races in a finite lifetime? Zeno claims Achilles will never catch up with the tortoise, and moreover that all movement is impossible.

T: I do not agree with Zeno's conclusion though I see no error in his argument. Socrates, can you help me resolve the dilemma?

S: Zeno's error is simple. He assumes that distance is infinitely divisible but will not grant a similar favor to time. For suppose swift Achilles can run ten paces in a single heartbeat. Then he runs the first five paces in half a heartbeat; he runs the next fraction of the race in a quarter of a heartbeat; he runs the next in an eighth of a heartbeat; and so on. Achilles therefore has an infinite number of ever-smaller time segments to run an infinite number of ever-smaller distance segments. In the limit, as the distance segments D go to zero, the time segments T also go to zero. Therefore there is no paradox.

P: Yet what of Achilles' speed? For speed is distance divided by time . . . and if both D and T go to zero, do we not have a case of zero divided by zero? You must realize, Socrates, that in Athens, advocating division by zero is a crime punishable by death. Do you wish to corrupt our youth with seditions against the very foundations of mathematical discourse?

S: I preach no seditions. My Socratic method is merely to slice ever more finely until I arrive at the truth. Do you realize my techniques can analyze all manner of phenomena? The fall of an apple. The movements of stars and planets. Why bubbles are round and how to calculate pi.

P: None of that matters, Socrates—not if you divide by zero! Such talk offends the gods. I beg you, abandon these notions. Do you wish to be executed?

[Silence.]

S [stiffly]: I do not divide by zero itself. Merely by values approaching zero.

P: That is an extremely delicate distinction, Socrates . . . and I am afraid the elders of Athens will not be able to differentiate.

The Death of Ideals (by Plato)

My mentor Socrates is dead. Compelled to take poison because his ideas transgressed the status quo.

Never mind that Athens pretends to venerate ideas. Our ambassadors have traveled the entire world—to Persia, the Indus, the court of the Chou emperor, and everywhere in between—deliberately seeking out systems of thought, to make our city a paragon of wisdom.

Yet we are incapable of honoring one of our own.

Now Socrates is dead. His writings have been destroyed. His knowledge is lost—his vast vast knowledge. For the notions that led to his death were infinitesimal compared to the greater body of work he never made public. The secrets known only to his most intimate students.

Those who loved him.

Like me.

I watched him die. I saw the best mind of my generation destroyed by intolerance, called heretical, stripped naked, dragged through the hemlock streets at dawn by angry fanatics.

An agile-headed trickster burning with an ancient Zoroastrian grasp of the fiery calculus running the machinery of night.

Who bared his brain to Heaven under the Parthenon and heard algebraic angels totaling Buddhist zeros into infinite chanted sums.

Who got arrested in pubescent years returning through Sparta with a contraband copy of Lao Tzu under his robe.

Who studied Aesop, Mahavira, Pythagoras, and fourteen forbidden Upanishads to find the cosmos instinctively ordering itself in probabilistic sample spaces.

Who read Daniel's writing on the wall, walked with saints and angels in the Babylonian furnace, slept in the lions' den, slept with all the lions, triangulated their manes to five decimals.

Who wept at his first glimpse of analytic geometry, wept copiously asymptotically exponentially logarithmically, all the while on his way to becoming a superior man.

Who took T to zero in the company of epsilon and delta, then worked backward as infinite Σ became smoothed-out, and slopes reversed themselves into areas-under-the-curve always always plus a constant or marks would be deducted.

Who journeyed to Athens, who differentiated in

Athens, who came back to Athens & integrated in vain, who factored over Athens & X-the-unknowned in Athens and finally went away to take Athens' measure, & now Athens is lonesome for her hero.

Who dreamed and made incarnate more secret things still: the transfinite aleph, the rank-clashing matrix transforms, the groups and the rings and the prime-power fields, the stretched deformations of bourgeois space into patchy coordinate manifolds, the torn topologies, the random walks, the bloom of cardinalities, series and sequences, the functors, the metrics, the lemmas, the postulates, the perfect perfections of perfected forms, now with the absolute magnitude of the poem of mathematics butchered in Socrates' body, gone and dead for the next two thousand years.

Light. Dark. Light. Then fire.
Light. Dark. Light. And fire.
Light. Dark. Light. Ahh, fire!
Fire is light. And fire, it burns. Burns the dark.
Fan . . . the . . . flames!

Revision Point

As noted at the beginning of the story, the Axial Age (600-400 BCE) was a sort of Renaissance wherein many old tribal beliefs were questioned and replaced. Throughout Europe and Asia, several generations of thinkers tried to make sense of the world in a way that had never been tried before. As a result, the Axial Age saw the birth of Zoroastrianism (the first religion that combined true monotheism with a strong belief in an afterlife), Buddhism, Taoism, Confucianism, Jainism, and modern Hinduism, as well as the late Jewish prophets and the most important Greek philosophers. The religions and philosophies created during this time set Eurasia's intellectual agenda for more than two thousand years.

What the Axial Age *didn't* give us was much advancement in science. A few small steps were taken, but nothing comparable to the great developments in philosophical thought. Why not? Perhaps because it was still the Bronze Age, and humanity hadn't yet invented useful things like telescopes, mechanical clocks, sextants, etc. People could think, but they couldn't *measure*. What kind of science could flourish in such an environment?

Well, there's one realm of science where abstract brainpower is all that counts: math. It occurred to me that if all those prophets and philosophers had just spent a little time putting their ideas into mathematical form, the Axial Age would have been a lot more fun . . . at least to a math geek like myself. Therefore, I've attributed the invention of various mathematical concepts (from positive and negative numbers, up to calculus and beyond) to appropriate thinkers of the Axial Age. It's scary just how easily the math and the people lined up. . . .

J.A.G.

THE TERMINAL SOLUTION

by Robin Wayne Bailey

IN the matter before us which now threatens us so direly we have relatively few facts, and the hypotheses and opinions we now offer are subject to so many caveats and arguments as to invite ridicule not just from numerous of our fellow colleagues, most notably Dr. Joseph Lister of the King's College Hospital and in Paris M. Louis Pasteur, but from clergy and from political circles throughout the empire as well.

Nevertheless, the facts are the facts, and I take no great pleasure in noting that the British Medical Association as well as leading figures within the Royal College of Surgeons, if somewhat slowly—indeed, and without leveling judgments, I might say too slowly—have come to concur with much of what I now report.

We can state as fact that the epidemic which now confounds and menaces us had its origins in the darkest heart of Africa, perhaps somewhere along the Ruvuma River or along the banks of the great lakes of Mweru and Bangweulu. It is impossible to more precisely determine where it first appeared. As fearful as this disease is to us, it has struck a far more devastating blow there. Many of the key settlements and villages where important clues might have been found are now either abandoned or completely wiped out. Ujiji and Kolobang were burned. Capetown has completely quarantined itself.

We know as fact, however, that the renowned explorer and writer, David Livingstone was already quite ill when he returned to London on July 23, 1864. His physician, one Doctor Samuel Overton, diagnosed his several maladies as symptomatic of malaria, and there can be no doubt that malaria was present. However, Doctor Overton also indicated the occurrence of several purplish lesions of an unknown and possibly cancerous nature upon Livingstone's torso. These lesions seemed to defy all treatment.

So, detracting no honor from his famous name, it is with David Livingstone that we find the first evidence of this plague, which I now call African Invasive Disease, upon our shores. And it is with David Livingstone that we begin to document a curious and notable progression of subsequent, and I might add inevitably fatal, occurrences. Most immediate among these are Dr. Overton, himself, and a number of his patients. Overton's copious notes describing his own symptoms and pathology provided useful groundwork for my investigations.

From this point, I must speak with some delicacy about matters that may shock or offend, for in charting the progress of this plague. . . .

Dr. Joseph Bell laid his pen aside, leaned his elbows on his writing table, and in the dim, yellowish light from a single gas lamp, rubbed his eyes. In his mind, he'd gone over this passage a dozen times and on paper at least half that many. He felt tired, so very deeply tired. The summary of his investigations at which he was working and which he would soon present to the British College of Physicians was proving difficult, requiring wording that was foreign to his blunt nature.

"Devil damn us all!" he grumbled, wadding his pages up and hurling them across the room of his cluttered apartment. He stared in disgust after the parchment ball as it bounced off a bookcase full of medical texts and settled into a shadowy corner. Then, recovering from his outburst, he settled back in his chair and rubbed his eyes a second time as he muttered to himself, "Indeed, he already has—damned us every bloody one."

Weary to the bone, he tried to push all thought from his mind. He knew he needed sleep, but there was no time for that. There were riots in Whitechapel, in Aldgate, and Spitalfields, demonstrations at the gates of Buckingham, itself.

He squeezed his temples as he rose and paced back and forth over the carpet which Mrs. Hudson, his housekeeper, had once kept so clean. Poor, sweet woman. She was dead, too, like so many others.

On the corner of his desk rested a small black case, and in it his hypodermic needle. Beside that, the cocaine bottle. In that vial of cobalt blue he might find a little rest. He ran his fingers over the case, a fingertip over the bottle's lid, feeling the hunger gnawing inside him. He pushed both farther back on the desk where the light didn't reach and where the little glass bottle didn't sparkle quite so interestingly. Perhaps later, but there was still so much to do.

Downstairs, the front door closed softly, but not so softly as to escape his hearing. Nudging back the edge of a lace drapery (more of Mrs. Hudson's handiwork), he peered down to watch a thin figure in top hat and black cloak descend the three stone steps and move with a quickly furtive gait into the damp, fog-enshrouded street. The silver head of a walking stick which he tucked under one arm flashed briefly.

A moment later, footsteps sounded on the seventeen steps that led from the first floor, where he and his assistant maintained medical offices, to the upper rooms which they shared in these troubled times. The door's brass knob turned. The door opened. Dr. Arthur Doyle, tall and slender, dark of hair, not yet thirty, stepped from the brighter hallway into the gloom of their living quarters. He closed the door in a thoughtful manner and leaned back against it. His slim-fingered hand lingered on the knob.

At Edinburgh University Hospital, Doyle had been Bell's finest student. His mind was keen, and Bell had quickly taken him on as a clerk. Now a doctor fully in his own right, he continued to work loyally at Bell's side.

"Even in this weak light," Bell commented as he settled into an overstuffed chair near the window and regarded the younger doctor, "you look quite ashen."

Taking a handkerchief from a trousers pocket, Doyle wiped his brow, nodding as he sank back into a chair opposite his mentor. He seemed at a loss for words, but Bell waited patiently. "An old friend," Doyle murmured distractedly. "Also from Edinburgh. I knew him at university. We . . ." he hesitated, biting his lip as he thrust the handkerchief back into his pocket. "We once shared an interest."

"In writing," Bell interjected. "I know. How was Mister Stevenson?"

Doyle's thick eyebrows shot up over his hawkish nose. "How did you . . . ? I promised him I wouldn't . . . !"

Bell waved a dismissive hand. "You didn't tell. He gave himself away with that ostentatious cane. He never appears or is photographed without it. And the very lateness of the hour suggested someone famous, or at least well-known, who preferred not to be recognized. There's also the fact that this person came to you, someone he knew and trusted." He picked at the nap of the chair's fabric and flicked away a bit of lint. "Even without the cane I would have recognized your friend, Robert Stevenson."

A moment of silence hung between them while both men stared toward the window and dark London beyond. Droplets of rain were beginning to splatter on the pane.

"I'm afraid he has it," Doyle said at last.

Between themselves they had stopped naming the damnable disease. It was only *it*. He has it. She has it. It's spread to Bombay. It's shown up in America. It is a germ. It isn't a germ. Why can't we cure it?

Bell closed his eyes briefly, then opened them. "What are his symptoms."

In the opposite chair, Doyle fidgeted uncomfortably. He sat with his hands on his knees and his head down, looking like a student being chastised by his teacher. "I'd rather not say," he answered. "It would be an embarrassment to him, and I daresay to you and me. Robert is a man of, well, two natures."

"Indeed," Bell replied. Rising from his chair, he crossed the room to a sideboard and poured two small glasses of cognac, one of which he delivered to Doyle. "My dear fellow, that certainly sheds new light on his most recent novel, that absurd *Jekyll and Hyde* silliness."

Doyle raised his glass to his lips, but did not yet drink. "I dreamed of writing once, myself," he murmured. "Detective stories, actually. Tell me, Doctor, do you ever regret leaving Edinburgh and taking up this impossible challenge?"

Bell thought for a moment, then tossed back the

contents of his glass. "I was Her Majesty's personal physician," he answered. "And London was still in shock from the cholera outbreaks of August and September, 1864. Victoria, herself, requested that I come and look into this new threat." He set his glass down beside the cognac bottle. "What man could ever resist Victoria?"

"But it's been twenty years!" Doyle thrust himself out of his chair, splashing his drink over his hand and wrist. "Twenty years, and what progress have we made? It continues to spread. The new railways that link our cities carry it from one end of the island to the other. Our soldiers and sailors, our merchants and businessmen, have transported it to all corners of the empire. On the continent it spreads like wildfire, and we are helpless!"

Doyle dashed his glass on the floor. Shards of crystal flashed and sparkled in the gaslight.

Bell watched dispassionately as the carpet soaked up the alcohol. "You've wasted a very expensive cognac," he noted.

Doyle's rage did not abate. Indeed, it bordered on hysteria. "I just administered paregoric and camphor for a friend's severe diarrhea, knowing full and damnably well it won't have any lasting effect!" He shoved his hands deep into his trousers pockets and began to pace. "This morning for another patient, a woman of some status, I made plasters from clover extract for a trio of lesions beneath her left arm. But we both know that will have no real effect, either! Laudanum will manage her pain, but the cancers will continue to grow!"

Ceasing his pacing, Doyle stopped before Bell's writing desk and slammed his hands down upon it, causing the small blue cocaine bottle to jump. "These frightening cases of trichinosis! Vermifuge has no effect at all! Calomel! Bromine! This new penicillin in which we placed so much hope! Nothing has an effect!''

Doyle spun about to face his mentor. His eyes almost glowed, wide and white in the dimness, and the look on his face was more than mere frustration. It was horror. "I think I'm treating a man for the grippe or loss of appetite. Then he's back the next week with the worst case of dysentery! Then the week after that with intestinal parasites! And it's not just one patient—it's hundreds!" He shook his fist at the walls, making it plain that he was raging at himself, perhaps barely aware that Bell was there at all. "I'm not a doctor, anymore! I'm an assembly line worker!"

Bell walked to his writing desk and set the cocaine bottle back in its place. "Are you quite finished?" he asked in a calm, yet stern voice.

His assistant and former student stared at him. Then, giving out with a deep sigh, he resumed his seat, unmindful of the broken glass around his feet. "Quite," he answered. He hung his head and rubbed his temples with the finger and thumb of his right hand. Over the years, he'd adopted that habit from Bell. "Perhaps Canterbury and Rome are right and this is God's Judgment upon us all."

"I think, my dear Doyle, that you should have drunk that cognac," Bell stooped to reclaim the wadded pages of his summary from the floor near the bookcase before Doyle should notice them. The tight little ball of paper was an irritating reminder that the estimable Dr. Joseph Bell could also have his little moments of pique and tantrum. "Alcohol provides such a ready excuse when a man speaks nonsense and balderdash."

Doyle looked up, and his eyes were tired and wet.

"Of course it's nonsense," he agreed in a somber tone. "Who cares what the Pope or the Archbishop says? We're men of science, aren't we? Just as John Snow solved the cholera problem, we'll solve this."

There was more than a hint of sarcasm in Doyle's voice, but Bell let it go. He completely understood his assistant's frustration. Dr. Snow's "problem" had been child's play compared to the mystery at hand. A mere six hundred lives within a two-month period, and once the source of the bacteria was found—a well pump in the Soho district—that epidemic was stopped in its tracks.

Terrible as that epidemic had been, this African nightmare had claimed far more lives and lasted far, far longer. Nor was Doyle alone in his exhaustion. It was exhausting the empire. Indeed, all of Europe. And still there was no end in sight, no meaningful treatment, no cure.

Yet Bell was not without some theories.

"Tell me," he said as he headed for the door and seized the brass knob, "did you administer the cup to your friend?"

Doyle turned in his chair to regard Bell over one shoulder as the older doctor opened the door. "Of course," he answered. "Two small incisions along the rectis abdominus . . ."

Bell moved into the hallway and began the descent down the stairs to the medical offices. Doyle gathered his strength and rose from his chair to hurry after his old teacher, pausing long enough at the sideboard to raise the cognac bottle to his lips and take a deep drink before setting it back in its place.

At the bottom of the stairs were a pair of doors on either side of a carpeted vestibule. One door opened into the rooms set aside for Bell's use, but Bell pushed

open the other door and entered Doyle's consulting
rooms. The gas lamp inside still burned with a bright
flame.

With narrowed gaze, he scrutinized the room.
Doyle's bloody apron lay across the examining table
where he'd discarded it after Stevenson's departure.
On a tray beside the table lay the scalpel with which
he'd made the aforementioned incisions, and next to
that, several glass vials which, when heated and applied to the merest incision, formed a vacuum and
drew forth blood. It was, Bell often reflected, only a
small improvement over common leeching, a practice
still followed in some parts of the empire. As for the
application of evacuated cups to draw forth blood
thought to be diseased, the treatment was so common
that most patients not only expected it, but insisted
upon it.

Bell considered the practice vaguely medieval and
of unproven value. Nevertheless, like all physicians of
the day, he understood the theory behind cupping and
frequently employed the treatment.

As Doyle came in behind him, Bell went to the tray.
He picked up the scalpel and turned it toward the
light. A fine, precision tool, of course—Doyle would
have no less. A red smear of blood still colored the
razor edge. Setting the scalpel aside, he next picked
up the vial that his former student had used. Blood
still colored the inside of the glass, and the rim as well.

He turned to a table against the wall near the head
of the examining table. Here sat the mortar and pestle
in which his student had mixed the clover extract poul-
tices. Beside that was a small pan containing a quantity of the crimson liqueur from Stevenson's flesh, and
possibly that from other patients of the day as well,
such was the amount of blood.

Turning again, he scanned the open cabinets and

the well-stocked shelves and bottles within: opium and laudanum for pain; tincture of mercury for syphilis; bromine and digitalis; morphine; penicillin; quinine for appetite and digestion; calumel, mercury chloride, and other purgatives; various expectorants, liniments, and camphors; carbolic acid for disinfectant.

In another cabinet next to the first, more vials and glass cups for bloodletting; sets of scalpels, clamps, spools of silk thread and catgut for surgeries; powders for plasters. On the centermost shelf, as if occupying a place of honor, and plainly visible through the glass of the closed cabinet door sat a microscope—Leeuwenhoek's marvel, and Doyle's prized possession.

Despite the presence of the microscope, it all seemed horribly primitive to Bell. He recalled how not all that long ago Londoners had hung sprigs of elderberry in their windows to ward off cholera. Useless superstition. In the face of this new pestilence, he wondered if the conglomeration on these shelves was any better.

He picked up the blood-smeared scalpel again and turned it before the light, noting its balance and its weight, turning it between his fingers this way and that. He ran a fingertip along the side of the blade, accidentally nicking the skin. Only the tiniest drop of blood welled near his cuticle, and he sucked it without a thought as he set the scalpel down again.

So many times before he'd thought that the answer, or at least part of the answer, that he sought must lie in a surgery just like this one. He considered Dr. Samuel Overton again and his cluster of patients, among the first to succumb to the mysterious contagion. He knew their names, the intimate details of their lives. He had suspicions—but he had no clear answers, not yet, and that rankled him.

And time was desperately short, for there was news

he had not yet dared to share with Doyle, nor with anyone. A small cobalt bottle in the open cabinet caught a gleam of light from the gas lamp. It drew his attention. He thought of another cobalt bottle on his writing desk and experienced a craving like he never had before.

"Doctor Bell?" Doyle spoke formally from the doorway. "Sir Charles Warren is here from the Metropolitan Police."

Bell had been so deep in thought that he had not even heard the doorbell, nor taken note of the voices in the vestibule. But for Mrs. Hudson, he thought sometimes that he would lose his head. No, that wasn't right. He squeezed his eyes shut briefly. Mrs. Hudson was dead, another victim of the African curse. He fought to push away her memory and focus his thoughts on the present. Straightening his jacket, he turned toward Doyle.

"Damn," he groused, "if Scotland Yard is here, that means there's been another murder."

Doyle turned toward the staircase and started up to their shared apartment. "I'll get our hats and overcoats," he said.

In the vestibule, Sir Charles Warren glanced through the office doorway at Bell, but called up after Doyle. "Better bring your revolver, too, if you have one," he advised as he pushed back the brown derby on his head. "Hell's very own ghosts are roaming the streets tonight. There's rioting in the East End and other parts of the city, and we're getting reports of looting in Carnaby. Nobody's safe, and particularly not where we're going."

Bell frowned at Sir Charles Warren. He didn't much like the commissioner of police. Not many people did. He was a bumbler and an incompetent, and dressed the part. His worn tweed suit was rumpled and considerably out of fashion, and his starched collar was dirty. The cuffs of his trousers were also wet, and the soles of his boots stained with mud. A graying mustache framed his mouth and drooped to either side of his chin. In all respects, he looked a sadly comical figure, but for the large-caliber American pistol he wore strapped in a holster to his right hip.

"It's unholy late," Bell grumbled at Sir Charles. He noted the sorry state of the commissioner's trousers again. "Is it still raining?"

"Later for some than others," Sir Charles shot back. "And of course it's still raining. This is London!"

Doyle hurried down the stairs. He wore an Inverness overcoat and handed a nearly identical garment to his former teacher. As Bell slipped it on, he felt a weight in the coat's right pocket. He wasn't at all surprised to reach his hand inside and find his pistol. He assumed Doyle had likewise armed himself. Clapping his hat upon his head and shouldering past Sir Charles, he opened the door to the street and descended the three stone steps. A hansom cab waited at the curb.

"Where are we going this time?" he demanded without glancing back at Sir Charles.

The surly commissioner pulled his derby lower upon his head as he nudged past Bell and flung open the hansom cab's black door. "Well, sir, you could go straight to hell if it were up to me, but it's come down from Her Majesty that you're to be brought in on these events. Seems some folks have a higher opinion of your abilities than I do."

Laying a light hand on Bell's elbow, Doyle helped him into the cab after the commissioner, then climbed in himself. "Perhaps they merely have a lower opinion of yours," he said as he settled back for the ride.

Sir Charles glared at him, then rapped on the roof of the cab. "Dutfield's Yard on Berner Street," he ordered the driver. "And make a damned hurry of it. This is police business!"

The hansom cab lurched into motion. At the sound of a whiplash, the horse sped forward. Sir Charles grabbed for the handle on the inside of the door to avoid being thrown into Bell's lap. Doyle's head bounced back against the cab's construction. All three men exchanged glares, then arranged themselves in their seats. No one spoke. The grim occasion for their meeting didn't lend itself to chitchat.

As they left London proper and entered the East End, Bell leaned closer to his window and lifted the edge of the rain curtain, his attention drawn by voices in the street. A pair of men on the curb dropped their conversation to watch with sullen eyes as the hansom cab passed by. It was well after midnight, but the men weren't alone on the streets.

The East End was a place of outcasts, a vast and dirty slum teeming with the poor and downtrodden, with immigrant masses, and with the sick. Economically and socially, it was a world apart from the rest of London and from the rest of Britain. Here, pigs and sheep and cattle were driven down the open streets to the stinking slaughterhouses. Excrement and rubbish and sewage filled the ditches that lined the dismal streets. Between the slaughterhouses and the filth, the most obnoxious miasma that not even the hardest rain could wash away hung perpetually over the district. The rows and rows of rotten, reeking tenements stood in the most deplorable conditions, often with more than one family occupying the meager rooms. The lodging houses were no better.

Looking out upon it, Dr. Joseph Bell felt sick to his stomach, and not from the stench. Such a place was a breeding ground for disease and all manner of contagion.

A raucous shouting suddenly surrounded them, and

the hansom cab lurched to a halt. The horse gave a loud whinny and crashed its hooves down upon the muddy cobbles. The driver let out a string of curses.

Sir Charles whipped out his immense revolver and pushed open the cab's door. Bell and Doyle both reached into their pockets, although neither drew a gun. Clinging to the side of the cab, the commissioner rose to stand upon the running board. "Get back! Get back, I tell you!" He brandished his weapon. "This is police business! Police business, I say! You! Unhand that bridle, or I'll shoot your damned eye right out of your head!"

Doyle raised the rain curtain on his side of the cab. A mob surrounded the conveyance. Desperate faces pressed closer and stared inside. A woman's hand reached inside, and fingers brushed lightly over Doyle's Inverness. "Please, yer lordship!" she said before someone shoved her out of the way. Rougher hands thrust through the window. With restrained calm, Doyle drew out his pistol, then returned it to his pocket, all the while meeting the bitter gaze of the leprous man who peered at him. Grudgingly, the unfortunate stepped away from the cab.

"Well played," Bell whispered. He held his own pistol out of sight in his lap, but he put it away at once.

A thunderous blast erupted from the commissioner's gun. Shouting, cursing, the mob fell away from the cab and in twos and threes melted back into shadow-filled doorways and alleys. Sir Charles Warren of the Metropolitan Police settled into his seat once more and closed the hansom cab's door. Acrid smoke still wafted from the barrel of his oversized revolver as he leaned back and shoved it into its holster. "Damned beggars! Packs of them! Like diseased wolves! They're everywhere, and not just in the district, either. Through all of London!"

Bell could barely repress his disgust for the commissioner. His mouth tightened into a lipless line as he reached into the breast pocket of his coat and took out his wallet. Without a word or a glance at either of his companions, he drew out a sheaf of pound notes and flung them out the window.

The streets grew darker, and the rain began to drum with an insistent rhythm on the hansom cab's roof. The rain curtains rustled and flapped as the wind picked up, and the cab itself rocked under the gusts.

In Berner Street, the cab slowed to a creaking stop. Sir Charles pushed open the door and the wind blew it closed, banging his head and his knee. With a curse, he kicked it open again and the driver, having dismounted, caught it and held it for them. Bell and Doyle climbed down. The thin rain stabbed at them, and the wind snatched at their coats. Bell pushed his hat lower on his head to keep it from flying off.

Another crowd had gathered close by, but this one was a mixture of ordinary citizens and policemen. The cab had stopped before a factory warehouse. The sign on the street-side of the building read, *A. Dutfield, Van and Cart Builders.* Close beside it stood another warehouse, and the faded white-paint sign above its entrance revealed it to be the business of one *W. Hendley, Sack Manufacturer.* A narrow black alley, utterly devoid of any light, separated the two businesses.

Someone called out, "Commissioner! Sir Charles!" A large man pushed his way through the crowd and hurried toward them. His face was concealed beneath a sodden hat that he wore pulled down over his eyebrows to shield off the rain, and his coat collar was turned up high around his neck. "Over here, Sir Charles. She's down the alley."

"Of course she's down the alley," Warren growled. "They're always down the damned alley! Why can't someone ever get murdered in a nice, clean street with decent lighting just for once?" He made a gruff gesture toward Bell and Doyle, "Inspector Abberline, these gentlemen with me are Dr. Joseph Bell and Dr. Arthur Conan Doyle. They're . . ." he hesitated, frowning, and seemed about to choke on the word. ". . . consultants." He waved a hand toward the alley. "Now lead on, man. Lead on!"

Inspector Frederick Abberline nodded to Bell before he turned to obey the commissioner. Bell had already met Abberline at the scene of the Annie Chapman murder three weeks' previous. Despite Abberline's failure to apprehend the killer, the inspector impressed him as one of the few competent detectives in the city.

A pair of constables carrying lanterns joined them at the entrance to the alley where yet another pair were positioned to keep the onlookers away. Taking one of the lights, Abberline led them into the darkness.

"Six paces," Bell muttered as the lamplight fell on the body. He squeezed passed Sir Charles and knelt down. "Eighteen feet at most. Who found her?"

"A passing wagoner heard three short screams and stopped," Abberline answered. "Claims he saw someone in a cloak and hat run away. We've identified her as Elizabeth Stride, but she was known on the streets around here as Long Liz. A prostitute like the others. Forty-five years old. Swedish immigrant. Lived in a lodging house off Devonshire and Commercial Streets."

"Looks like your wagoner scared the monster—this so-called *Jack the Ripper*—away before he could finish his grisly work," Doyle said between clenched teeth.

"He finished it well enough," Bell replied. Yet he knew what his former student meant. Elizabeth Stride was quite dead, but she hadn't suffered the same butchery as the madman's other victims. She lay on her side exactly as she had fallen, with her face to the wall of Dutfield's warehouse. Mud caked the fur trim of her black cloth coat and one side of her face. A cheap penny-corsage made from a single red rose and a sprig of white maidenhair fern adorned her shoulder. A few curls of brown hair spilling out from under her crepe bonnet stirred in the breeze that whispered over the ground.

"Lots of men have it in for these old whores!" Sir Charles Warren scoffed. "Are you sure this one's the same as the others?"

"There's no blood on the front of her clothing," Bell noted as he turned her gently onto her back. "He knocked her down first." He pointed to a dark bruise on Elizabeth Stride's chin, then he loosened the neck of her brown velveteen bodice and the white blouse beneath that to expose marks on her collarbone and chest. "Then he held her down to cut her throat with a left-handed stroke. Same as the others."

Abberline leaned closer with the lantern so the commissioner could see the violent gash for himself. "We found this clutched in her left hand," he said to Bell, proffering a small bottle.

In the lamplight, Bell studied the fine printing on the bottle's label. *Doctor Gull's Life-Saving Pills*! it proclaimed. *A Triumph of Science! The Light of the World!* There was more, but he didn't need to strain his eyes to read it. "Patent medicine. Quackery," he said, returning the bottle to Abberline. "Charlatans are everywhere offering cures for what cannot be cured."

Sir Charles Warren recoiled. "She has the pox?" he cried, eyes widening. He whipped a handkerchief from his coat pocket and pressed it to his mouth and nose.

Bell rose to stand. Gull's Pills, like a hundred other

patent medicines, were marketed to the gullible and the poor as a remedy for the African curse. "You're a blithering fool, Warren," he said, turning. "If it could be caught by breathing, we'd all be dead long ago."

With Doyle at his shoulder, he made his way back to the curb. The onlookers parted to let him pass. Without saying a word, he leaned his head on the side of the waiting hansom cab, squeezed his eyes shut, and rubbed his temples.

"Did she have it?" Doyle quietly asked.

Bell nodded. "As I turned her over I noted the lymph glands in her neck and under her arms. They were quite swollen. And on the muddy side of her face, shingles. Then there are the pills." Recovering himself, he straightened and drew a deep breath. He still couldn't quite get Elizabeth Stride's face out of his mind. He opened the hansom cab's door. "An autopsy will confirm it. Let's get out of this rain."

Inside the cab, Doyle sat facing his old teacher and his friend. "Then it seems this Jack the Ripper is systematically killing infected prostitutes," he said.

"So it seems," Bell agreed. "But why? Is it some twisted idea of public service? Or is it out of revenge because he, himself, is infected? The violence of the deeds suggests a tremendous anger." He sighed again and put his chin on his fist as he stared out the cab's window.

Then, for a moment he straightened. On the opposite side of the street away from the crowd, something moved in the shadow of a doorway. The wind rustled the hem of a cape, and some stray bit of light touched something silvery. "A knife!" he thought at once, and his hand plunged into the pocket of his overcoat for his gun. But then, the figure stepped out of the shadow and hurried on by.

Not a knife. Only a walking stick.

Some gentleman, a noble perhaps, slumming with the Whitechapel ladies and not wishing to be seen. Catching contagion, carrying it home to wives, to other lovers and mistresses who passed it to their husbands and lovers, from the lowest Whitechapel doxy on up to the throne itself.

He'd just examined Victoria that morning, and her philandering husband, Albert. He hadn't told them yet, nor Doyle, nor anyone.

He closed his eyes again. Twenty years wasn't such a long time, but he was so tired. He rapped on the roof of the cab. "Two-twenty-one Baker Street," he told the driver.

"What about Sir Charles?" Doyle said.

Bell looked out the window again, but the cloaked figure was gone. "Devil take him," he answered. "Let him get another cab."

The hansom cab rocked in the wind as they journeyed home, and the rain beat down upon it with a growing determination. The beggars left them alone, whether because the hour was too late even for them, or because the driver took a different route, Bell couldn't say, nor did he care. He closed his eyes, and thought of what he would try to say in his speech to the College of Physicians, and he wondered if any of it would matter or make a difference.

London, the empire, the world as they knew it was coming down around their ears. In Paris, Capetown, New York, even Hong Kong, the story was the same, and the tale only ended in darkness. He laughed soundlessly at himself, recalling the earlier drafts of his speech in which he'd dared to give a name to a disease that defied him. He glimpsed the answer sometimes, or so he told himself, but he couldn't grasp it.

He had suspicions, and he had hypotheses. But no proof and not even a clue as to how to go about finding proof.

The science just didn't exist yet that could show him the way.

He opened his eyes and stared out into the rain and the fog. "It's beaten me," he said. Doyle looked back at him with tired eyes. When the hansom cab let them out at their address, they went by the consulting rooms which still had not been cleaned from the day's appointments, and climbed the stairs to their apartments. Doyle sank down in one of the overstuffed chairs, then leaned forward and wearily began to pick up the pieces of the broken cognac glass. Nicking his thumb as he gathered the pieces, he said nothing, just wiped the fine line of blood on his trouser.

Bell went to his writing table, and took out a sheet of paper to write. But there at hand was the black case with his needle, and the damnably pretty blue cobalt bottle containing the only paradise he ever expected to know. Pushing back the paper, he opened the case, the bottle, and prepared his injection. Just a seven-percent solution, he reminded himself. But perhaps tonight just a little more.

Doyle dropped the pieces of the broken glass into a wastebasket near the sideboard and turned as his mentor pushed the point into the proper vein. "Does it really give you any release?" he asked.

Bell hesitated for a moment, savoring the needle's sting, waiting for the first cold rush. "No, but it dulls the pain," he answered as he withdrew the instrument and set it aside. "And at least for a little while, it eases the fear." He closed his eyes, and his head rolled back between his shoulders. "You don't know."

He smiled to himself. Doyle didn't know, because

he disdained the needle and disapproved of his old
teacher's use of cocaine. Bell didn't blame him. It was
a weakness, if only a small one, but still a weakness.

Soft footsteps on the carpet made him open his
eyes. With dreamlike slowness, his student, his friend,
and his colleague walked across the carpet and picked
up the hypodermic which still contained a measure of
the damnable drug.

"Maybe it's time I found out," Doyle said. He
pressed the point deep into his arm.

Beyond the lace curtain (poor Mrs. Hudson!), beyond the window, the wind moaned and the rain
drove down.

Revision Point

The genesis of "The Terminal Solution" isn't
easy to relate. It sprang from a dream, a nightmare, actually, very complete and very detailed. The premise was simple enough on the
surface: what if AIDS had emerged from the
African continent 125 years early, brought
back by David Livingstone, the African explorer, in 1864 to Victorian England? How
would the medical science of that time have
dealt with such a disease?

Consider that "cupping," or bleeding a patient, was still a common practice and that
basic sterilization techniques were not. Joseph
Lister didn't propose the idea of using carbolic
acid as an antiseptic until 1867. Frederich Loef-
fler and Paul Frosch didn't suggest the existence of viruses until 1898. Medicine and
medical science were, to say the least, still
quite primitive.

Social conditions throughout London would

have contributed to massive and rapid spread of the infection. Poverty and a huge influx of immigrants were contributing to the swift growth of slums. Prostitution was widespread. So was drug use. Opium and morphine were perfectly legal, cheap, and available. Anyone could buy a hypodermic needle on the corner. Rail lines were also springing up all over Britain, linking major cities and smaller ones, and British forces and culture were spreading across the world.

In modern times, after twenty years of effort, our science and medicine have barely made inroads against Acquired Immune Deficiency Syndrome. What chance would the Victorian world have had?

None at all.

R.W.B.

THE ASHBAZU EFFECT

by John G. McDaid

In the course of its growth and development, the school came to be the center of culture and learning in Sumer. Moreover, unlike present-day institutions of learning, the Sumerian school was also the center of what might be termed creative writing.

—Samuel Noah Kramer
History Begins at Sumer

There was no question that Enzu had performed all the required actions, and yet his manuscript had been rejected. He had brought an *arua* gift to the temple of Nanna, paid the divination priest to prod a reeking sheep's liver, and, much to his wife's annoyance, he had hired a professional omen reader to untie his dreams.

"And what did she tell you, Enzu-dumu? 'Opportunities exist, but there are challenges.'" Mari, who made a few coins on the side by reading dreams for friends, shook her head.

"Something like that," he muttered. In truth, he thought ruefully, the *shailtu* had said his petition would be granted.

144

"You don't really believe in that nonsense," Mari persisted.

"No, beloved." Enzu sighed. "What's important is that influential elders still do, and one does well to be seen adhering to the forms."

"*Lum*." She gave him the eye of death and stormed off into the kitchen where he heard her busily re-arranging jars.

Her anger was understandable. He brushed dust from his robe and set down the heavy leather bag holding his tablets. Approaching the temple for sponsorship had been expensive, and their savings were nearly exhausted. The high life he'd enjoyed as a school-father had evaporated. Gone were the hordes of aspiring scribes paying cash—and offering up delicious and exquisite bribes for good grades.

Gone with the invention of printing.

After months of *arua* and wheedling from Yadidatum, his Introducer, Enzu had finally set up a meeting with the financier-priestess at the temple of Nanna. It had been a frustrating wait since he'd sent the tablets, then, finally, today he had been summoned to meet Ningal-ummi.

Trudging up the impressive stone steps, he noticed once again the profound changes. Ten years ago, the lower temple square would have been full of circus acts to entertain the masses: dancing bears, snake charmers, transvestites, the whole nine *iku*. Now, narrow paths snaked through a huckster's barrow of tablet stalls, some bare wood tables, the higher-end draped in fabric and shaded with awnings. A continuous trickle of Ur's citizens wandered the twisty passages amid racks of texts old and new, and the clink of commerce was constant.

Enzu waited in the inner courtyard. Here there was shade, cool pitchers of water, and the fragrant smell of cedar. Around him strolled and chatted the deal-makers of Ur, dressed in fine-spun clothes, with neatly trimmed beards. Merchants seeking capital for trade voyages down the Gulf rubbed shoulders with engineers looking to publish canal-building texts. He felt isolated and noticed, and wished he'd been able to talk Yadidatum into accompanying him.

When the page called, he was relieved to be led into the dim stone hallways and directed, wordlessly, into a small audience room.

Ningal-ummi sat on a lush cushion, lit from a courtyard door behind, surrounded by stacks of tablets. She offered food and water, and nodded as Enzu presented her with a small silver stylus. Her eyes narrowed as he thanked her for the meeting, formally and correctly, in liturgical idiom.

"You speak *Emesal* well," she said.

"You are kind. What little I know I learned transcribing for Ugazum, one of your tax collectors."

"He says your hand followed his mouth accurately."

"Again, you are too kind."

"Well, to business." She frowned. "You speak and write capably. So why, scribe, are these tablets so strange?"

"I'm sorry you find them so. I mean only to tell an interesting story."

"Do you? But this story *lies*," said Ningal-ummi tightly. "You talk of real places, people who still live. But then you describe things which did not happen. The story claims that printing was never invented. It says that the Sons of the Left invaded us and took over our temples, our cities, even our language."

"Your displeasure shames me," said Enzu, bowing. "I mean only to show what might have been, had things happened differently. I call it 'fiction-that-continues-a-line.' What if Ilammadu had not invented molded text? How quickly things might have gone horribly wrong! It serves to show the greatness of our city and our goddess, and the rightness of our path.''

"And you believe that Sargon's daughter would now be high priestess in this very temple?''

"It is, apologies, merely a continued line. A logical next step for the Bin-Shimal, to install one of their own, to try to subvert our people's strong faith.''

She looked at him wordlessly for a long time. Flies buzzed, and tallow crackled and sputtered in the sconces.

"You are a strange one, Enzu,'' she said finally. "Despite my protests, I do like this idea of continued lines. But your work is not something we can take up. This is not what the people in the lower courtyard want to read. And certainly not something which can come from the temple, in a year when Sargon's minions still harass the outskirts of Nippur.''

Enzu felt like a hammered ox. He stood, but the world wavered darkly.

"You write well,'' she said, "And your thought is true. We do always live trapped inside our narrow everyday world until something—a vision, new learning, tragedy—knocks us out of it. It is intriguing to imagine how things might be different. With your mind, perhaps you should think about teaching.''

"I was a school-father. With less copy work, fewer seek training.''

"There might be other opportunities . . .''

Enzu summoned his courage. "You are very knowledgeable about the printing houses. Do you have any thoughts about who might be interested?''

With a look of dismissal, she clapped for her servant. "I can suggest, but not recommend, that you offer this continued-line idea to the printing house of Beretegal."

Her page scooped up his tablets and guided him out.

"You might think about a different story line, though," she called after him. "Some might think it a bit obvious for an unemployed scribe to imagine that his nemesis had never been invented."

"Don't take it so hard, Enzu," Yadidatum consoled. "This isn't about making the word of Utu manifest, this is about moving product."

They sat amid accountants and bureaucrats in a beer parlor in the temple sector. A half-empty crock waited in front of him, and a pleasant warm buzz had at least partially whitewashed his despair.

"So what do you think of her suggestion. Who do you know at Beretegal?"

Yadidatum studiously played with his straw.

"You taught math as well as writing; you know it's all about numbers. I love your work, but it's just too different. Tablet houses need to sell 500 copies to break even. Bronze for plates doesn't jump out of the river into your basket."

"Well, suppose I publish it myself. Copy it by hand, take tablets around and sell them out of a cart."

Yadidatum shook his head. "You've seen people who do that. How do you think readers see them?"

Enzu sighed. "Hopeless losers who couldn't find a publisher."

"Finish that beer, let's have another round," said Yadidatum brightly, waving to the barkeep. "Say. You know what I *could* sell? Have you seen these new children's tablets? Stories with simple words and pictures, made for teaching kids to read. Got any ideas that might work?"

"No."

"How about trying your hand at *tesh*? There's a lot of action around the New Year's ceremony. If you could give me two tablets on the king plowing the sacred harlot, it would make a great seasonal tie-in. I work with a top cylinder-seal carver who could do a couple of images."

"Not interested."

"Look, Enzu-dumu, you need to build up a track record. Right now, you're an unknown scribe with a couple of tablets in the local library, and nothing on the market. There's always series work. I can get you a slot writing for Gilgamesh."

"*Gishtu*! What else can Gilgamesh possibly *do*?"

Yadidatum glanced around, then leaned over. "Well, now that you ask. You want to talk about fiction that continues a line? Well just suppose Gilgamesh and Enkidu were, you know, different. Different *together*. There's a market for that, too."

"You would want me to write about the gods coupling just to get your ten percent?"

"Hey, Enzu-dumu. That's my job." The server set down two fresh *silas*. "I want to make you a success. We'll get past this small roadblock." He lifted his jar. "Beer to you."

"Beer to you."

Mari noted that he "stank like a Gutian," and suggested he spend the night in the tablet room. He didn't argue, and fell asleep at his table, trying to read. His head felt like broken pottery the next morning when Mari shook him awake, announcing a well-dressed visitor waiting in the guest room.

"He says it's business—about your writing." She handed him a basin of water and some aromatic oil. "Make yourself presentable."

The visitor was dressed in bright, dyed robes, and

sported a fistful of ornate silver rings. When Enzu
entered, Mari was filling his goblet from their last
good bottle of date wine. She bowed, and on the way
out, gave Enzu a look that had only one meaning:
don't mess this up.

But Enzu saw trouble as soon as the stranger introduced himself.

"I am Ikuppi-Adad, chief administrative scribe of
Badizi, *ensi* of Kish."

"I'm honored to have you visit me." Scribe of the
mayor of Kish. Ally of Sargon. Not good. "How might
I be of service?"

"I'd like to talk about your writing. A friend of
mine at the Temple of Nanna shared with me a copy
of a most intriguing and fanciful story, which he said
was your work."

Here was what Enzu had been expecting, but he
was shocked at the brazen disclosure. A spy within
the temple?

"Your kind words far exceed the merits of my humble text."

"For someone like me," Ikuppi smiled, "A mere
scribe, your work is a revelation. You must have a
rabisu who speaks such visions to you, no?"

"A *mashkim*?" Enzu detected no reaction to his
insistence on Sumerian. "No, no spirit voices. I call it
fiction-which-continues-a-line. Like following the
curve in a geometric figure; I look at events and project the world. I make it up."

"So. From your mouth to your hand," Ikuppi stared
intently into Enzu's eyes, then, "And does the speaker
believe in what he makes up?"

"I . . . I . . . write . . ." Enzu stammered.

"Relax, Enzu. Please. Where are my manners? I
sound like a lawyer." Ikuppi laughed. "Let us sit to-

gether. Here, here, sit with me, let us enjoy this excellent wine. Praise to Geshtinana."

"Praise be," he echoed automatically, and drank to cover his confusion and horror. Was his fiction being taken as an expression of support for the Bin-Shimal?

"What a challenging land we live in, eh, Enzu?" Ikuppi leaned back against the wall, smiled engagingly. "Ten thousand *buru* of flat earth, with no minerals, no stone, and no trees. In the summer, the fields are baked dry, and no rain for three-quarters of the year."

"Yes," Enzu tried a note of irony. "The Land is a truly a paradise."

"Who would want to be ruler of this? Just one bad harvest from starvation, in fields that only produce because we sentence people to perpetual labor maintaining canals. And harassed on all sides by nomads and poachers, barbarians from the rims of the world."

"They probably look at *us* as poachers when we send troops up to cut their trees," said Enzu.

"They are savages. Jackals."

"The jackal is a lion in his own neighborhood."

"Well put," said Ikuppi. "Speaking of lions. Do you know where your king is? Lugalzagesi's out shooting lions this week. Well, actually, he doesn't do a lot of the shooting. He has archers and spearmen for that. He mostly does the posing in the chariot for the artists."

Enzu let his mounting rage slip. "And where might *Sargon* be?"

"Sargon?" Ikuppi replied mildly. "For all I know, he might be reading your story by now. He is an educated man with a taste for literature."

That stopped Enzu cold.

"This isn't about politics, Enzu, this is about mar-

kets. As you say in your story, without printing, the
fall of Sumer would have been an inevitability. Printing brought your cities together around common standards: language, measurement, law. And those
standards reduced the risk in travel and transporting
goods, so your markets prospered.

"We're no fools, we did the same up in Akkad. But
now we both have reached the limits of what we can
do alone. We live in the same Land, along the same
rivers, facing the same enemies. Ultimately, it's about
unifying the Left and the Right.

"You and I, Enzu, we're scribes, we know the
power of the word. And you have used this power in
a new way that can help us think through, and shape,
the future. If Sumer can't appreciate your vision, Bu-
di-zi would be happy, I think, to sponsor such a tal-
ented hand as yours."

"I will consider it."

Ikuppi smiled. "I know you are both an honest man
and a careful thinker, so I will leave you to 'continue
the line.' "

When he returned from showing Ikuppi-Adad to the
door, Mari was hunched under the courtyard awning,
staring blankly at the water basin. The noon sun beat
mercilessly in the still air of the atrium. She looked
up as he sat next to her and he shook his head.

"With them," he said sadly, "There would only be
danger and fear."

"But could you do it for a while? To make some
money?"

"Mari, we have enough to live . . ."

"To live?" She spat. "To live in a barren
netherworld."

Enzu sighed, put an arm around his wife. "We will
find a way to have a child."

"Useless amulets and boxes of centipedes are all we can afford. The only real solution is beyond our means."

"Beloved, we've talked about this. It's not as simple as buying a host concubine. How could we support her?"

"We could sell this house. My father says we are welcome to move back to their farm. That would give us enough room," said Mari, pleading.

"Room, yes. But where could we find work? And what happens when your brother takes over? Would we just become field hands?"

"It would be worth it."

He looked into her eyes for a long time. "Yes," he said, "Yes, it would be worth all of that. But you know your father's fields are becoming less productive. Each year, the white lands expand. And the taxes to support the war in the north grow. How much longer would they be able to afford us?"

"More of your 'continued lines'? Must we live every day in fear of your imagination?" Tears began to leak from her eyes.

"I'm sorry. I have no way to ignore the possible futures which present themselves."

"I'm sorry, too. I know you only look for what's best for us."

"And I'm willing to consider your father's offer. But before that, I have one last thing to try."

"What's left?" said Mari. "You've been denied by all your former pupils. The temple has turned you down. And that fool Yadidatum is a useless parasite."

"For a long time, I've been convinced that there might just be one person in Sumer who would really understand my work. One man who might believe in it and sponsor me. I have to at least try."

"Try with who?"

"The inventor of printing."

*   *   *

Everyone knew where Ilammadu lived: an enormous estate just outside Eridu, a three-hour walk south from Ur. So Enzu awoke before dawn, packed his tablets, kissed Mari, and headed out with only the stars and the desert wind for company.

The stars, the wind—and incessant thoughts. Could he really give up writing? Go back to working the land? Given the choice between a comfortable and secure life as a scribe for Sargon, and eking out a hardscrabble existence on a farm, would he be able to make a decision he could live with?

He felt that he finally understood Enkidu's final curse. Civilization was more than humans could bear.

Columns of smoke from Ilammadu's compound were visible a long way off. Even this early in the morning, big kilns were already busy firing the day's production of tablets.

Before he could even see the bakehouse chimneys, guards intercepted him. Half expecting to be immediately turned back, he was surprised that they recognized his name. He was even more surprised when he was welcomed and bundled into a cart for the ride to the main house.

It was bigger than his whole schoolhouse had been back in its heyday. The walls were mudbrick, baked and painted to the height of a man, with glazed terra-cotta insets of lions and snake-dragons. Above the entrance rose wooden roof beams that seemed the thickness and length of whole trees. Enzu had never seen such construction outside of the temple and the palace. The guard led him through a maze of passageways, and into an inner courtyard, open to the sky.

In the center of the square stood an enormous stone *apzu*, an ornately sculpted ceremonial water tank, waist-high and dozens of cubits square. To the side was a table, shaded by an awning, and it was here the guard deposited the thoroughly dazed scribe.

"How much does a tablet weigh?" came a voice from the tank.

Incapable of more amazement, he simply answered. "A standard administrative text weighs about 4 *mina*."

"Not easy to carry around. And you appear to have several in your bag."

"Thirteen."

A hand appeared on the lip of the tank, then the head and shoulders of Ilammadu rose, dripping. A crinkled, sun-baked face; Enzu was startled at how young he was, then realized his mistake. The clean-shaven chin was deceptive.

"In just ten years, we have enhanced reading speed by standardizing on left-to-right order. We have made obsolete the crabbed, stuff-it-in-one-tablet stylus-work of the scribe. And we have retrieved the simplicity and beauty of our signs. All byproducts of printing."

"Your invention has been most successful."

"And yet, no fundamental change in the tablet. The costs to prepare and move all that heavy clay." Ilammadu nodded at the table. "What do you make of that material?"

Enzu looked next to him. Piled there was a stack of thin sheets, yellowish matter shot through with rough fibers. The top one was decorated with a series of small, ornate images.

"Paintings. On a substance I don't recognize."

"You will. That is papyrus, Enzu. And those are no paintings—that is written language from the kingdom of the Nile."

"A painted language . . ." Enzu was intrigued.

"But you see the problem," said Ilammadu.

"Of course," said Enzu, distractedly, staring at the papyrus. He picked up a corner and rubbed it with his fingers. "You could never print into this."

"The priestess was right about you, Enzu. You're a sharp one." Illamadu climbed out of the tank, slipped on a smoothly-woven loincloth. "I'd like to hear your thoughts on something. Come, let me show you my printing room."

Enzu reached for his bag, but Illamadu checked him. "No need—I've already read it."

"Ningal-ummi?"

"Yes, she provided a copy. Most intriguing. I like your voice. It's fresh."

"Thank you. Most of all, I detest repetition and formula. How often can you say, 'His face was like that of a man who walks a long road.'"

"Indeed. Tired phrases from the spoken world of yesteryear."

Ilammadu motioned him into a low, square building, open on both ends, with laborers ferrying materials in and out. To the right, workers hauled wooden trays of freshly smoothed clay to a low, flat stone in the center of the room. Above, two print-men wrestled with an enormous cylinder, balanced with pulleys and counterweights, wrapped with a thin bronze printing plate. As he watched, the sweating men swung the cylinder down and rolled it into the clay, rotating it as it moved, pressing the signs into the soft surface. When the plate reached the end, workers whisked out the tray and began trimming clay with knives, wipers cleaned the bronze plate, and the print-men swung it back into position to start again.

Even though Enzu had been in print houses many times, he still marveled at the speed and efficiency of the process. He knew how much organization went into preparing for this deceptively simple act; the coordinated efforts that prepared the clay, stoked the kilns, and moved finished tablets out to the cities.

"What types of tablets do you print here? Do you produce any fiction?"

"Enzu, I know you are anxious, but what I'm going to show you will explain much." They walked out, past the kiln to a smaller building, guarded by two husky men with gleaming copper knives.

In the narrow entrance room was a table, on which sat three small bronze cubes, a little bigger than a thumbnail. Enzu had a moment of doubt. What could be of such value here? Had Ilammadu lost touch with reality?

"Look at these blocks." Ilammadu presented the three cubes, and Enzu saw raised signs reversed on their faces, clearly tiny printing plates.

"Three different plates. The signs for Ash. For Ba. Zu."

"Suppose they weren't three different plates?" He held the blocks together and Enzu read them.

"Zu-ba-ash. That's what? Not a word."

"Try this." He rearranged the blocks.

"Ba-ash-zu. To be ashamed . . . of sweat? That doesn't make sense."

Ilammadu scrambled the blocks. "Again."

"Ash-ba-zu. A unique house of knowledge?" He frowned, thinking. "I'm not . . . how to say it, seeing your point."

"Continue this line. Ten years ago, we were inscribing words in wet clay with reeds, sign by sign. Then, I borrowed from cylinder seals the idea of molding a plate with a full tablet of signs and rolling it out. Now, suppose, instead of having to cast those plates whole, you could assemble them," he held up the bronze blocks, "from these?"

Enzu's mind spun. "You would need dozens—hundreds of the sign-blocks."

"In here." Through the door was a printing room—but smaller than any he had seen. A compact stone sat in the center, with a rectangular wooden frame suspended above it, and, lining the walls, rack after rack of identical sign plates. A servant carried in a freshly prepared tray of clay, and Illamadu strode to the table, where the wooden frame hung suspended. He motioned Enzu to look, and from beneath, he saw that the frame was packed with rows of the cubes, held in place with screw-presses from the side.

"It's flat!" Enzu exclaimed. "A flat printing form."

"Yes," said Illamadu. He nodded, and the servant slid the clay beneath the frame. "In order to hold the sign-cubes, I've had to give up the cylindrical plate."

Illamadu lowered the frame into the clay; when he cranked it back up, the new tablet had taken a crisp impress. The servant slid out the clay, and began wiping the plate with a blackened rag.

"Amazing," said Enzu. "This will make it possible to set up and change texts at will. With a ready store of the sign-cubes, it could be done anywhere, and cheaply." He thought for a moment. "But, it still doesn't address the weight of the tablets. What about that?"

"Suppose, Enzu, the plate did not have to press the signs *into* the surface?"

The servant had slid a sheet of papyrus onto the stone, and Illamadu lowered the frame. Even before it was raised, Enzu knew what he would see.

Neat rows of signs, imprinted in black, across the surface of the papyrus.

"Continue this line, Enzu. Cheap, portable writing. Texts that can be cast and printed in minutes. We have broken words down into bits. If the word is made of bits, why not the world? I could use a scribe who can help me imagine this world."

Enzu saw it at once, entire. "This is what will make it all possible. The breaking to pieces, the explosion of texts, the world of multiple voices, that's what will create readers who can envision with relish change points and alternatives."

"I admire your single-mindedness," Ilammadu laughed, "But such fiction is still a long way off. There are many painstaking, necessary steps, innumerable small battles to fight, and an enormous weight of tradition to overturn. In the meantime, would you work with me? Move your family down here, become my scribe, and help me make this change happen."

There was no question in Enzu's mind. Fiction could wait, for now. It *was* only a matter of continuing the line. For he could see, branching out into the future, not only a limitless ocean of texts, but a strange, unknowable pantheon of possible readers, there, latent, in the simple bronze blocks of the Ash-ba-zu.

Revision Point

Media are tools, and it is axiomatic in media theory that such tools are profound shapers of the cultures which employ them. By around 2350 BCE, the Sumerians had a rich scribal tradition, an increasingly abstract inscription system, some level of general literacy, and a language well suited to phonemic—as opposed to phonetic—representation.

Suppose, at this point, someone discovered that the technique used for reproductions of small texts (the carved cylinder seal) could be scaled up to produce full "pages." The invention of printing would likely have been as explosive for this culture as it was for Europe in the years before the Renaissance.

The title is an homage to a book by one of Marshall McLuhan's collaborators, Dr. Robert K. Logan, called "The Alphabet Effect." McLuhanesque theorists—sometimes called media ecologists—are particularly interested in the impact of the highly abstract alphabet on culture; my deviant assumption here is that simplified cuneiform might have exerted a similar force.

Who knows? Perhaps a print tradition built around the phonemic—rather than phonetic— might even have avoided some of the worst excesses of Aristotelian logic. At least, one can hope.

J.G.McD.

A WORD FOR HEATHENS

by Peter Watts

I AM the hand of God.

His Spirit fills me, even in this desecrated place. It saturates my very bones, it imbues my sword arm with the strength of ten. The cleansing flame pours from my fingertips and scours the backs of the fleeing infidels. They boil from their hole like grubs exposed by the dislodging of a rotten log. They writhe through the light, looking only for darkness. As if there could be any darkness in the sight of God—did they actually think He would be blind to the despoiling of a place of *worship*, did they think He would not notice this wretched burrow dug out beneath His very *altar*?

Now their blood erupts steaming from the blackened crusts of their own flesh. The sweet stink of burning meat wafts faintly through my filter. Patches of skin peel away like bits of blackened parchment, swirling in the updrafts. One of the heathens lurches over the lip of the hole and collapses at my feet. *Look past the faces*, they told us on the training fields, but today that advice means nothing; this abomination *has* no face, just a steaming clot of seared meat puckered by a bubbling fissure near one end. The fissure splits, revealing absurdly white teeth behind. Something between a whine and a scream, barely audible over the roar of the flames: *Please,* maybe. Or *mommy*.

I swing my truncheon in a glorious backhand. Teeth scatter across the room like tiny dice. Other bodies crawl about the floor of the chapel, leaving charred bloody streaks on the floor like the slime trails of giant slugs. I don't think I've *ever* been so overpowered by God's presence in my life. I am Saul, massacring the people of Amolek. I am Joshua butchering the Amorites. I am Asa exterminating the Ethiopians. I hold down the stud and sweep the room with great gouts of fire. I am so filled with Divine Love I feel ready to burst into flame myself.

"Praetor!"

Isaiah claps my shoulder from behind. His wide eyes stare back at me, distorted by the curve of his faceplate. "Sir, they're dead! We need to put out the fire!"

For the first time in what seems like ages I notice the rest of my guard. The prefects stand around the corners of the room as I arranged them, covering the exits, the silver foil of their uniforms writhing with fragments of reflected flame. They grip not flamethrowers, but dousers. A part of me wonders how they could have held back; how could *anyone* feel the Spirit in this way, and not bring down the fire? But the Spirit recedes in me even now, and descending from that peak I can see that God's work is all but finished here. The heathens are dead, guttering stick figures on the floor. Their refuge has been cleansed, the altar that once concealed it lies toppled on the floor where I kicked it just —

Was it only a few minutes ago? It seems like forever.

"Sir?"

I nod. Isaiah gives the sign; the prefects step forward and spray the chapel with fire suppressants. The flames vanish; the light goes gray. Crumbling, semicremated corpses erupt in clouds of wet, hissing steam as the chemicals hit.

Isaiah watches me through the smoky air. It billows around us like a steam bath. "Are you all right, sir?" The sudden moisture lends a hiss to his voice; his respirator needs a new filter.

I nod. "The Spirit was so—so . . ." I'm lost for words. "I've never felt it so strong before."

There's a hint of a frown behind his mask. "Are you—I mean, are you *sure?*"

I laugh, delighted. "Am I *sure?* I felt like Trajan himself!"

Isaiah looks uncomfortable, perhaps at my invocation of Trajan's name the very day after his funeral. Yet I meant no disrespect; if anything, I acted today in his memory. I can see him standing at God's side, looking down into this steaming abattoir and nodding with approval. Perhaps the very heathen that murdered him lies here at my feet. I can see Trajan turning to the Lord and pointing out the worm that killed him.

I can hear the Lord saying, *Vengeance is mine.*

An outcast huddles at the far end of the Josephus platform, leaning across the barrier in a sad attempt to bathe in the tram's maglev field. The action is both pointless and pitiful; the generators are shielded, and even if they weren't, the Spirit moves in so many different ways. It never ceases to amaze me how people can fail at such simple distinctions: shown that electromagnetic fields, precisely modulated, can connect us with the Divine, they somehow conclude that *any* coil of wire and electricity opens the door to redemption.

But the fields that move chariots are not those that

grace us with the Rapture. Even if this misguided creature were to get his wish, even if by some perverse
miracle the shielding were to vanish around the tram's
coils, the best he could hope for would be nausea and
disorientation. The worst—and it happens more than
some would admit, these days—could be outright
possession.

I've seen the possessed. I've dealt with the demons
who inhabit them. The outcast is luckier than he
knows.

I step onto the tram. The Spirit pushes the vehicle
silently forward, tied miraculously to a ribbon of track
it never touches. The platform slides past; the pariah
and I lock eyes for a moment before distance discon-
nects us.

Not shame on his face: dull, inarticulate *rage*.

My armor, I suppose. It was someone like me who
arrested him, who denied him a merciful death and
left his body lingering in the world, severed from its
very soul.

A pair of citizens at my side point at the dwindling
figure and giggle. I glare at them: they notice my insignia, my holstered shockprod, and fall silent. I see nothing ridiculous in the outcast's desperation. Pitiful, yes.
Ineffective. Irrational. And yet, what would any of us
do, cut off from grace? Would any straw be too thin
to grasp, for a chance at redemption?

Everything is so utterly clear in the presence of
God. The whole universe makes sense, like a child's
riddle suddenly solved; you see forever, you wonder
how all these glorious pieces of creation could ever
have confused you. At the moment, of course, those
details are lost to me. All that remains is the indescribable memory of how it felt to have *understood*, absolutely and perfectly . . . and that memory, hours old,
feels more real to me than *now*.

The tram glides smoothly into the next station. The news feed across the piazza replays looped imagery of Trajan's funeral. I still can't believe he's dead. Trajan was so strong in the Spirit we'd begun to think him invulnerable. That he could be bested by some *thing* built in the Backlands—it seems almost blasphemous.

Yet there he rests. Blessed in the eyes of God and Man, a hero to both rabble and elite, a commoner who rose from Prefecthood to Generalship in under a decade: killed by an obscene contraption of levers and pellets and explosions of stinking gas. His peaceful face fills the feed. The physicians have hidden all signs of the thing that killed him, leaving only the marks of honorable injury for the rest of us to remember. The famous puckered line running down forehead to cheekbone, the legacy of a dagger that almost blinded him at twenty-five. The angry mass of scars crawling up his shoulder from beneath the tunic: a lucky shock-prod strike during the Essene Mutiny. A crescent line on his right temple—a reminder of some other conflict whose name escapes me now, if indeed I ever knew it.

The view pulls back. Trajan's face recedes into an endless crowd of mourners as the tram starts up again. I barely knew the man. I met him a few times at Senate functions, where I'm sure I made no impression at all. But he made an impression on me. He made an impression on everyone. His conviction filled the room. The moment I met him, I thought: *here is a man untroubled by doubt.*

There was a time when I had doubts.

Never about God's might or goodness, of course. Only, sometimes, whether we were truly doing His will. I would confront the enemy, and see not blasphemers but people. Not traitors-in-waiting, but children. I would recite the words of our savior: did not the Christ Himself say *I come not bringing peace, but*

a sword? Did not Holy Constantine baptize his troops
with their sword arms raised? I knew the scriptures,
I'd known them from the crèche—and yet sometimes,
God help me, they seemed only words, and the enemy
had *faces*.

None so blind as those who will not see.

Those days are past. The Spirit has burned brighter
in me over the past month than ever before. And
this morning—this morning it burned brighter still. In
Trajan's memory.

I get off the tram at my usual stop. The platform is
empty but for a pair of constables. They do not board.
They approach me, their feet clicking across the tiles
with the telltale disciplined rhythm of those in authority. They wear the insignia of the priesthood.

I study their faces as they block my way. The memory of the Spirit fades just enough to leave room for
a trickle of apprehension.

"Forgive the intrusion, Praetor," one of them says,
"but we must ask you to come with us."

Yes, they are sure they have the right man. No, there
is no mistake. No, it cannot wait. They are sorry, but
they are simply following orders from the bishop. No,
they do not know what this concerns.

In that, at least, they are lying. It isn't difficult to
tell; *colleagues* and *prisoners* are accorded very different treatment in this regime, and they are not treating
me as a colleague. I am not shackled, at least. I am
not under arrest, my presence is merely required at the
temple. They have accused me of nothing.

That, perhaps, is the most frustrating thing of all:
accused, I could at least deny the charges.

Their cart winds through Constantinople, coasting
from rail to rail with a click and a hum. I stand at the
prow, in front of the control column. My escorts stand

behind. Another unspoken accusation, this arrangement; I have not been ordered to keep my eyes front,
but if I faced them—if I asserted the right to look
back—how long would it be before a firm hand came
down on my shoulder and turned me forward again?

"This is not the way to the temple," I say over
my shoulder.

"Origen's blocked to Augustine. Cleaning up after
the funeral."

Another lie. My own company guarded the procession down Augustine not two days ago. We left no
obstructions. These two probably know this. They are
not trying to mislead me. They are showing me that
they don't care enough to bother with a convincing lie.

I turn to confront them, but I am preempted before
I can speak: "Praetor, I must ask you to remove
your helmet."

"You're joking."

"No, sir. The bishop was quite explicit."

Stupefied and disbelieving, I undo the chin strap
and lift the instrument from my skull. I begin to tuck
it under my arm, but the constable reaches out and
takes it from me.

"This is insane," I tell him. Without the helmet I'm
as blind and deaf as any heathen. "I've done nothing
wrong. What possible reason—"

The constable at the wheel turns us left onto a new
track. The other puts his hand on my shoulder, and
firmly turns me around.

Golgotha Plaza. Of course.

This is where the Godless come to die. The loss of
my helmet is moot here; no one feels the presence of
the Lord in this place. Our cart slides silently past the
ranks of the heretics and the demon-possessed on
their crosses, their eyes rolled back in their heads,
bloody rivulets trickling from the spikes hammered

through their wrists. Some have probably been here since before Trajan died; crucifixion could take days even in the days before anesthetics, and now we are a more civilized nation. We do not permit needless suffering even among our condemned.

It's an old trick, and a transparent one; many prisoners, paraded past these ranks, have chosen to cooperate before interrogation even begins. Do these two think I don't see through them? Do they think I haven't done this *myself*, more times than I can count?

Some of the dying cry out as we pass—not with pain, but with the voices of the demons in their heads. Even now, they preach. Even now, they seek to convert others to their Godless ways. No wonder the Church damps this place—for what might a simple man think, feeling the Divine Presence while hearing sacrilege?

And yet, I almost *can* feel God's presence. It should be impossible, even if the constables hadn't confiscated my helmet. But there it is: a trickle of the Divine, like a thin bright shaft of sunlight breaking through the roof of a storm. It doesn't overpower; God's presence does not flood through me as it did earlier. But there is comfort, nonetheless. He is everywhere. He is even here. We do not banish him with damper fields, any more than we turn off the sun by closing a window.

God is telling me, *Have strength. I am with you.*

My fear recedes like an ebbing tide. I turn back to my escorts and smile; God is with them, too, if they'd only realize it.

But I don't believe they do. Something changes in their faces when they look at me. The last time I turned to face them, they were merely grim and uncooperative.

Now, for some reason, they almost look afraid.

*　　*　　*

They take me to the temple, but not to the bishop. They send me through the Tunnel of Light instead. They tell me it is entirely routine, although I went through the tunnel only four months ago and am not due again for another eight.

My armor is not returned to me afterward. Instead, they escort me into the bishop's sanctum, through an ornate doorway embellished with the likeness of a fiery cross and God's commandment to Constantine: *In hoc signo vinces.* In this sign, conquer.

They leave me there, but I know the procedure. There will be guards outside.

The sanctum is dark and comforting, all cushions and velvet drapes and mahogany bones. There are no windows. A screen on one wall glows with a succession of volumetric images. Each lingers for a few moments before dissolving hypnotically into the next: the Sinai foothills; Prolinius leading the charge against the Hindus; the Holy Grotto itself, where God showed Moses the Burning Bush, where He showed all of us the way of the Spirit.

"Imagine that we had never found it."

I turn to find the bishop standing behind me as if freshly materialized. He holds a large envelope the color of ivory. He watches me with the faintest trace of a smile on his lips.

"Teacher?" I say.

"Imagine that Constantine never had his vision, that Eusebius never sent his expedition into Sinai. Imagine that the Grotto had never been rediscovered after Moses. No thousand-year legacy, no technological renaissance. Just another unprovable legend about a prophet hallucinating in the mountains, and ten commandments handed down with no tools to enforce them. We'd be no better than the heathens."

He gestures me toward a settee, a decadent thing, overstuffed and wine-colored. I do not wish to sit, but neither do I wish to give offense. I perch carefully on one edge.

The bishop remains standing. "I've been there, you know," he continues. "In the very heart of the grotto. I knelt in the very place Moses Himself must have knelt."

He's waiting for a response. I clear my throat. "It must have been . . . indescribable."

"Not really." He shrugs. "You probably feel closer to God during your morning devotionals. It's . . . unrefined, after all. Raw ore. It's astounding enough that a natural formation could induce *any* kind of religious response, much less one consistent enough to base an entire culture on. Still, the effect is . . . weaker than you might expect. Overrated."

I swallow and hold my tongue.

"But then, you could say the same thing about the whole religious experience in principle," he continues, blandly sacrilegious. "Just an electrical hiccup in the temporal lobe, no more *divine* than the force that turns compass needles and draws iron filings to a magnet."

I remember the first time I heard such words: with the rest of my crèche, just before our first Communion. *It's like a magic trick,* they said. *Like static interfering with a radio. It confuses the part of your brain that keeps track of your edges, of where you* stop *and everything else* begins—*and when that part gets confused, it thinks you go on* forever, *that you and creation are one. It tricks you into believing you're in the very presence of God.* They showed us a picture of the brain sitting like a great wrinkled prune within the shadowy outline of a human head, arrows and labels drawing our attention to the most important parts.

They opened up wands and prayer caps to reveal the tiny magnets and solenoids inside, subtle instrumentality that had subverted an entire race.

Not all of us got it at first. When you're a child, *electromagnet* is just another word for *miracle*. But they were patient, repeating the essentials in words simple enough for young minds, until we'd all grasped the essential point: we were but soft machines, and God was a malfunction.

And then they put the prayer caps on our heads and opened us to the Spirit and we knew, beyond any doubting, that God was real. The experience transcended debate, transcended logic. There was no room for argument. We *knew*. Everything else was just words.

Remember, they said afterward. *When the heathens would tell you there is no God, remember this moment.*

I cannot believe that the bishop is playing the same games with me now. If he is joking, it is in very bad taste. If he is testing my conviction, he falls laughably short. Neither alternative explains my presence here.

But he won't take silence for an answer. "Don't you agree?" he asks.

I tread carefully. "I was taught that the Spirit lives within iron filings and compass needles as much as in our minds and our hearts. That makes it no less Divine." I take a breath. "I mean no disrespect, Teacher, but why am I here?"

He glances at the envelope in his hand. "I wished to discuss your recent . . . exemplary performance."

I wait, not taken in. My guards did not treat me as an *exemplary* performer.

"You," he continues, "are why we prevail against the heathens. It's not just the technology that the Spirit provides, it's the *certainty*. We *know* our God. He is empirical, He can be tested and proved and experienced. We have no doubt. *You* have no doubt. That is why we have been unstoppable for a thousand years, that is why neither heathen spies nor heathen flying machines or the very breadth of an ocean will keep us from victory."

They are not words that need corroboration.

"Imagine what it must be like to have to *believe*." The bishop shakes his head, almost sadly. "Imagine the doubt, the uncertainty, the discord and petty strife over which dreams are divine and which are blasphemous. Sometimes I almost pity the heathens. What a terrible thing it must be, to need *faith*. And yet they cling to it. They creep into our towns and they wear our clothes and they move among us, and they *shield* themselves from the very presence of God." He sighs. "I confess I do not entirely understand them."

"They ingest some sort of herb or fungus," I tell him. "They claim it connects them with their own *God*."

The bishop *mmmm*s. Doubtless he knew this already. "I would like to see their *fungus* move a monorail. Or even turn a compass needle. And yet, surrounded by evidence of the Lord's hand, they continue to cut themselves off from it. This is not widely known, but we've recently received reports that they can successfully scramble entire rooms. Whole villas, even."

He runs one long fingernail along the envelope, slitting it lengthwise.

"Like the room you purged this morning, Praetor. It was scrambled. The Spirit could not manifest."

I shake my head. "You are mistaken, Teacher. I've never felt the Spirit more strongly than I did in that—"

The grim-faced escorts. The detour through Golgotha. The shaft of inexplicable sunlight. Everything falls into place.

A yawning chasm opens in the pit of my stomach.

The bishop extracts a sheet of film from the envelope: a snapshot of my passage through the Tunnel of Light. "You are possessed," he says.

No. There is some mistake.

He holds up the snapshot, a ghostly, translucent image of my head rendered in grays and greens. I can see the demon clearly. It festers within my skull, a malign little lump of darkness just above my left ear. A perfect spot from which to whisper lies and treachery.

I am unarmed. I am imprisoned: I will not leave this place a free man. There are guards beyond the door, and unseen priest holes hidden in the dark corners of the room. If I so much as raise a hand to the bishop, I am dead.

I am dead anyway. I am possessed. I am condemned.

"No," I whisper.

"*I am the way, the truth, and the light*," the bishop intones. "*None can come to the Father except through me*." He stabs at the lump on the plate with one accusing finger. "Is *this* of the Christ? Is it of His Church? How then can it be real?"

I shake my head, dumbly. I cannot believe this is happening. I cannot believe what I see. I felt the Spirit today. I felt the *Spirit*. I am as certain of that as I have been of anything.

Is it me thinking these thoughts? Is it the demon, whispering to me?

"It seems there are more of them every day," the bishop remarks sadly. "And they are not content to corrupt the soul. They kill the body as well."

They force the *Church* to kill the body, he means. The Church is going to kill me.

But the bishop shakes his head, as though reading my mind. "I speak literally, Praetor. The demon will take your life. Not immediately—it may seduce you with this false rapture for some time. But then you will feel pain, and your mind will go. You will change; not even your loved ones will recognize you by your acts. Perhaps, near the end, you will become a drooling infant, squalling and soiling yourself. Or perhaps the pain will simply grow unbearable. Either way, you will die."

"How—how long?"

"A few days, a few weeks . . . I know of one poor soul who was ridden for nearly a year before she was saved."

Saved. Like the heretics at Golgotha.

And yet, whispers a tiny inner voice, *even a few days spent in that Presence would be easily worth a lifetime. . . .*

I bring my hand to my temple. The demon lurks in there, festering in wet darkness only a skull's thickness away. I stare at the floor. "It can't be."

"It is." Then, after a moment: "But it does not *have* to be."

It takes me a moment to realize what he's just said. I look up and meet his eyes.

He's smiling. "There is another way," he says. "Yes, usually the body must die that the soul can be saved—crucifixion is infinitely kinder than the fate that usually awaits the possessed. But there's an alternative, for those with—potential. I will not mislead you, Praetor. There are risks. But there have been successes as well."

"An . . . an alternative . . . ?"

"We may be able to exorcise the demon. We may be able to *remove* it, physically, from your head. If it works, we can both save your life and return you to the Lord's presence."

"If it works . . ."

"You are a soldier. You know that death is always a possibility. It is a risk here, as it is in all things." He takes a deep, considered breath. "On the cross, death would be a certainty."

The demon in my head does not argue. It whispers no blasphemies, makes no desperate plea against the prospect of its extraction. It merely opens the door to Heaven the merest crack, and bathes my soul in a sliver of the Divine.

It shows me the Truth.

I *know*, as I knew in the crèche, as I knew this morning. I am in the presence of God, and if the bishop cannot see it, then the bishop is a babbling charlatan, or worse.

I would gladly go to the cross for just such a moment as this.

I smile and shake my head. "Do you think me *blind*, Bishop? You would wrap your wretched plottings up in Scripture, that I would not see them for what they are?" And I *do* see them now, laid bare in the Spirit's radiance. Of course these vile Pharisees would trap the Lord in trinkets and talismans if they could. They would ration God through a spigot to which only they have access—and those to whom He would speak without their consent, they would brand *possessed*.

And I *am* possessed, but not by any demon. I am possessed by Almighty God. And neither He nor His Sons are hermit crabs, driven to take up residence in the shells of idols and machinery.

"Tell me, Bishop," I cry. "Was Saul wearing one of your *prayer caps* on the road to Damascus? Did Elisha summon his bears with one of your wands? Or were *they* possessed of demons as well?"

He shakes his head, feigning sadness. "It is not the Praetor that speaks."

He's right. God speaks through me, as he spoke through the Prophets of old. I am God's voice, and it doesn't matter that I am unarmed and unarmored, it doesn't matter that I am deep in the devil's sanctum. I need only raise my hand and God will strike this blasphemer down.

I raise my fist. I am fifty cubits high. The bishop stands before me, an insect unaware of its own insignificance. He has one of his ridiculous machines in one hand.

"Down, devil!" we both cry, and there is blackness.

I awaken into bondage. Broad straps hold me against the bed. The left side of my face is on fire. Smiling physicians lean into view and tell me all is well. Someone holds up a mirror. My head has been shaved on the left side; a bleeding crescent, inexplicably familiar, cuts across my temple. Crosses of black thread sew my flesh together as though I were some torn garment, clumsily repaired.

The exorcism was successful, they say. I will be back with my company within the month. The restraints are merely a precaution. I will be free of them soon, as I am free of the demon.

"Bring me to God," I croak. My throat burns like a desert.

They hold a prayer wand to my head. I feel nothing.

I feel *nothing*.

The wand is in working order. The batteries are fully charged. It's probably nothing, they say. A temporary aftereffect of the exorcism. Give it time. Probably best to leave the restraints on for the moment, but there's nothing to worry about.

Of course they are right. I have dwelt in the Spirit, I know the mind of the Almighty—for, after all, were not all of the chosen made in His image? God would

never abandon even the least of his flock. I do not
have to believe this, it is something I *know*. Father,
you will not forsake me.

It will come back. It will come back.

They urge me to be patient. After four days they
admit that they've seen this before. Not often, mind
you; it was a rare procedure, and this is an even rarer
side effect. But it's possible that the demon may have
injured the part of the mind that lets us truly know
God. The physicians recite medical terms which mean
nothing to me. I ask them about the others that preceded me down this path: how long before *they* were
restored to God's sight? But it seems there are no
hard and fast rules, no overall patterns.

Trajan burns on the wall beside my bed. Trajan
burns daily there and is never consumed, a little like
the Bush itself. My keepers have been replaying his
cremation daily, a thin gruel of recorded images
thrown against the wall; I suspect they are meant to
be inspirational. It is always just past sundown in these
replays. Trajan's fiery passing returns a kind of daylight to the piazza, an orange glow reflecting in ten
thousand upturned faces.

He is with God now, forever in His presence. Some
say that was true even before he passed, that Trajan
lived his whole life in the Spirit. I don't know whether
that's true; maybe people just couldn't explain his zeal
and devotion any other way.

A whole lifetime, spent in the Spirit. I'd give a lifetime now for even a minute.

We are in unexplored territory, they say. That is
where they are, perhaps.

I am in Hell.

Finally they admit it: none of the others have recovered. They have been lying to me all along. I have been cast into darkness, I am cut off from God. And they called this butchery a *success*.

"It will be a test of your faith," they tell me. My *faith*. I gape like a fish at the word. It is a word for heathens, for people with made-up gods. The cross would have been infinitely preferable. I would kill these smug meat-cutters with my bare hands, if my bare hands were free.

"Kill me," I beg. They refuse. The bishop himself has commanded that I be kept alive and in good health. "Then summon the bishop," I tell them. "Let me talk to him. Please."

They smile sadly and shake their heads. One does not *summon* the bishop.

More lies, perhaps. Maybe the bishop has forgotten that I even exist, maybe these people just enjoy watching the innocent suffer. Who else, after all, would dedicate their lives to potions and bloodletting?

The cut in my head keeps me awake at night, itches maddeningly as scar tissue builds and puckers along its curved edges. I still can't remember where I've seen its like before.

I curse the bishop. He told me there would be risks, but he only mentioned death. Death is not a risk to me here. It is an aspiration.

I refuse food for four days. They force-feed me liquids through a tube in my nose.

It's a strange paradox. There is no hope here; I will never again know God, I am denied even surcease. And yet these butchers, by the very act of refusing me a merciful death, have somehow awakened a tiny spark that wants to live. It is *their* sin I am suffering for, after all. This darkness is of *their* making. I did not turn away from God; they hacked God out of me like a gobbet of gangrenous flesh. It can't be that they want me to live, for there is no living apart from God. It can only be that they want me to *suffer*.

And with this realization comes a sudden desire to deny them that satisfaction.

They will not let me die. Perhaps, soon, they will wish they had.

God damn them.

God damn them. Of course.

I've been a fool. I've forgotten what really matters. I've been so obsessed by these petty torments that I've lost sight of one simple truth: God does not turn on his children. God does not abandon the faithful.

But *test* them—yes. God tests us all the time. Did He not strip Job of all his worldly goods and leave him picking his own boils in the dust? Did He not tell Abraham to kill his own son? Did He not restore them to his sight, once they had proved worthy of it?

I believe that God rewards the righteous. I believe that the Christ said *Blessed are those who believe even though they have* not *seen.* And now, at last, I believe that perhaps *faith* is not the obscenity I once thought, for it can give hope when one is cut off from the truth.

I am not abandoned. I am *tested*.

I send for the bishop.

Somehow, this time I know he'll come. He does.

"They say I've lost the Spirit," I tell him. "They're wrong."

He sees something in my face. Something changes in his.

"Moses was denied the Promised Land," I continue. "Constantine saw the flaming cross but twice in his lifetime. God spoke to Saul of Tarsus only once. Did *they* lose faith?"

"They moved the world," the bishop says.

I bare my teeth. My conviction fills the room. "So will I."

He smiles gently. "I believe you."

I stare at him, astonished by my own blindness. "You knew this would happen."

He shakes his head. "I could only hope. But yes, there is a—strange truth we are only learning now. I'm still not sure I believe it. Sometimes it isn't the *experience* of redemption that makes the greatest champions, but the *longing* for it."

On the panel beside me, Trajan burns and is not consumed. I wonder briefly if my fall from grace was entirely accidental. But in the end it does not matter. I remember, at last, where I once saw a scar like mine.

Before today, the acts I committed in God's name were pale, bloodless things. No longer. I will return to the Kingdom of Heaven. I will raise my sword arm high and I will not lay it down until the last of the unbelievers has been slaughtered. I will build mountains of flesh in His name, one body at a time. Rivers will flow from the throats that I cut. I will not stop until I have earned my way back into His sight.

The bishop leans forward and loosens my straps. "I don't think we need these any more."

They couldn't hold me anyway. I could tear them like paper.

I am the fist of God.

Revision Point

Contrary to what you may have heard, God isn't everywhere. The only place He reliably hangs out is in the temporal lobes—at least, that's where Vilayanur Ramashandran found Him when he went looking in the brains of hyper-religious epileptics at UC-San Diego. You'll *never* find the Almighty slumming in the parietal cortex, judging by radioisotopes Andrew Newberg tracked through the heads of a meditating Buddhist monk at the University of Pennsylvania. Most spectacularly—and controversially—Michael Persinger of Laurentian University claims to be able to induce religious experiences using a helmet which bathes the brain in precisely-controlled electromagnetic fields.

We begin to understand the mechanism: Rapture is as purely neurological as any other human experience. With that understanding, inevitably, comes the potential for control. Religious belief—that profound, irrational disorder afflicting so many of our species—may actually have a cure.

Of course, a cure is the last thing many would want. Religion has been a kick-ass form of social control for millennia, even absent any understanding of its neurology. It seems likely that these new insights will be used not to free us from the Rapture, but to tweak it to maximum effect—to make us even more docile, even more obedient, even less skeptical of our masters than we are now.

Today we're just taking our first steps down that road—but what if we'd taken them back in the third century, instead of the dawn of the twenty-first? That was the time of Constantine, the Roman Emperor who legitimized Christianity after a religious vision promised him victory in battle. It's not much of a stretch to posit a subsequent expedition to the Holy Land, in search of ancient miracles.

I see a vein of magnetic ore in the Sinai Hills. I see it speak to Constantine's pilgrims as it spoke to Moses, sixteen centuries earlier. I watch it seed a renaissance in neurotheology—inevitably, in all manner of electromagnetic physics—and then I jump forward a thousand years and tell you a story. . . .

It's an unbelievable gimmick, of course, a natural miracle filling in for Persinger's God Helmet. But given that conceit, the social consequences seem more than plausible; they almost have a ring of inevitability to them. Perhaps, in all these stories about parallel universes, we've focused too much on chaos and too little on inertia. Perhaps it doesn't matter where the butterfly flaps its wings.

Perhaps human nature pulls all time lines back to same endpoint.

P.W.

A GHOST STORY

by Jihane Noskateb

"*H*OW *did it happen, for you?" she asks me. She won't look at me; her voice is so soft, it would be easy to ignore her request. She would understand, I know, that the wounds are too fresh. She only told me how she fell from time to let me know I wasn't alone.*
    That's why I tell her everything.

I was sentenced to a month of isolation at the end of April 2103 for trying to build a net interface. The fact that I built it for scientific purposes made no difference to the judge. Net interfaces were under the strict dominion of the Five Firms' Council.

They stripped me of my wrink, the wrist link interface everyone is given upon reaching adulthood, thus cutting me off the net. Then, they locked me in a cell with only four white walls, and my thoughts.

One of their techs, Angriess, came to see me on my first day there. The only gentle person in the nightmare my life had become.

She brought me net-interface-free paper books and told me they had put my antiquarian shop under seal. She also had to supervise the one on-line chat I was allowed, and heard when my friend and business partner, the archaeologist Sabine van Saragreg, said it would be best if we weren't in contact, "until all is forgotten."

One week later, on May 4th, 2103, I was going crazy from white walls and silence. *You don't know how it is, to be part of a Net* . . . The wrink, like every other receiver, is also a relay. A small one. But there are larger ones made up of so many satellites above the Earth's atmosphere that from there it looks as if a globe of switching plates protects the planet.

All those relays make the Net accessible from anywhere. At least, as long as you have a key.

What Angriess brought into my week-long isolation was, I thought then, even better than that.

"How are you feeling today?"

I glanced up from the already worn-out book.

Angriess stood on the other side of the transparent door. Behind her, I could see the now familiar faces of my midday guards, in a room as white, stark, and empty as mine.

"Bored," I informed her. "Why?"

"I . . ." She glanced back. The guards didn't move. "I have something for you."

After a week of silence, and only three choices of readings, I was on my feet before I knew it. "What?"

She turned again toward the guards, "Please, let me in."

Their voices came muffled by the distance through the interphone embedded next to the door.

"Have you been checked for links?"

"Those kinds of security measures are for visitors. I'm a first-rated member of Youhen."

And in answer the door opened.

A movement caught my eyes. She must have noticed: she lifted the bag she held in one hand, and came to sit on the floor at my side.

I slid down, my eyes still on the black leather backpack and the knot that held it closed. I had had to sew the leather thong on when I broke the plastic lock, some weeks ago. I always carried too much. Today, it looked almost empty.

"Sir. You're an antiquarian."

With an effort, I looked up, nodded.

Her eyes were kind and sad, too.

"You're the one who repaired old themed coffee mugs and replicated them, aren't you? I bought some of those replicas."

"I don't always succeed in bringing objècts back to life."

"But most of the time you do."

"I try."

She smiled. It lit up her eyes, almost enough to erase the sadness. "I'm an engineer. With the rhythm with which technologies evolve, I sometimes feel like a builder of sand castles. I care for each and every one of them, but tomorrow'll have forgotten my creations. Except if someone like you finds them. . . ."

She paused. I had no answer for her, but she didn't seem to mind.

I think she's one of the people I'll miss the most. I wonder what became of her, if she still exists.

She went on, after a while, "This is why you tried to build your own net interface, isn't it? To bring some technology of the past back to life, and make it part of our present."

"Yes."

"I thought you'd like to keep working on it."

Angriess got up in one fluid motion and went to the door. She didn't look back.

I never saw her again.

In the bag, I found most of my tools, and the two artifacts Sabine had sent me from her digs at Crotona, sealed in plastic.

The first was an old, worn-down plastic casing that fit easily in the palm of my hand, with empty sockets where numbered keys used to be and a broken screen above. I didn't have to look inside to know from its weight that the secondary interface I'd been building inside the ancient mobile phone was still there. Either Angriess had put it back, or they hadn't checked, believing they had discovered my only illegal interface embedded in my desk. The one that had brought me here to be punished.

I could make this one work, I knew it. It would bring the ancient phone to life.

Even if I couldn't "make a call," I would hear static, maybe more.

The second object had yielded little of its mysteries since Sabine had sent it for authentication. Even its true form, that of a hyperoctahedron, had been difficult to ascertain.

Its constant shifting under my gaze owed more to technical prowess than to optical illusion, and was my only clue to its origin. Who would conceive a solid octahedron from which stretched braids of silken material woven so tight they sketched around it the fleeting, three-dimensional image of an octahedron?

Who would be interested in creating a three-dimensional image of a four-dimensional hyperoctahedron? I'd wondered, until the white paint of the solid core told me that it was more than two thousand and fifty years old. The time of the Pythagoreans.

The Pythagorean school, fascinated with numbers and their relationship to music, associated the octahedron with air—and recognized the octave as the first natural harmony. They had dwelled in Crotona, where the hyperoctahedron had been found.

If they had created this geometric representation out of worship or interest for the number eight, what was its use? It played no sound I cared to hear.

Out of frustration, I had nicknamed it my "octofuss."

Others would give it other names. But no one would have such an intimate relationship with it, and to this day, I grant myself the right to name it as I feel fit.

That day, I didn't care much for it, though. I unsealed it, put it carefully on the floor next to me, and turned my attention back to the phone.

A glance at my guardians.

They weren't paying attention.

I started working.

Three hours later, I was done, the inner circuitry either reconfigured or replaced.

I pressed the "on" button. I held it to the side of my face, making believe I was one in a crowd of self-talkers, like those we saw in old flat-screen movies.

"I can't hear you!" I said into it, and, still hurting from Sabine's forsaking, "Crotona, Crotona!"

A voice answered, in bad English.

"Yes? Who's there?"

"Who's there?" I echoed in a silly manner.

My palms were damp with sweat, my hand trembling. I tried to get a better grip on myself and the phone.

In a steadier voice, I asked, "Who are you?"

"I'm Saturnin Ferrault. One of the archaeologists of Crotona. Who are you?"

I am not proud of what I felt then.

I remembered that Sabine didn't want anyone to know she knew me, especially not her esteemed colleagues. Too bad for her, I thought: I was actually on the "phone" with one of them, and I would make my voice heard.

That, I did.

"I am Sabine's antiquarian," I said. "The precious finds you made in the creek? I'm the specialist authenticating—"

"What are you talking about?"

Static and a French accent made him hard to understand.

I turned my back to the guards, and talked louder.

I gave him every detail I could remember about the dig's latest discoveries to prove my claim, and concluded: "From the inscriptions Sabine discovered, the date, and some veiled references in Plato and Plotin, I'm almost positive the hyperhedron, like the cave itself, dates back to Pythagoras himself, and his school. We always believed they dwelled only on numbers, music, and that their geometry was purely theoretical, but it's clear that . . ."

I glanced at the object in question. It quivered with each sound, lay quiescent for each breath between words.

That's the last I saw of my world.

My voice faded out. My breath, too.

My cell was no more.

I was facing a man dressed in an early twentieth century suit. He looked right past me, as if I wasn't there, and talked into an antique radio post.

"What is clear? Who is this *fichue* Sabine? *Monsieur!*"

My first thought was: I have brought both objects to life!

My second, darker one, was: I, on the other hand, don't feel that much alive anymore. . . .

"Why was it so important to you, to make this thing work?"

"I'm an antiquarian. Bringing life . . ."

I pause; her gray eyes, upon me, are sad. Beyond her, beyond the bulk of the space station we chose to attach ourselves to, the stars burn the night of space with promises.

Suddenly, I remember.

"I mean, I was. Bringing the past to life . . ."

"Is it why you talk to me?" Her voice is small, cold, and far away. Like the stars.

"What? You mean . . . some morbid . . . No!"

She doesn't believe me, despite everything we have shared. I never realized how much she had been hurt before by trust unduly placed.

So I force the truth out. "I speak with you, not the others like us, because I can. With you at my side, even remembering . . ."

Words fail me. As I lapse into silence, my eyes search her face for answers I don't have.

She's smiling a small private smile that lights up her narrow face. Brown wisps of hair shadow her eyes into calm dark pools.

"What happened then?" she asks.

"When?"

"When you ceased to exist."

Oh.

"You don't understand what I am saying! The Pythagorean school was thought lost after the death of its creator in 548 BCE. But all we know for sure is that secrecy was important to them, that they worked on polyhedrons, numbers, music, as parts of a whole that would unlock the universe's mysteries!"

"And I'm telling you, you're too damn gullible! Why would a total stranger speak in English to a French archaeologist, and reveal to him . . ."

"His English wasn't that good," the French epigraphist pouted.

"Neither is yours," replied the Tunisian engineer.

They were both quite drunk by then. Youssef Bin Ines. Saturnin Ferrault, who had answered my phone call, and whom I had continued to follow, unwillingly, invisibly, all along this hot, dusty day in Crotona, Sicily—May 4, 1923.

They staggered out of the bar at midnight, convinced that the only way to settle their argument was to prove one—or the other—right.

And so we went, me a mere thought, them noisy shadows, to the empty dig to get whatever they thought they would need, then to the creek I had described thoughtlessly.

I tried not to be here, tried to gather my wits, to shake off this vivid yet immaterial hallucination. But each breath Saturnin took shuddered inside me, and I found myself, or what was left of me, following his every move as if tethered to his muscles by invisible cords.

I even felt cramps from his rhythmic digging.

They searched for hours. At first, it seemed like a fool's errand, until they discovered among the rubble a stone with an inscription Saturnin translated. It was part of a mysterious vow of secrecy.

They dug further.

I was starting to fear what was happening, that I

wouldn't wake up, when Saturnin stopped to answer the call of nature—one I shared, but would experience no more.

Dawn broke when they found the entrance. They took one step inside the man-made cave, and stopped.

Unable to go forward until Saturnin did, all I could do was stare with them at the perfect replica of my octofuss; this one carved from crystalline stone and half as high as a man of my time.

It stood in the exact center of the room. The room itself was half a sphere, the floor the only plane surface. The hyperhedron's edges reached the walls.

I was dragged forward as Saturnin took soundless steps inside. Youssef followed, and stopped before the hyperhedron. But Saturnin's attention had been caught by the walls themselves. With him, I came close enough to realize inscriptions ran everywhere.

He read for a long while, his eyes huge with wonder.

Finally, he said, "This changes everything we thought about the technology-poor Greeks. . . ."

A snapping sound almost deafened me. I looked around in amazement. I immediately noticed that the others hadn't reacted. And that I wasn't tethered to Saturnin anymore.

Youssef was commenting, "It looks like an acoustic device of some kind. . . ."

"It is," Saturnin confirmed.

Is it how I heard the past?

"According to this," the epigraphist gestured toward the wall's inscriptions. "Other chambers existed, linking every disciple of Pythagoras together. They managed to communicate over great distances, if the inscriptions are to be believed. I wonder how many other chambers might still exist."

I wonder what will come of that.

* * *

No sooner had I thought the question than the world whirled around me, as if my asking was taking me in search of the answer.

I no longer stood—or floated, or existed disembodied—in the cave, but in what looked like a laboratory. It wasn't the 1920s, but not my time either.

1972.

The knowledge had come, unbidden, to my mind.

I didn't question it, though. My attention was caught by the room in which I had appeared. Very large with white walls. Not a single straight line, nor a roof.

But what of rainy days?

With the question, the answer again. It was the strangest sensation, as if I only had to become aware to have always known. At the time, it was one more insane thing that distanced me from the reality of it all.

Chimes hung above the wall and sang a soft but complex harmony along three octaves. The sound made a field of some kind, on which rain played, changing the sound into a very different kind of melody that pulled the threads of the field tighter.

There was an equation for it, of alien beauty. Mathematics made tangible through sound and giving rise to an EM field. This was possible because of . . .

A man sighed. I turned.

He was seated at a desk, poring over some papers.

A name came with the sight. Anis Korbous. No older than me, he was already a physicist of renown.

His brows furrowed in concentration. He spoke softly as he worked. A flute hung from his chest, and, from time to time, he took it to his lips and played a series of notes. A recorder, not unlike those I had repaired except for a dishlike antenna, responded to it by stopping, rewinding, and replaying his last arrangement.

Listening, I learned why my question had brought me here.

One look at the artifact he was working on confirmed it.

My *octofuss*. Its condition was as pristine as the first time I had seen it. Somehow I knew it had been dubbed "the Saturnine Enigma," because its use hadn't been identified yet.

Korbous was convinced that sound could be transformed into a form that could exist forever, and the octofuss was the key to proving that.

His only problem was what sounds he had to play to activate it.

Research is fascinating. But done by someone else, it's also a very tedious process. My attention wandered the room, its materials, alien no more than a second.

Only the lone *cube*, at the center of the room, rising from the floor, with incense burning on its surface, refused to yield its secret immediately.

What is inside?

The mere thought brought me in. There was no light, and yet I could sense the presence of walls, set at wild angles. They didn't reflect in any way the outer shape of this place.

But I didn't have to wonder about its function. A single tone played, its echo growing into a continuous, complex chord. And from that, pressure waves of sound converted to electromagnetic energy, accessed as needed by the different devices of the house.

I watched Korbous for hours, trying to unravel a mystery that would explain my own, fascinated by the way knowledge kept popping into my head about this different time period. This new path of time.

*   *   *

I wonder if it wasn't then that I started to appreciate what I had become.

"Your wife and I missed you at lunch. I guess you missed lunch altogether, didn't you?"

We both jumped, one of us real, the other an immaterial presence still learning to control its bodiless movements.

The voice emanated from the walls. Anis turned slightly toward a curve in the wall. Sound came from there, and a face was appearing, fuzzy, and slightly out of synch with the voice. I stepped *inside*. And saw that the inside of the wall was hollow, but with wood and more complex material built into a complex maze that led to different, smaller chimes. The walls, powered by a central polyhedron.

Wavecatchers.

Sound programmed, or filtered, I'm not sure, what came in and out. Machinery changed the nature of the waves. Sound waves were turned into electromagnetic waves and traveled through a relay as light, carrying the two *phones'* signatures.

Where does the light go . . . ?

The speed of a thought. Amazing, isn't it? I think I will like experimenting with that. . . . And how we can sense without touch or sight, solids that we can stand upon or pass through . . . but that's . . . well, that's not my story, is it?

"Nisea asked me to check on you. She had to go back to the Academia, but as soon as she dispatches her students, she'll come and feed you." The voice wasn't out of synch anymore; a dimple added humor to its warmth. "I thought I should warn you!"

This time, my questing thoughts had tethered me to a woman named Myrib. Myrib Zrirey, her full name was.

I walked away from her, curious again.

Her room, unlike the scientist's, was full of colors and clutter. Only the same bare polyhedron at the center reminded me of Anis'.

Differences and underlying similarities caught my attention.

Here, there was a roof, but small colonnades held it at least ten centimeters above the end of the walls. It was larger than the room itself; the corners caved in, slightly. Floating closer, I saw smaller water balls used as chimes.

The work itself was beautiful to behold.

This was, I discovered, an artist's home. There was peace and quiet. *It was easy to forget what I was and wasn't.*

All afternoon, she worked on a new kind of wave field, designed to generate a lighter gravity for small objects.

Wave fields were created by combining compatible waves, each building upon the other in a feedbacklike reaction. They didn't travel, but kept interlacing until they became impermeable to a third kind of wave that sometimes created a specific state around them.

Myrib didn't understand the reactions, nor did she care. She understood, barely, the complex harmonies that made it possible, and while she played them in the background, she gave the result a superb, aesthetic form.

She believed that the world never had enough beauty and that by revealing some, she helped people see it everywhere.

She didn't only paint wave field equations or symphonies, I discovered. She sculpted *wavecatcher ghosts*, as she called them.

That returned me to myself.

Electronic relays were scattered between houses, catching electromagnetic signals translating them into electrical impulses and storing their representations in chips not unlike those I repaired as a kid, then sending them back to wavecatchers.

Except that, from time to time, unsent waves were caught, and got past the signal recognition filters. It had happened once during Myrib's chat with Anis.

When my thoughts brought me from his place to hers.

Most people erased those, or recalibrated or sent for a tech. Myrib unplugged a small red memory cube, no larger than a single die, from under the belly of her phone, and replaced it with a clean white one. She had asked Anis to make them specifically to catch ghosts.

She played it afterward on a sensitive plate where sound became image. On the other side of the plate, using touch and sound, she enhanced and transformed the image.

She never recognized the slightly slanted eyes in the dark thin face, made somber by its mien and framed by unruly dark hair.

I did. I had seen the face for years, in the mirror.

Memories, feelings, flooded back. Fears and grief.
And a sudden hatred for the mysterious artifact that had deprived me of mirrors forever.

The thought brought me back to Korbous' side, but years later, as he gave a lecture in an amphitheater.

So I traveled through the ages, following my octo-fuss, until its mystery unraveled.

As fate, or whatever, would have it, it happened on May 4, 2103. Because of me.

By that time, EM waveforms had been mastered, mathematical music was taught in school, called mathic, and inspired no wonder anymore. Because humankind had set foot in space, with veils that caught no wind, but waves of a special kind.

But I didn't care about the recently discovered aquantic waves, didn't marvel at those particles that weren't packed together, but truer to older calculations, could emit infinite warmth, on a line so thin it was almost nonexistent—the ultimate power source if created inside a wave field that could contain it, or harvested in its natural environment of interstellar space.

Wonder at that came later, with you.

Then, nothing mattered to me. At least to my disembodied self who watched, with a sinking feeling of doom, his own doppelganger.

He was an antiquarian, too. The similarity ended there. Even his voice, quieter, more sure than mine. His brown hair hadn't grown dark, nor had it faded with maturity. Maybe he dyed it. He didn't seem to need glasses or contact lenses, never stumbled, never seemed to say anything inappropriate. He understood science.

And he wasn't working alone.

I couldn't help but think he had more right to an existence than I.

"Today," my doppelganger claimed in his adult, alien voice. "We will prove our theory."

Around him, people applauded.

In the center of the room, my octofuss lay.

"The Saturnine Enigma has been lent to us for one

day. One hour will suffice to prove, as Anis Korbous theoretically proved more than a century ago, that sound waves can be transformed into electromagnetic waves in such a way that this hyperoctahedron, if activated with adequate mathic input, can reproduce it as easily as my cat does a ball of fur."

This elicited laughter all around. The sound of it was muffled, though.

I glanced around. The room, I discovered, was wave field-proofed. Soundproofed, light-proofed walls. Knowledge came to me again, unbidden and welcome: more and more people chose to do this, for privacy. "And, using Anis Korbous' algorithm," my doppelganger concluded, "let us hear his first lecture on the subject, the one he wrote, but refused to record in any other way, so that one day, that is today, Humankind might learn, literally, from the past!"

He put a complex instrument before the cube, programmed with mathic equations derived from the Korbous Formula.

Its circuitry looked familiar, but only to me since this time line never created its close cousin: the mobile phone.

Beside it, my octofuss started to vibrate in a sickening, unforgettable way.

So this is real.

As I heard, for the second time, the long tedious lecture, the thought turned round and round in my head. This is real.

This time, my thoughts took me nowhere.

When everyone had left the room, I tried an experiment of my own. ·

I had, by now, enough practice with my new self to sense the object's edges with insubstantial fingers that trace their way to each meeting point.

Softly, I asked, "Octofuss, Octofuss, tell me who isn't real anymore. . . ."

And it answered, "Crotona!"

I froze. The cube, shrouded in its mysterious vibrations, went on, "Who are you?"

Could I change it all back?

Go back to my life—or stay in this one, whatever it was?

I stood there for a long time, until the voice died out and my chance to change it all back had passed.

I had no regret; I had made my choice. Who knew what other terrible consequences my trying to change time would create?

This time it wouldn't be by accident, I knew what I was doing. This *time*, I would have been responsible.

But more than that. I had already become what I now was. Undoing it would be trying to move backward.

Moving forward is the only way in which life makes any sense.

Life, or whatever state of existence passes for it.

We are neither sitting nor standing. We are, I reflect, both answer and proof. Intangible, but no less real.

"You look at peace," she informs me, with a ghost of a smile.

I laugh at the thought.

I have lost everything, even myself. It feels wrong to feel good about it. But . . .

"Do you realize how many answers I thought I'd never learn are now part of my life?"

"Like what? Me?"

There's mischief now in her eyes, not the broken truth I saw when she finished her own tale of how, as one of the few "historical figures" to fall off time, she only met with questions at best, critical rejection, or adoration from every other time orphan she met. She must have felt even more adrift than I. . . .

I tease her, gently,

"You? Don't forget, you're not the only one anymore who heard voices." I wink. "I was thinking of ghosts. And the time travel grandfather paradox. We're living answers. . . ."

"Who said you were alive?"

I extend my translucent hand. Beneath the palm of hers, I still see the stars, and part of the hulk of the station the future has built. Yet, it's flesh that I feel entwining with mine.

"You did, Joan."

I can't believe she is blushing.

But I no longer need to believe in order to live.

Revision Point

In the sixth century BCE, Pythagoras founded a school in Croton to study geometry, music, philosophy, as part of the same mysterious whole that is our universe. Harmonies like the octave were studied as another expression of mathematics—or the reverse. Indeed, Pythagoras held that everything was numbers given form, and that to understand them was to bridge the gap between humans and the divine.

We are told that polyhedra were just such a bridge, because they symbolized numbers, elements, and the link between them.

Legends also tell us Pythagoras was able to be at two places at once, that he managed miracles.

Legends . . . for little is known for certain

about him or his school. His followers were sworn to secrecy, and the price for breaking that vow was death. Much like Socrates, his contribution to history left little trace . . . little written trace, that is.

But when his school was finally destroyed and his followers hunted down, Pythagoras had already accomplished what he believed to be the duty of a philosopher: to change the world. If not in the political field, as he would have wished, in the mathematical. We know what we remember of his work, theorems, real and unreal numbers. What we forget, we can only dream of . . . and hope that one day an archaeological discovery might add one more piece to the puzzle.

J.N.

THE EXECUTIONER'S APPRENTICE

by Kay Kenyon

WHEN the obsidian blade fell upon the king's neck, tears streamed down Pacal's face.

Altun Ha performed the execution himself, in full regalia. As he straightened from delivering the blow, blood droplets fell from his mask of quetzal feathers. Amid the pounding of Tunkul drums, an apprentice came forward to take custody of the blade, and others adjusted King Bahlum Kuk's body for proper drainage into the blood reservoir.

Pacal stood with the other Temple apprentices in a steep row from the bottom stair to the summit, witnessing the king's sacrifice, his atonement for defeat in battle against the Eastern army. From the pyramid's summit, Pacal looked out over the tree canopy, imagining enemy warriors stomping the jungle to the ground. But they were still far away, and they were not giants. Indeed, their religion proved how small they were.

The hard sun dried Pacal's tears—a good thing, because he didn't want Master Altun Ha to think him weak. As the solemn odor of blood soaked the air, Pacal sucked in a deep breath. With his investiture in eight days, he would wield the black knife for the first time, sanctifying once more the people, and the city of Tikal with the immemorial ritual.

Well, actually, he would rid the populace of another violent criminal. Looking out over the thousands gathered in the plaza below, Pacal knew that many of them saw Temple sacrifice in just those terms: as societal cleansing. Knowing each citizen's genotype did allow some purging of villainy. As Tikal's population geneticists read the citizens' genomes, the sequencers would search for the genetic variations associated with violence, and those with the V-gene fell to the obsidian blade. But of course, the Temple's ceremonies meant more than mere justice.

He watched as apprentices carried Bahlum Kuk's body through the portal of the Temple, the doorway framed by stone snake jaws, symbolizing the threshold between the Middleworld and the Underworld, over which Heaven arched. Through these three worlds the Tree of Life rose, symbolically linking the domains.

Pacal was a modern student, trained in single nucleotide polymorphism analysis. But his cultural roots went deep, and he felt their tug. The sacred blood metaphorically nourished the three worlds, bringing prosperity to all. The king's sacrifice was especially noble since he was no criminal, but the city's highest symbol. Blood was the purifying sacrifice, and had been for a hundred twenty-year cycles of Mayan progress. Pacal looked at his bare toes and fingers, a sum of twenty, the logical basis of Mayan numbers. The numbers of the Eastern tribe were based upon half the number of human digits—another sure sign that their culture was inferior.

Poking through the jungle canopy was the summit of a neighboring Temple—by its presence helping to sanctify the landscape, physically linking geography and ritual. In this profound moment, Pacal felt tears accumulate again, but blinked them away as Altun Ha strode past, his face beaked and feathered, pocked here and there with the king's blood.

Pacal followed his master into the robing room, deep and cool in the pyramid recesses, where he helped Altun Ha remove the feathered cape and regalia of office.

As Altun Ha removed the quetzal mask, Pacal could see a lingering trace of ecstasy on the old man's face. Altun Ha and Bahlum Kuk had long been friends, but the master spoke with only the slightest quaver in his voice: "He was a good king," he said. Such was the professionalism Altun Ha could command.

"A good king," Pacal repeated in hushed tones.

The king's sacrifice proved that.

Nighttime was a good time for sex. So Pacal had been told by those who'd lain with women. Nighttime was the intoxicating reign of Xibalba, when the dark underworld rotated above the earth. It was also the time when thugs lurked in waiting to slit throats and steal the clothes off your corpse. So this night, to find Pacal a woman, his friends accompanied him well armed and in a group.

They sped along the branching canals in a power boat, with his friend Chel at the helm, dodging other traffic with ease, flying the pendant of the Temple, and commandeering the lanes by right of their Order. Overhead, Jupiter lay in alignment with Chicchan's star, a fine configuration for first sex. It was nearly the same alignment that would, in six days, smile on Pacal's investiture. He was eager to begin his purification rituals instead of carousing with friends, but it was a tradition that no executioner be a virgin, and Pacal was one who followed tradition.

Arriving in the grotto, Chel and the others found their girlfriends, leaving Pacal with a voluptuous older woman. The night's magic settled over him as she poured their wine. Then a slim hand snatched the cup from the woman, and Pacal turned to face a beautiful girl with hair cut evenly at chin level.

She cocked her head to dismiss the other woman, and handed Pacal the wine. "I thought you'd be taller," she said. It was a rude thing to say, but her eyes smiled over the edge of the cup she was draining.

"I am taller when I do my duty." He meant when he stood on the Temple stairs, but her mocking grin informed him what she interpreted as "duty."

"I also thought you grew feathers from your face. Glad to see you don't." One side of her mouth curled up. "I'm Kina."

He drank quickly, trying to think of a retort, or how to escape this arrogant girl who mocked his Order.

Laughter rose and fell in the grotto like the chatter of birds. He noted Kina's dark beauty, and her half smile. He wondered which side of her smile was meant for him. She resolved that question, taking him by the hand, and leading him into the forest.

Wet leaves slapped at his face as the path narrowed. He followed her, drunk with the prospect of unwinding the cloth that tightly bound her hips. When at last she stopped, they stood before a dark cave entrance, a portal exhaling a cold breath. Distant sounds of the grotto's revels merged with the nearer jungle chitter.

"I've been watching you at the Temple ceremonies," Kina said.

Pacal had known that his role was public, yet it startled him to think that she had noticed him as an individual.

"We all know the apprentices' names. My girlfriends have their favorites. You're mine."

"Why?"

The half smile reappeared, mocking, beguiling. "Because you cry at the executions."

"I don't."

Her dark eyes held him. "It's all right to cry. What the Temple does is murder."

She had taken his hands in her own, and now he pulled away. "It's not murder. And you can't see that high up."

Kina shrugged. "Binoculars."

Despite the cool draft from the cave, his face grew hot. "Those are wondrous moments. You couldn't understand."

Her smile flattened. "Never mind, then." She walked into the mouth of the cave, disappearing like a stone dropped in a pool.

Did she want him to follow her, or had he driven her from him? He peered into the cave, into what might be a black portal to Xibalba. Then he walked inside, where his skin sprouted an icy sweat. "Kina?" The cave's version of his voice was pitifully small. No answer. She had shed him like an old garment.

He spoke into the blackness. "What would happen if we didn't remove criminals from our land?" If she was there, she could hear. "If we let those with the violence gene procreate and transmit their violence to future generations? You see how criminals prey on decent folk. How a few hoodlums terrify us with killings and rape. Isn't it better to cull such things from our genomes? Or would you rather have us dispatch undesirables in secret? Would you feel more pure if you didn't observe?"

Her silence was her verdict. "You think I'm a monster," he whispered.

An arm slithered along his waist. "No," Kina said

from close behind him. "I think you can change, that's all." She pressed her naked skin against his back.

He found himself quite willing to save moral discussion for another time. Pacal followed her to a bed of palm fronds on the cave floor. "I'll never change, you know."

"We will change together," she said.

Hearing this, he thought she might be as new to sex as he was. To spare her the embarrassment of his fumblings, he said, "I'm supposed to lie with someone who knows what they're doing."

"Well, let's not do what we're supposed to."

And then they didn't.

The realm of Xibalba stripped their inhibitions, setting its dark powers loose in their blood. She kept pulling back from him, helping him last, sharpening his desire. During that hour Pacal fell deeply in love with this stranger who now knew his body better than anyone.

It was with some disgust, then, that he learned why she had lain with him. She rumpled the fronds to refresh them, and lay back in his arms. From the darkness she brought out a small square and held it aloft at arm's length.

"It's The Book," she said.

His heart sinking, he reached out and touched it, feeling the bumpy leather, the tissue-thin pages. "Tell me this is not the Book of the Eastern god." Tikal's enemies called themselves the People of The Book, and they were intent on converts, whether by war or stealth.

Her pause made him sick. Rising up on one elbow, he stared at her, a dark soul in a world of blackness. He stood, snatching up his clothes and throwing them on. "Bahlum Kuk lost 15,000 warriors to the barbarians. How could you love them?"

Shadows stirred as she fumbled with her own

clothes. "Pacal, what would happen if we didn't allow all books to be read? Wouldn't *we* be the barbarians?" Insufferably, her tone mimicked the one he had used earlier to defend his Order.

At the cave opening he paused. "How could you turn sex into preaching? Is this what your Eastern god commands?" He strode from the cave, feeling debased by what they had done together.

From the darkness her voice came, even clearer than when she lay next to him: "Your Temple doesn't kill those with the violence gene, you know. They kill the People of The Book. That's how they get rid of us. Not such a high calling after all, is it?"

"Is that why you lay with me? To change me?" he asked, feeling foolish for exposing that, even now, he cared what she thought.

"No. But I think you're better than what you do."

He laughed, though it was far from what he felt. How could he be better than Master Altun, or the Order that tried to eradicate cruelty from their lives? With ritual cruelty. It was better so. *Better*, he said with each stomp of his feet through the underbrush. *Better*.

As Xibalba occupied the sky, the brazier's smoke carried Pacal's blood to the Heavens. The strips of paper that had caught his few drops of blood curled on the embers. Pacal reached down to cut himself one more time.

"Enough," came the voice from the western portal. Altun Ha stood there, dressed now in the simple tunic of an educator and scientist. "It's supposed to be purification, not torture," the master said.

"Some need more purification than others," Pacal dared to say. Though his investiture was only three days away, his former devotion was receding from him. Kina's voice needled at him: *Not such a high calling, is it?* She had given him her body, but taken his certainty. It was not worth the trade.

Pacal rewound his loin wrap as Master Altun stood beside him, staring at the coals.

Altun Ha said, "Let us be the judge of who is pure and who is not." With more warmth he added, "I cut myself a lot when I was your age. I felt responsible for what our Order must do." He turned to gaze at his student. "But I learned that I am not that important. Only the Temple, our city, our people have that importance."

Pacal had used a desensitizer, but his loins began to hurt. He managed to stay professional, keeping expression from his face.

Altun Ha motioned for an apprentice to remove the brazier, lest Pacal attempt further mortification. "Tonight I go to sit by the new king's bedside, to soothe his dreams. He, too, doubts his worthiness of office." He smiled. "It's contagious, perhaps. Get some sleep, boy."

Pacal obeyed for a while. Then he rose from his bed, and walked the Temple halls. His aimless steps led him to the Repository. Flickering lights threw shadows on the walls storing the genomes of the 700,000 residents of Tikal. Though all the genomes had been sequenced, not all had been read. It was the difference between a library and a deepened scholar, between information and knowledge.

The genomes were organized by birth year and designated by engraved names: Kan-Xul, Lady Zak-lay, Uayeb, Mah-Cit, Yax-Ikal . . . and so on, across the vast wall, displaying the work of the last five cycles of Mayan scholarship. The implications of this knowledge were terrible and profound. Once knowing the trajectory of a life, Pacal's Order could prevent its fruition. For the sake of the larger society.

It was terrible. It was fair.

Just ahead in the dim hall was Master Altun's domain, a small stone cubicle with a simple chair and several digital machines. A light still burned, although the master was gone for the evening.

Gone for the evening. It was as though Kina herself whispered in his ear. Pacal entered the master's room.

It took only a moment to find the data files for the next Temple ceremony. A person named Wac Chanil Ahau would meet the obsidian blade tomorrow.

Pacal glanced through the portal toward the Repository, but all remained quiet. Quickly, he scanned for the V-gene. He missed it the first time through. Hands slick with sweat, he keyed in a closer look at the genetic code, then scanned more deliberately for the telltale segment. Still nothing.

Xibalba held the heavens, and the Temple slept. Altun Ha could return at any moment, or the guards come checking, but Pacal persisted. Next he looked up the last person to require sacrifice, just a few days ago. No V-gene. Nor the one before that. He checked a dozen names.

Then, selecting the date of his investiture, he searched for the identity of the intended sacrifice. When the name appeared on the screen, he paused, his hands like claws on the keyboard. Here was a young woman who could not have the slightest violence in her. Her only unkindness had been her half smile, when he had wanted the full one. So he was to sever her neck for the crime of reading The Book. His world tipped out of balance.

In his intense concentration, he didn't notice that he had company. The master. Pacal looked up. No, not the master. It was Chel.

Chel moved to Altun Ha's machine and shut down the program. "So, then," he said, "you know."

Pacal could barely look at this young man that he thought he'd known, a man of the Temple's highest Order, his friend Chel—his corrupt friend.

"You would have been told before your investiture. It is the next level of initiation."

"The initiation that began when I slept with a woman whom I am to murder?"

Chel closed his eyes for a moment. Then: "It is unusual. But Altun Ha doubts you." He glanced away, saying the next thing with as much dignity as he could muster: "He saw your tears at Bahlum Kuk's ceremony." Then, meeting Pacal's gaze, he added, "You have another chance. Kina will be your test of loyalty. Sometimes we must perform the ceremony on those we know. It does happen. We have to be professional."

Pacal shoved past Chel into the Repository. "She has no violence gene. We're not saving society, we're ruining it."

Chel caught up with him, grabbing Pacal's elbow and spinning him around. "Listen to me. The Temple is the glue that holds society together." He pointed past the stone walls, toward the kingdom of jungle and temples. "How long before the masses run riot in the streets, overtaking the king, the Temple, all that keeps order? Even if they have no violence gene, they're doing a fine job of running riot."

"So you cook up a story that we're doing a big job keeping society orderly?"

Chel shrugged. "It's working, isn't it?"

"By killing people who follow other religions?"

Chel frowned. "Who said we were? We read the genomes, but so far we can't figure out how *beliefs* are encoded." He paused. "We're culling those *without* the V-gene."

At Pacal's look of consternation, he went on: "Tikal needs to be strong. The Eastern army is only one predator. There's Calakmul and Uaxactun, both drooling at the prospect of our fields and temples." He held up his hands against Pacal's objections. "How do you think Tikal stays strong? Through violence, that's how. Matching our strong warriors against theirs. Only a courageous people send their young fighters against invaders. We can't afford the gene variants that make us soft."

Pacal leaned against the wall holding the genomic Repository. He rubbed at the etched name under his fingertips, thinking that all this should be erased. No one had the right to know so much. The notion surprised him. He was a scientist. He'd never thought there should be a limit to knowledge.

Chel put his hand on Pacal's shoulder. "*Soft* will kill us."

"I think *hard* is killing us."

"Go to bed, Pacal. We all have this reaction, at first. It's only natural."

Pacal turned to leave, desperate to be alone, to turn off Chel's voice.

"One more thing," Chel said. "About Kina. If you don't follow through with the ceremony, someone else will. You can't save her, any more than Altun Ha could save the king. The difference between Kina and Bahlum Kuk is that he knew he had to die for his city. Kina is not so wise."

Pacal staggered off to his bed.

Close to dawn on his investiture day, Pacal had slept little. In the sweltering predawn, he sat alone on the altar at the head of the Temple stairs, where the massive stones pumped out their stored heat. The day that he had anticipated for so long now began to color the sky. But he would rather hurl himself down the endless stairs than wear the feathered mask.

Kina waited in the cells beneath the Temple, along

with all the other innocents. She was one of Tikal's best, one of the soft ones. Pacal looked at the obsidian blade in his hand, its edge one molecule thick. Turning it on himself, his death would be swift. But it wouldn't save Kina.

Bird cries arose from the jungle, as they began their daily plea for mates, calling their songs to demonstrate their genetic superiority. And the female birds, what sequencers did they have, to judge worthiness?

"The ceremony is still hours away, my boy."

Altun Ha stood in the portal, a mere shadow.

Without turning around Pacal said. "No, it's closer than that, really." He had never said *no* to the master before, and its sound now charged the silence between them. Pacal turned to face his old teacher.

Altun Ha noted the black knife that Pacal held loosely at his side. "Do you love the girl that much?"

Balanced on the edge of the stairs, Pacal planned to tumble down before he would relinquish the blade to this man. "No. I love what she is."

The old man drooped his head. When he raised it again, his face had sagged with age. "Oh, Pacal, I worried about you from the start. Yet I hoped . . ."

"Hoped? Hoped that I would follow in your steps, execute the peaceful?"

Altun Ha stepped forward, but Pacal shoved out a hand, warning him. Still, the old man advanced. "Give me the blade, son."

Pacal felt tears welling. He clutched the knife so close to his chest that it nicked his tunic. "Why, Altun? Why not just develop a micro-reservoir of the kind of genes you want, and infuse them into the peaceful? Why kill them?" He waved his bladed hand at the Temple. "Is it just for showmanship? All this blood, just for show?" He was crying openly. And the tears this time were true, not some whipped-up allegiance to culture.

Altun Ha was close enough now that Pacal could see the anger hardening his features. "You of all people should know that keeping power requires a commitment to violence. You, Pacal, have the V-gene. As do I." Seeing the expression on Pacal's face, he shook his head. "Why else were you drawn to this Order?"

The man's words ran into him, water through cold stone. "No," Pacal whispered.

Altun Ha shook his head with infinite weariness. "It's not a bad thing. We need it to do our job. Who else could stand to kill friends?" He looked down at the altar, perhaps remembering his own tests.

The sun sprayed its first light through the screen of the jungle, lighting up Altun Ha's face. Pacal saw him clearly for the first time in his life: the easy grace, the good will, the evil. But he was no worse than Pacal himself.

Altun Ha knew what was coming a moment before Pacal himself. A look of alarm, like a frightened bird, lit in his face for a moment, replaced by the shock of the blade slicing in, as Pacal threw his weight behind the thrust. Altun fell forward, collapsing on the altar, sheltering the blade with his body.

V-gene, indeed. Pacal had it, in full. As he trembled, sweat ran from his body, releasing the accumulated poisons. Every cell in his body was contaminated. And not just genetically, but by all that he had done, by the ceremonies he had witnessed, by the apologies he had made for his Order. Everything was overturned, like the Underworld crawling into the sky at night.

Leaving Altun Ha's body, he walked through the portal to the Temple's inner world. He paused at a fountain, rinsing the blood from his hands and arms. A few drowsy acolytes were now afoot, but hardly noted him. Pacal found himself walking into the lower reaches of the Temple near the holding cells. There he roused a guard and, pointing to the stairs and the upper levels, babbled of murder and evil.

It was no more than the truth.

Their only chance was to travel swiftly toward the encroaching army, hoping for asylum. Pacal and Kina paddled unceasingly through the morning, using not the great canals, but the waterways overhung with jungle, too shallow for power boats.

The river current was with them, flowing into the ocean, the great half circle gulf that separated the great peninsula lands from the northern lands. Kina had spoken of life on those vast plains, filled with bison and the tribes she called "close cousins," but Pacal hardly cared. It was only for Kina that he paddled. Because her life should not be forfeit.

Before long they did encounter the Eastern forces, who let them pass because Kina had The Book, and could quote it. They looked askance at Pacal, but during the last few days he had learned to lie, among other things.

They came to the blue gulf, where Kina said they could paddle north, hugging the coast. Pacal would leave her now that she was safe. Surely he could no longer be her favorite. He hadn't changed as she'd hoped—in fact he had proved his violence. But he was unwilling to convert to a religion. Religion had ruined so much. Could the Eastern religion be far different?

As night fell, they made their camp on the beach. It was just an ordinary night, no great myth of antiquity. The stars poked through, their alignment a matter of indifference.

Kina drew near, opening The Book.

"Please, no preaching," Waves hit the sand in a comforting drumbeat, healing his troubled thoughts.

Kina said, "It's not religion as you know it, Pacal. It's science."

He sighed. She would preach no matter what.

She held the pages toward the campfire, illuminating a diagram. "The Tree of Life," she said.

Pacal jerked away. "We had a tree of life in Tikal—the one that grows between the three worlds. It was full of rot. So is this one."

Kina's smile dented one cheek. "That was a symbol. This one is a diagram."

Pacal looked more closely. It looked like a tree, but it had tiny writing all over it.

"The Maya aren't the only ones that have been working on gene analysis. Across the ocean, our sisters and brothers have been working on genomes, too. All the genomes." As Pacal took The Book in his hands, he peered more closely at the branches depicted there. Each one held not a leaf, but a species of plant or animal.

Kina went on, "They've finished it, Pacal. The Tree of Life. Look." She sidled closer to him, pointing to the center page, one so large it had to be folded out. "Here's what the genomes—all the genomes—teach us: the unique pattern of evolutionary branching. On these branches and twigs you can read the names of every creature, every plant known to us, and how closely each is related to each." She looked at him squarely, without a zealot's fire, but with a firm resolve. "It's our kinship system. This is what we revere now. This is the new religion."

"Haven't we had enough of religion?"

She shrugged, turning the pages of The Book, showing yet more diagrams, more details of the links between and among creatures. "Maybe it's not a real religion. But it's something to honor. We honor each other, because we're kin to each other. And to every living thing." She stirred the fire, and it burned brighter. "The human genome isn't the only one that matters. It all matters. It's all part of a grand progression. We have to revere that."

"Have to?"

"Well, it's nothing to spit at, anyway."

The surf pounded, somehow louder now that it was cloaked in darkness. Pacal had to wonder if the lessons nature taught were violent or peaceful ones. He asked, "With all this reverence, why are the Eastern armies trying to destroy Tikal?"

"They're not. They're protecting their boundaries from Tikal's armies. Eventually the Eastern tribes will bring news of The Book to Tikal. Maybe it will compete with the Temple. Maybe it won't." She looked at him with mischievous dark eyes. "But meanwhile, you and I will be heading north to spread the word on the northern plains."

"We will?" Did that mean she would go with a man who had the violence gene? He asked her.

She turned the pages of The Book. "Pacal, do you see any individual genomes here? Any attempts to say what an individual is or may do?" He saw the branches of cousinship, but no personal genomes. Kina went on, "The Book says that reading a genome isn't the same as understanding that animal."

Although she offered him a way out, he couldn't help but pursue the topic. "But Kina, I have the V-gene, and I did kill Altun Ha."

She nodded. "Yes. But I think you're better than what you've done."

She forgave him his crimes. But was that a fatal softness in her, or a deeper wisdom? He had to admit that just because the V-gene and the murder of Altun Ha happened together, it didn't mean that one caused the other. He wanted to believe he could change. And so he resolved to justify her faith in him, to be better than what he'd done so far. To be worthy of her. To prove his genome didn't rule.

He watched Kina as she closed The Book. She carefully wrapped it in heavy cloth, and tucked it into their knapsack. "The Book is a good size for traveling," she said, smiling with both sides of her mouth. "Nice and small."

When she had finished, she asked. "Will you journey north with me, Pacal?"

He wanted to say he would go anywhere with her. But all he said was, "Yes. If you'll have me."

Her answer was in her arms, as she pulled him down to lie with her in the sand, to watch the stars and listen to the surf.

Lying next to Kina, Pacal thought about the Temple's Repository, with its 700,000 names. He was glad they would be traveling light.

Revision Point

In May, 1995, the bacterium that causes meningitis became the first free-living organism to have its entire DNA sequence revealed. On June 26, 2000, a draft sequence of the human genome was announced by the Human Genome Project led by Francis Collins, and Celera Genomics, led by Craig Venter. In the twenty-first century, what if functional genomics, identifying what specific genes do, provides the basis for extraordinary new knowledge of the machinery of life, and perhaps the gene variants that influence behavioral differences in individuals?

K.K.

SWIMMING UPSTREAM IN THE WELLS OF THE DESERT

by Mike Resnick and Susan R. Matthews

SERI stood at the observation port, watching intently as Mushir—his khaki-clad back to the one-
way mirror—emptied the hikers' packs out one by one
on the broad table. The hikers themselves were seated
in folding chairs along the cinder-block wall of the
bleak room, nervously watching both Mushir and the
guard at the door.

"United States government maps," Mushir announced, shaking a laminated document out to open
it. "You don't trust the tourist office in Bishkek?" He
paused and stared at them. "It's been years since we
purged those maps. The trek maps are perfectly up
to date."

No answer from the hikers, but of course none had
been expected. "They don't look like a hard lot," offered Prizmak. "Tough, certainly, they'd have to be to
have gotten this far. But terrorists?"

"What does a terrorist look like?" mused Seri
aloud. Prizmak was an older man, but idealistic; still,
Seri had always found his idealism to be of a harmless
sort—disposing him to doubt evil where it seemed to

manifest, rather than becoming fanatical about the justice of his politics and religion.

"They're young people from the Demon States, with no purpose to their lives," he continued. "Seduced by the offer of excitement. I could almost feel sorry for them."

"I don't understand the need for these . . . these *Gestapo* tactics," one of the hikers said forcefully, with the air of a woman who had been pushed past the limits of her patience. "We came here to climb a mountain, that's all."

"You're a long way from Khan Tengri. You know that." Mushir made the observation as though it was of general interest and no particular importance, sorting through the contents of the packs. "Cameras. Yes. Very nice. Thirty-gigabyte disk storage? Never mind, they'll have a look later."

"Khan Tengri," one of the other hikers muttered under his breath, but not so softly that the room's microphones didn't pick it up. "Done to death since the zeros. Almost as bad as Denali." Seri had to stifle her smile of recognition; she'd heard that rant from Paul before. Climbers could be so elitist . . . but he was very good at almost everything he'd ever put his mind to.

"And yet Khan Tengri's the permit you've got. How did you get that past your guide? Or did you come across the border from Xinjiang?" Mushir continued looking. "GPS device, disabled, old model. I wonder whether that's actually all it does." He turned to the hikers. "What do *you* think?"

"I think this is just a misunderstanding. We're sorry if we've trespassed. It's inadvertent. We haven't done anything wrong. Well, maybe we've stretched our permits a bit. That's all." That was Georg, calm, reasonable, appealing for understanding, for a little flexibility in an unfortunate situation. "The cameras don't matter, though we'd hate to lose the documentary for our trek. Will our permits be revoked?"

It was almost too innocent a question. Seri couldn't see Mushir's face, of course; she could imagine, though, the quick sharp glance from beneath his black eyebrows, the dangerous light in his dark eyes. "With extreme prejudice."

Georg exchanged looks with one of the women, someone Seri didn't know. "In that case," Georg said. "I expect we'll want to contact our government representatives. Except for Conners, of course, but there's a British representative in Karakul, I think."

It was actually farther to Karakul from here than back to the capital at Bishkek, but if they were lucky that would help present the appearance of having been simply off course on an attempt at some lesser-known peak, rather than on their way to their true destination: the nuclear plant at Iskamir.

Prizmak shook his head, smiling. "Of course you want to contact your governments," he said, folding his arms with an expression of satisfaction. "You always do. You're not going to get away with it, you know." Although they couldn't hear him, he was talking to the hikers, Seri reminded herself, firmly. Prizmak was the administrator here at the nuclear plant. He had no interest in what was going on in maintenance. Time to take a risk . . .

Seri coughed, gently, to attract attention, waiting for Prizmak to give her permission to speak. Finally he nodded.

"I know one of them, Administrator," said Seri. "We were in school together. The American—Conners."

"Really?" For a moment Prizmak looked eager and interested; then he collected himself. "We should tell

Mushir, when he comes out. You think they came to sabotage the plant?"

He couldn't really ask where, exactly, that had been, without exposing the charade on which the entire plant depended for trained engineers. There were colleges within the Wells of the Desert client states that accepted women, and many of them had excellent engineering programs. For maintenance of increasingly aged nuclear plants in earthquake zones, however, not even the Wells of the Desert dared rely on anything less than the very best training—training still available only in the Demon States. It was a small deception, but necessary. As far as the administration was concerned, Seri had taken her degree in Kabul, not Michigan.

"We'll get an escort together to send you all back to Bishkek," Mushir was saying. "Consider your personal effects confiscated. They'll be returned to you in Bishkek after security analysis. Go with the guards when they come, and you'll get a hot meal and a shower." He was packing things as he spoke; maps, cameras, cell phones. Luxury goods from the Demon States. Seri knew what kind of a temptation they represented. Such things could be got in Kyrghyzstan, but only for an almost irrationally inflated price.

The single guard at the door came forward with a box, to help; the hikers stirred restlessly on the bench, but there was no sense in trying anything rash. They didn't have their gear. It was summer, but that didn't mean that anybody could try to walk down out of Iskamir in their hiking boots and not be dead of exposure by morning. And they had no papers; they couldn't get out of the country unless there was a prearranged drop somewhere, and if it existed, the air security forces would spot it.

Mushir left the room and joined Seri and Prizmak

a moment later. He set down the equipment he'd collected on the table in the observation room that mirrored the one in the interrogation room.

"No question in my mind," Mushir said, motioning to the guard to put the box of residual gear down. "Greenies, maybe worse. Look at this camera. How much would you like to wager that the office in Bishkek is going to find a complete scale model of the plant in there?"

"Seri went to school with one of them," Prizmak said. "Seri?"

"I don't think they're any worse than greenies." She had to tread very carefully. "But I don't think they came just to bag an unclaimed peak. I know that John Conners used to go mountain climbing on the weekends. But I also remember that he was opposed to nuclear power, back when I knew him."

Mushir turned cameras and phones over on the table, contemplatively. He would know about the open secret of her schooling; he was from the security forces, and she'd checked in with her local administration on her return from abroad. They had given her forged papers a cursory examination and signed her off as having lawfully returned from a legal absence.

"Well, there certainly don't seem to be any explosive devices here," remarked Mushir. "That much is in their favor. We'll see what the police have to say about it, once they have a chance to question each of them separately. I may send someone back to talk to you, Seri, if that's all right."

She nodded; it had been so easy for her to revert to the habits of her childhood, not speaking unless she was spoken to, and making sure that she didn't say anything at all that wasn't necessary. A woman's virtue, her mother and aunts had told her frequently, lay in her modesty. She wore her head scarf here in the plant because it helped keep her warm, but it served the purposes of modesty as a disguise just as well.

"You'll take them back under escort, then, Mushir?" Prizmak asked. "We don't really have an adequate holding facility here. Those storerooms are secure, but there's no heat."

Mushir made a face. "It'll be a few days before I can arrange an escort for them. The Numingar bandits, you know. Do you need me to sign a chit for extra rations?"

Prizmak shook his head. "No. We can feed them— and if you don't think they're a threat, I suppose we'll be able to keep them comfortably enough. But I won't be happy until they're out of my custody."

Nodding, Mushir escorted Seri and Prizmak out of the room—so that the hikers' gear could be secured, Seri assumed.

His wink was so quick and so subtle that she wasn't sure she even saw it.

Three days later Seri stood at the loading docks at the end of the long road leading to the Iskamir reactor, looking out over the steep slopes of the Tian Shan into the hazy yellow obscurity of the valley below. Mushir had sent vehicles and an escort. Seri was to ride with the convoy into Bishkek to provide her statement, and Mushir had thoughtfully sent along two female police officers to keep her company and preserve her modesty.

Beside her John sniffed deeply of the cold morning air, and wrinkled up his nose. "Even up here it stinks," John said. "Does anybody remember what these mountains are supposed to look like? Even the snow is dirty."

"It's Kyrgyz business, not yours," she said frostily. "If the Demon States were so concerned about the welfare of mere hot-fueled nations, they know what they could do about it."

John shook his head. This was an old argument. "There's no excuse for trying to run one of these old Soviet-era reactors, Seri; none at all. How old is Iskamir? Sixty years? And in a geologically active area."

"We will not be the spaniel of the Demon States!" she snapped. It always came down to that. Yes, the United States was willing to share its cold fusion technology. Yes, all of Western Europe and much of Central Europe, the North American continent, Australia, Southeast Asia, all those places had the cold fusion, and no longer needed more than a steadily decreasing fraction of their former requirements for crude oil.

It didn't make the world any better for nations whose infrastructure had not been developed to the point where they could exploit the new technology, when the breakthrough had come—1997. The year of the Great Technological Divide. The year in which the impoverished nations of central Asia had become hostage to the oil of increasingly extremist Islamic states, oil they could only obtain by pledging to shun all contact with the hated Demon States.

Seri had been to the Demon States. She had seen what life could be like with an abundant supply of clean energy. She didn't like to be reminded, especially when she looked down from the mountains with their no-longer-pristine snowpack into the poisonous smoggy haze of the valleys. This used to be one of the most beautiful places in all of the world; she'd seen pictures.

She'd pledged to do her part in restoring it to its former beauty, whatever the cost might be.

"It doesn't have to be this way, Seri," John said quietly, after a contemplative pause. One of the policewomen who stood nearby shifted a little closer, in order to be able to catch his words. "You don't live in a theocracy. You could work to change the policy. The choice your country made thirty years ago doesn't have to define its future. You can change the rules. The political landscape isn't chiseled in stone. This is Kyrghyzstan. Not Saudi. Not Iraq."

"No." Their police escort had settled the rest of the party in cars, two police, two prisoners—detainees—to a limo. There was no shortage of what had once been luxury automobiles in Kyrghyzstan. It was regarded as a pledge of loyalty to the Wells of the Desert to consume the bountiful blessing of cheap oil as conspicuously as possible, a constant public admission of absolute dependence; which was why the existence of the Iskamir reactor was such a sensitive political issue, as well as a serious environmental one. "No, we don't have to work loyally in the shadow of the Wells. We could just as easily break our treaties and realign ourselves. Look how well that's worked out in Tajikistan."

He had no answer for that, because there *was* no answer. All of Tajikistan a wasteland, a poisoned battlefield where oil and cold fusion had been struggling for supremacy for the past eight years; a political prize in name only, because there was nothing left to win.

He made a face instead. She'd won, and they both knew it. He let her have the last word in acknowledgment of that fact, and followed the policemen into the limo that was waiting for him.

The bandits ambushed the convoy just at the curve of the road down through a steep glacial ravine, less than thirty kilometers from the foot of the mountains and civilization. Numingari, an ancient tribe of freebooters and mercenaries, adapted to modern times with all-terrain attack vehicles from the last days of the last Iraqi wars; when the limo in which Seri was riding with the two policewomen for company slid suddenly to a sickeningly slewed stop on the gravel road she knew.

She held out her hand for the hand of the police-woman nearest her; she couldn't help it. The police-woman squeezed her hand reassuringly, but made no move to flee the vehicle: let the bandits come to them.

There were stories about the Numingari. Terrible stories. Enemies mutilated and left not to die but to live in a world where devalued oil wealth could no longer buy the best in reconstructive surgery. Women deprived of head scarf and dressed in inappropriate attire, estranged from their families, their names ex-cised from the public records, their honor destroyed.

Closing her eyes, Seri tried to calm herself: stories are to frighten children and tourists. *I am not a child and I am not a tourist. I am a respectable scientist. They will rob us and let us go*.

The policewomen drew their weapons. Seri listened. Loud voices, shouting, the sound of breaking glass. Then relieved voices. What was going on? No shots, no cries of pain, not yet.

The window nearest Seri burst from the impact of a rifle butt. She cringed, but did her best to emulate the calm policewomen. "There are women here," said one of them. "Have respect."

Someone's brown scarred hand reached in through the window for the door latch, pulling the door open; "I'm a woman," the Numingari said. "You can come out on this side. The men are over there. Out, please."

Yes, she was a woman. And she had three soldiers with her, all with weapons. The policewomen put their weapons back on safe and left the vehicle, one of them behind Seri and one of them before, and the Numing-ari soldiers searched them—with odious familiarity, but no shaming exposure—and sent them back into the limo, minus only the side arms they had carried.

The woman who had broken the window closed the door and smiled through the broken frame. "They'll have the road cleared in an hour or two," she said. "Wait here. You won't be bothered again." In the background Seri could hear men exclaiming over their booty. *Look, look, twelve-gigabyte storage camera. We love the Demon States. At least their technology we love.* One of the policewomen took a deep breath, as though to calm herself.

After some minutes it was quiet, and one of the policewomen got out of the limo. Seri followed her, anxious to see what had happened. She could see the captured hikers gathered in a little knot, and counted them as she hurried toward them. All of them there. All of them standing. Nobody hurt, not that she could see, but the convoy commander was coming toward them as well, so Seri hung back a bit to preserve her modesty.

"Everyone uninjured?" demanded the commander, sounding deeply disgusted—at having been ambushed, Seri supposed, not at the absence of casualties. "Good! I'm sorry to inform you that your equipment is gone, all of it. You'll be feeding bandits in these mountains for weeks."

"Damn it!" said Georg. "That's expensive gear! We were under your protection!"

"Hold your tongue," said the convoy commander sharply. "Without your recording devices we have no evidence that you spied on our industry, and no reason to risk an incident by holding you. The government will put you on a commercial flight out of Bishkek. You can complain to your governments when you get home, though personally I think you should be grateful."

He was clearly not interested in engaging in any further conversation. Turning from the little group of hikers he caught sight of Seri standing there with a policewoman beside her, and climbed the few steps of the little slope to join her.

"You've had a scare for nothing, I'm afraid," he said. "But there's no reason to ask you to come in to Bishkek now. No evidence, no case, no statement. We'll probably have someone up in a week or two to interview you, but for now you might as well go back to your workstation. We'll probably still be waiting for the road to clear when your driver gets back."

"Thank you, Commander." It was a long and tiresome trip into Bishkek. She was anxious to get back to her lab; she had work to do. "Could I say goodbye to them? I thought I'd be speaking to them again before I left Bishkek, you see."

He caught the policewoman's eye, and she shrugged. "Don't be too long," he said, then added: "I do not envy them, returning home to the Demon States. It must be terrible to live there."

"Yes, terrible," lied Seri.

The policewoman didn't bother to come with her. Since she was in plain sight, there was little danger of her being compromised, and now that there was to be no case, the police had lost interest in what the hikers might say.

"Damn it, Seri, we could have been killed!"

"Oh, yes, and you climb mountains," she retorted. "On purpose. Still, it's been nice to see you again. You'll be out of the country in no time. Relatively speaking."

"I can't say it's been a particularly fascinating trip," Paul said, looking at her more directly than she was accustomed, now that she was home. "What do you do for amusement up here, anyway?"

She knew what he was trying to find out. "We have plenty to do," she assured him. "Reading material. Technical manuals. Flow diagrams. Wonderful stuff. I never tire of it. Trust me. Why, I've got some specifications waiting for me in my lab right now that will keep us going for months."

That was the message: *Trust me. I've got it.*

He smiled. "I'm glad to hear it. I don't believe you," he said in a voice loud enough to be overheard, "but I'm glad to hear it."

But he'd caught the message. He *did* believe her. Those cameras had had thirty-gigabyte storage disks when Mushir had examined them, not the twelve-gigabyte disks that currently resided within them. Everything had hinged upon Mushir examining only the three cameras, without bothering with the disk-magazine, and thankfully, he'd done just that.

With the information that they had smuggled into the country Seri could have the Iskamir reactor safely converted to cold fusion within a matter of months, so long as Mushir's party remained in control of intelligence and procurement in Bishkek.

Prizmak would notice; he wasn't stupid, but with luck he'd draw his own conclusions and keep quiet. They needed him there. As long as Prizmak was there, the government still had deniability if the Wells of the Desert discovered the defiance of its client state too soon.

If that happened—if the secret came out—Seri would die, and most of her staff would be purged, but it wouldn't stop the Demon States from conspiring with the clients of the Wells of the Desert to replace fossil fuels with cold fusion across the globe.

"I'd better go," Seri said diffidently, looking back over her shoulder to where the policewomen were waiting for her by the limo. "I can't say I'll be seeing

you." *Don't come back; it would just arouse suspicions.*
"Take care of yourselves."

"And you, Seri," John answered for the group.
"Take very good care." *Be careful.*

Smiling, Seri turned away, to go back to her work
up on the mountain. *We didn't come this far by
being careless.*

It had been thirty years since the Demon States had
mastered the first crude elements of cold fusion. Thirty
years of economic chaos in the Middle East. Thirty
years of polarization between the privileged states and
the have-not states that were too undeveloped to be
able to exploit the new discovery, remaining totally
dependent on the Wells of the Desert while the
Demon States closed its own oil fields down.

But a country could not embargo knowledge, and
ideas could not be stopped by ideology. Cold fusion
would come to the Tian Shan. If it should mean her
life, she would gladly surrender it, because whether
the snow that fell in the year of her death covered an
honored grave or a dishonored corpse, it would fall
clean again from Heaven, and the shadow of the Wells
of the Desert would no longer fall across the Kyrgyz
steppe.

Revision Point

We have postulated that cold fusion became
possible, practical, inexpensive, and widespread in the late 1990s, which led us to wonder what effect it would have on the oil-rich
and everything-else-poor countries of the Middle East.

Cold fusion for the purposes of this story
refers to the claim that a nuclear (fusion) reaction can be initiated and sustained in a very

basic, stable environment available to almost anybody with a fully chopped chemistry lab set; something that would solve the world's needs for clean, safe, cheap energy. Greeted with a mixture of exultation and ferocious skepticism when its attainment was announced in March of 1989 (by Fleishmann and Pons, University of Utah), discredited in the popular and scientific press since, its true believers continue to chip away at the "proofs" of its implausibility—if ever there was a subject fit for what-if speculation, cold fusion is it. What impact might a successful demonstration have had on economic and political structures currently supported by conventional fuel economies? It takes infrastructure to configure infrastructure to take advantage of advances in technology. Maybe a successful demonstration of cold fusion would have ushered in the Golden Age of peace and prosperity on this planet—or maybe it would have looked something a little more like this.

                                        M.R. and S.R.M.

UNWIRER

by Cory Doctorow and Charles Stross

THE cops caught Roscoe as he was tightening the butterfly bolts on the dish antenna he'd pitoned into the rock face opposite the Canadian side of Niagara Falls. The crunch of their boots on the road-salt and the creak of their cold holsters told him they were the law, but they were only state troopers, not fed radio cops.

"Be right with you, officers," he hollered into the wind. The antenna was made from a surplus satellite rig, a polished tomato soup can, and a pigtail with the right fitting for a wireless card. All perfectly legal, mostly.

He tightened the last of the bolts, squirted them with lock-tite, and slid back on his belly, off the insulated thermarest. The cops' heads were wreathed in the steam of their exhalations, and one of them was nervously flicking his—no, *her*—handcuffs around on her belt.

"Everything all right, sir?" the other one said, in a flat upstate New York accent. A townie. He stretched out his gloved hand and pulled Roscoe to his feet.

"Yeah, just fine," Roscoe said. "I like to watch winter birds on the river."

"Winter birds, huh?" The cop gave him a bemused look.

"Winter birds."

The cop leaned over the railing and took a long look down. "Huh. Better you shouldn't do it by the roadside, sir," he said. "Never know when someone's going to skid out and drive off onto the shoulder— you could be crushed." He waved at his partner, who gave them a hard look and retreated into the steamy warmth of the cruiser. "All right, then," he said. "When does your node go up?"

Roscoe smiled and dared a wink. "I'll be finished aligning the dish in about an hour. I've got line of sight from here to a repeater on a support on the Rainbow Bridge, and from there down the Rainbow Street corridor. Some good tall buildings there, line of sight to most of downtown."

"My place is Fourth and Walnut. Think you'll get there?" Roscoe relaxed imperceptibly, certain now that this wasn't a bust.

"Hope so. Sooner rather than later."

"That'd be great. My kids are e-mailing me out of house and home." The cop looked uncomfortable and cleared his throat. "Still, you might want to stay home for a while. DA's office, they've got some kind of hotshot from the FCC in town, uh, getting heavy on bird watchers."

Roscoe sucked in his lower lip. "I may do just that," he conceded. "And thank you for the warning."

The cop waved as he turned away. "My pleasure, sir."

Roscoe drove home slowly, and not just because of the compacted slush on the roads. *A hotshot from the*

FCC sounded like the inquisition. Roscoe's lifelong mistrust of radio cops had blossomed into hatred three years ago, when they busted him behind a federal telecoms rap.

He'd lost his job and spent six months inside, plus two years' probation, during which he wasn't allowed to program a goddamn microwave oven, let alone admin the networks that had been his trade. And he'd gotten off lightly—on paper. While he was inside, Janice filed for divorce. She kept the small house and he got the big house.

Roscoe was in a bad mood as he climbed the front steps of the house he and Marcel rented.

"Slushy boots! For chrissakes, Roscoe, I just cleaned."

Roscoe stared at the salty brown slush he'd tracked over the painted floor and shook his head.

"Sorry," he said lamely. He sat down on the floor to shuck his heavy steel-shank Kodiaks. "Just ease back, all right? It didn't go so good."

Marcel set his machine down on the hearthrug. "What happened?"

Roscoe related his run-in with the law quickly. Marcel shook his head.

"I bet it's bullshit. Ever since Tijuana, everyone's seeing spooks." The ISPs on the Tijuana side of the San Ysidro border crossing had been making good coin off unwirer sympathizers who'd pointed their antennae across the chain-link fence. La Migra tried tightening up the fence gauge to act as a faraday cage, but they just went over it with point-to-point links. Finally, the radio cops had Ruby-Ridged the whole operation, killing ten "terrorists" in a simultaneous strike with Mexican narcs who'd raided the ISPs under the rubric of shutting down narcotraficante activity.

Roscoe shook his head. "Bullshit or not, you going

to take any chances? Believe me, there's one place you don't want to go. Listen, when I was your age, I thought it couldn't happen to me either. Now look at me." He started thumbing his way through the stack of old magazines on the coffee table.

"I'm looking at you." Marcel grinned. "There was a call while you were out."

"A call?"

"Some woman, said she wanted to talk to you. I took her number."

"Uh-huh." Roscoe put the magazine back down. *Heads it's Janice, tails it's her lawyer*, he thought. It was shaping up to be that kind of day; a tire slashing and an hour of alimonial recriminations would complete it neatly. "Ah, shit. Get it over with."

The number was unfamiliar. That didn't mean much—Janice's frothingly aggro lawyer seemed to carry a new cellular every time he saw her—but it was hopeful. Roscoe dialed. "Hello? Roscoe here. Who am I talking to?"

A stranger's voice: "Hi there! I was talking to your roommate about an hour ago? I'm Sylvie Smith. I was given your name by Buzz—he told me you put him on the backbone."

Roscoe tensed. Odds were that this Sylvie Smith was just looking to leech a first-mile feed, but after this morning's run-in with the law he was taking nothing for granted.

"Are you a law enforcement officer federal employee police officer lawyer FCC or FBI agent?" he asked, running the words together, knowing that if she was any of the above she'd probably lie—but it might help sway a jury toward letting him off if he was targeted by a sting.

"No." She sounded amused. "I'm a journalist."

"Then you should be familiar with CALEA," he said, bridling at the condescension in her voice. CALEA was the wiretap law that required switch-vendors to put snoopware into every hop in the phone network. It was bad enough in and of itself, but it made the snoop-proof code built into the BeOS access points he had hidden around town doubly illegal.

"Paranoid, much?" she said.

"I have nothing to be paranoid about," he said, spelling it out like he was talking to a child. "I am a law-abiding citizen, complying with the terms of my parole. If you *are* a journalist, I'd be happy to chat. In person."

"I'm staying at the Days Inn on Main Street," she said. "It's a dump, but it's got a *view of the Falls*," she said in a hokey secret-agent voice, making it plain that she meant, "It's line of sight to a Canadian wireless repeater."

"I can be there in twenty. Turn left out the front door and meet me at the diner that's fifty yards down the road," he said, hanging up.

Marcel looked up from his machine. "What?"

"I'm out. See you later."

Roscoe took a booth by the window and was halfway down his first mug of coffee when someone leaned over him. "Hi," she said.

"You must be Sylvie." He registered a confused impression of bleached blonde hair, brown eyes, freckles. *Must be straight out of J-school*. "Have a seat. Coffee?"

"Yes, please." She put down something like a key ring then waved a hand, trying to catch the waitress' eye. Roscoe looked at the key ring. Very black, very small, very Nokia.

"Suppose you tell me why you wanted to meet up," Roscoe said quietly. "Up front. I'm on parole, and I've got no intention of violating it."

Sylvie ordered a coffee from the waitress. "What'd you do?"

Roscoe snorted. "I was *accused* of infringement with a side order of black crypto, but plea-bargained it down to unlawful emissions. Strictly a no-collar crime." It was the truth, though he'd originally been looking at a five-year stretch for contributory infringement, compounded to twenty by the crypto running on the access point ("use a cypher, go to jail"), until the ACLU mugged the judge with an amicus brief. The eventual plea bargain took it down to criminal trespass and unlawful emission, six months and two years, so that it merely cost him his home, his job, his savings, his wife. . . .

He took another mouthful of coffee to cover his feelings. "So what are you doing here?"

"I'm working on a story about some aspects of un-wiring that don't usually make the mainstream press," she said, as the waitress came over. Roscoe held up his mug for a refill.

She pulled out a notepad and began scribbling. "*This* is my editor's name and address. You can look it up. If you ask for him, you'll get put through—you're on a list of interview subjects I sent him. Next, here's my e-mail address." Roscoe blinked—it was a handle on a famous Finnish anonymous remixer. "Get a friend to ping it and ask me something." It was worth five to twenty for black crypto—anonymity was the FCC's worst nightmare.

"Okay, I'll check these out." He met her eyes. "Now, why don't you tell me why the *Wall Street Journal* is interested in a burned out ex-con and ex-unwirer?"

She dangled her key ring again, a flash of matte

black plastic. "These are everywhere in Europe. Like these," she opened her purse and he caught a glimpse of a sliver of curved metal, like a boomerang. Or the Motorola batwing mark. "Meshing wireless repeaters. Teenagers are whacking them up on the sides of buildings, sticking them to their windows. The telcos are screaming: their business is way down. Wired infrastructure is on the way out. Even the ISPs are nervous."

Roscoe tried to hide his grin. To be an unwirer in the streets of Paris, operating with impunity, putting the telcos, the Hollywood studios, and the ISPs on notice that there was no longer any such thing as a "consumer"—that yesterday's couch potatoes are today's *participants*!

"We've got ten years' worth of editorials in our morgue about the destruction of the European entertainment and telco market and the wisdom of our National Information Infrastructure here in the US, but it's starting to ring hollow. The European governments are *ignoring* the telcos! The device and services market being built on top of the freenets is accounting for nearly half the GDP growth in the French economy. To hear *my* paper describe it, though, you'd think they were starving in the streets.

"I just got back from a month in the field in the EU. I've got interviews in the can with CEOs, with street thugs, with grandmothers and with regulators, all saying the same thing: unmetered communications are the secret engine of the economy, of liberty. The highest quality 'content' isn't one-hundred-million-dollar movies, it's conversations with other people. Crypto is a tool of privacy not piracy.

"The unwirers are heroes in Europe. But here, you people are pirates, abettors of terrorists. I want to change that."

* * *

Marcel picked a fight over supper: "What are you planning this week?"

"More dishes. Got a couple of folks to splice in downtown if I want to hook up East Aurora—there're some black spots there, but I figure with some QOS-based routing and a few more repeaters we can clear them up. Why?"

Marcel toyed with a strand of cooling pizza cheese. "It's boring. When are you going to run a new fat pipe in?"

"When the current one's full. The more we've got, the more there are for the Feds to cut."

"I could take over part of the fiber-pull," Marcel said.

"I don't think so." Roscoe put his plate down.

"But I could—" Marcel looked at him. "What's wrong?"

"Security," Roscoe grunted. "Goddamnit, you can't just waltz up to some guy who's looking at twenty-to-life and say 'Hi, Roscoe sent me, howzabout you and me run some dark fiber over the border, huh?' Some of the guys in this game are, huh, you wouldn't want to meet them on a dark night. And others are just plain paranoid."

"You could introduce me," Marcel said after a brief pause.

Roscoe laughed, a short bark. "In your dreams."

Marcel dropped his fork, clattering. "You're going to take your pet blonde on a repeater splice and show her everything, but you won't let me help run a new pipe in? What's the matter, I don't smell good enough?"

"Up yours." Roscoe finished the meal in silence, then headed out to his evening class in conversational French. Marcel was just jealous because he wasn't get-

ting to do any of the secret agent stuff. Being an unwirer was a lot less romantic than it sounded, and the
first rule of unwiring was *nobody talks about unwiring*.
Maybe Marcel would get it one day.

Sylvie's hotel room had a cigarette-burns-and-must
squalor that reminded Roscoe of jail. "Bonjour,
m'sieu," she said as she admitted him.

"Bon soir, madame," he said. "Commentava?"

"Lookee here, the treasures of the Left Bank." She
handed him the Motorola batarang he'd glimpsed earlier. The underside had a waxed-paper peel-off strip
and when he lifted a corner, his thumb stuck so hard
to the tackiness beneath that he lost the top layer of
skin when he pulled it loose. He turned it over in
his hands.

"How's it powered?"

"Photovoltaics charging a polymer cell. The entire
case is a slab of battery plus solar cell. It only sucks
juice when it's transmitting. Put one in a subway car
and you've got an instant ad hoc network that everyone in the car can use. Put one in the next car and
they'll mesh. Put one on the platform and you'll get
connectivity with the train when it pulls in."

"Shitfire," he said, stroking the matte finish in a
way that bordered on the erotic.

She grinned. She was slightly snaggletoothed, and
he noticed a scar on her upper lip from a cleft-palate
operation that must have been covered up with concealer earlier. It made her seem more human, more
vulnerable. "Costs three Euros in quantity. Some Tai-
wanese knockoffs have already appeared that slice
that in half. Moto'll have to invent something new
next year if it wants to keep that profit."

"They will," Roscoe said, still stroking the batarang.
He transferred it to his armpit and unslung his lugg-

able laptop. "Innovation is still legal there." The laptop sank heavily into the bedspread.

Sylvie's chest began to buzz. She slipped a tiny phone from her breast pocket and answered it. "Yes?" She handed it to Roscoe. "It's for you."

He clamped it to his ear. "Who is this?"

"Eet eez eye, zee masked avenger, doer of naughty deeds and wooer of reporters' hearts."

"Marcel?"

"Yes, boss."

"You shouldn't be calling this number." He remembered the yellow pad, sitting on his bedside table.

"Sorry, boss," Marcel said. He giggled.

"Have you been drinking?" Marcel and he had bonded over many, many beers when they'd met in a bar in Utica, but Roscoe had cut back lately. Drinking made you sloppy.

"No, no," he said. "Just in a good mood is all. I'm sorry we fought, darlin', can we kiss and make up?"

"What do you want, Marcel?"

"I want to be in the story, dude. Hook me up! I want to be famous!"

Roscoe grinned despite himself. Marcel was good at fonzing dishes into place with one well-placed whack, could crack him up when the winter slush was turning his mood to pitch. Good kid, basically, but impulsive. Like Roscoe, once.

"C'mon c'mon c'mon," Marcel said, and he could picture the kid pogoing up and down in a phone booth, heard his boots crunching on rock salt.

He covered the receiver and turned to Sylvie, who had a bemused smirk that wasn't half cute on her. "You wanna hit the road, right?" She nodded. "You wanna write about how unwirers get made? I could bring along the kid I'm 'prenticing up." Through the cellphone, he heard Marcel shouting "Yes! Yes!

YES!" and imagined the kid punching the air and
pounding the booth's walls triumphantly.

"It's a good angle," she said. "*You* want him
along, right?"

He held the receiver in the air so that they could
both hear the hollers coming down the line. "I don't
think I could stop him," he said. "So, yeah."

She nodded and bit her upper lip, just where the
scar was, an oddly canine gesture that thrust her chin
forward and made her look slightly belligerent.
"Okay."

"Marcel! Calm down, twerp! Breathe. Okay. You
gonna be good if I take you along?"

"So good, man, so very very very very good, you
won't believe—"

"You gonna be *safe*, I bring you along?"

"Safe as houses. Won't breathe without your permission. Man, you are the *best*—"

"Yeah, I am. Four PM. Bring the stuff."

"We're heading for East Aurora." Roscoe looked
over his shoulder as he backed the truck into the
street, barely noticing Sylvie watching him. "There's
a low hill there that's blocking signal to the mesh near
Chestnut Hill. We're going to fix that."

"Great!" Marcel said. "Hey, isn't there a microwave
mast up there?"

"Yeah." Roscoe saw Sylvie making notes. "Could
you keep from saying exactly where we're placing the
repeaters? In your article? Otherwise FCC'll take
'em down."

"Okay." Sylvie put down her pocket computer. It
was one of those weird Brit designs with the folding
keyboards and built-in wireless that had trashed Palm
all over Europe.

"We should only need two or three at the most,"

Roscoe added. "I figure an hour for each and we can be home by nine."

"Why don't we use the microwave mast?" Marcel said.

"Huh?"

"The microwave mast," he repeated. "We go up there, we put one repeater on it, and we bounce signal *over* the hill, no need to go 'round the bushes."

"I don't think so," Roscoe said absently. "Criminal trespass."

"But it'd save time! And they'd never look up there, it'll look just like any other phone company dish—"

Roscoe sighed. "I am so not hearing this. Listen, if I get caught climbing a tree by the roadside I can drop the cans and say I was bird-watching. But if I get caught climbing a phone company tower, it's criminal trespass, *and* they'll nail me for felony theft of service, and felony possession of unlicensed devices—they'll find the cans for sure, it's like a parking lot around the base—and violate my parole. Enough about saving time, okay? Doing twenty to life is not saving time."

"Okay," Marcel said, "we'll do it your way." He crossed his arms and stared out the window at the passing trees under their winter cowl of snow.

"How many unwirers are working the area?" Sylvie asked, breaking the silence.

Marcel said, "Just us," at the same moment as Roscoe said, "Dozens." Sylvie laughed.

"We're solo," Roscoe said, "but there are lots of other solos in the area. It's not a *conspiracy*, you know—more like an emergent form of democracy."

Sylvie looked up from her palmtop. "That's from a manifesto, isn't it?"

Roscoe pinked. "Guilty as charged. Got it from

Barlow's *Letters from Prison*. I read a lot of prison-lit. Before I went into the joint."

"Amateurs plagiarize, artists steal," she said. "Might as well steal from the best. Barlow talks a mean stick. You know he wrote lyrics for the Grateful Dead?"

Marcel came out of his sulk when they got to the site. He set up a surveyor's tripod and was the model of efficiency as he lined up the bank shot to bounce their signal around the hill.

Sylvie hung back with Roscoe, who was testing the gear using his laptop and two homemade antennae to measure signal strength. "Got to get it right the first time. Don't like to revisit a site after it's set up. Dog returning to its vomit and all."

She took out her key chain and dangled it in the path of the business end of the repeater Roscoe was testing. "I'm getting good directional signal," she said, turning the keychain so he could see the glowing blue LEDs arranged to form the distinctive Nokia "N."

Roscoe reached for the fob. "These are just *wicked*," he said.

"Keep it," she said. "It's just a Nokia freebie."

Roscoe felt obscurely embarrassed—like an American hick. "Thanks," he said. "Hey, Marcel, you got us all lined up?"

"Got it."

They lined up the first repeater and tested it, but there was no signal. Bad solder joints, interference from the microwave tower, gremlins . . . Who knew? Sometimes a shot just didn't work.

"Okay, pass me another one." It worked fine, but they needed two to make the shot. "Didn't you bring a third?" Roscoe asked.

"What for?" Marcel shrugged. "They worked back home."

"Shit." Roscoe stamped his feet and looked back at the road. Sylvie was standing close to the truck, hands in her pockets, looking cold. He glanced at the hill and the microwave mast on top of it.

"Why'n't we try the hill?" Marcel asked. "We could do the shot with only one repeater from up there."

Roscoe stared at the mast. "Let me think." He picked up the working repeater and shambled back to the truck cab. "Come on."

"What now?" asked Sylvie, climbing in the passenger seat.

"I think." Roscoe turned the ignition key. "Kid has a point. We've only got one unit. If we can stick it on the mast, it'll do the job." He stared at Marcel. "But we are *not* going to get caught." He glanced at Sylvie.

She whistled tunelessly. "It's your ass."

"Okay. You guys keep an eye out for any sign of anyone following us." He drove with excruciating care.

The side road up to the crest of the hill was dark, shadowed by snow-laden trees to either side. Roscoe took it slowly; a couple of times there was a whine as the all-wheel drive cut in on the uncleared snow. "No fast getaways," Sylvie noted.

There was an empty parking lot at the end of the driveway. The mast rose from a concrete plinth behind a chain-link fence, towering above them like a giant intrusion from another world. Roscoe parked. "See anything?"

"No," said Marcel from the back seat.

"Looks okay—hey, wait!" Sylvie did a double take. "Stop! Don't open the door!"

"Why—" Marcel began.

"Stop. Just stop." Sylvie seemed agitated, and right then, Roscoe, his eyes recovering from headlight glare, noticed the faint shadows. "Marcel, *get down!*"

"What's up?" Marcel asked.

"Crouch down! Below window level!"

Roscoe looked past her. The shadows were getting sharper and now he could hear the other vehicle. "Shit. We've been—" He reached toward the ignition key and Sylvie slapped his hand away. "Ouch!"

"Here." She leaned forward. "Make it look like you mean it."

"Mean what—" Roscoe got it a moment before she kissed him. He was hugging her as the truck cab flooded with light.

"*You! Out of the*— Oh, geez." The amplified voice, a woman's voice, trailed off. Sylvie and Roscoe turned and blinked at the spotlights mounted on the gray Dodge van as its doors opened.

Sylvie wound down the side window and stuck her head out. "I don't know what you think you're doing, but you can fuck right off!" she yelled. "Voyeurs!"

"This is private property," came the voice. Boots crunched on the road salt. A holster creaked. Roscoe held his breath.

"Sorry," Sylvie said. "All right, we're going."

"Not yet, you aren't," the voice said again, this time much closer. Roscoe looked in the rearview at the silhouette of the woman cop, flipping her handcuffs on her belt, stepping carefully on the ice surface.

"Go go go," hissed Marcel from the back seat.

"Sit tight," Sylvie said.

From the back seat, a click. Roscoe mumbled, "Marcel, if that is a gun I just heard, I am going to shove it up your fucking ass and pull the trigger."

He rolled down his window. "Evening, officer," he

said. Her face was haloed by the light bouncing off her breath's fog, but he recognized her. Had seen her, the day before.

"Evening sir," she said. "Evening, ma'am. Nice night, huh? Doing some bird-watching?"

Made. He couldn't have moved if he tried. He couldn't go back—

Another click. A flashlight. The cop shone it on Sylvie. Roscoe turned. The concealer was smudged around her scar.

"Officer, really, is this necessary?" Sylvie's voice was exasperated, and had a Manhattan accent she hadn't had before, one that made her sound scary-aggro. "It was just the heat of the moment."

"Yes, ma'am, it is. Sir, could you step out of the car, please?"

The flashlight swung toward the back seat. The cop's eyes flickered, and then she slapped for her holster, stepping back quickly. "Everyone, hands where I can see them *now!*"

She was still fumbling with her holster, and there was the sound of the car door behind her opening. "Liz?" a voice called. The other cop, her partner. Fourth and Walnut. "Everything okay?"

She was staring wide-eyed now, panting out puffs of steam. Staring at the rear window. Roscoe looked over his shoulder. Marcel had a small pistol, pointed at her.

"Drive, Roscoe," he said. "Drive fast."

Moving as in a dream, he reached for the ignition. He slammed it into gear, cranking hard on the wheel, turning away from the cop, a wide circle through the empty parking lot that he came out of in a fishtail.

He regained control as they crested the ridge. Behind him, he heard the cop car swing into the chain-link fence, and in his rearview mirror, he saw the car whirling across the ice on the parking lot, its head-lights moving in slow circles. Sylvie's gasp snapped him back to his driving. They were careening down the hill now, tires whining for purchase.

He touched the brakes, triggering another skid. The truck hit the main road still skidding, but now they had rock salt under the rubber, and he brought the truck back under control and floored it, switching off the headlights.

"This isn't safe," Sylvie said.

"You said, 'Drive fast,' " Roscoe said, hammering the gearbox. He sounded hysterical, even to his own ears. He swallowed. "It's not far."

"What's not far?" she said.

"We've got about five minutes before their backup arrives. Seven minutes until the chopper's in the sky. Need to get off the road."

"The safe house," Marcel said.

"Shut up!"

Roscoe hadn't been to the safe house in a year. It was an old public park, closed after a jungle gym accident. He'd gone there to scout out a good repeater location, and found that the public toilet was unlocked. He kept an extra access point there, along with a blanket, a change of clothes, a first-aid kit, and a fresh license plate, double bagged and stashed in the drop ceiling.

He parked the truck outside the fence, between the bushes and the chain-link. They were invisible from the road. He got out quickly.

"Marcel, get the camper bed," he said, digging a crowbar out from under his seat and passing it to him.

"What are you going to do?" Sylvie asked.

He passed her a tarpaulin. "Unfold this on the ground there, and pile the stuff I pass you on top of it."

He unloaded the truck quickly, handing Sylvie the unwiring kit. "Make a bundle of it," he said, once the truck was empty. "Tie the corners together with the rope."

He snatched the crowbar away from Marcel and attacked the nuts holding down the camper bed. When he'd undone them, he jammed the pry end of the bar between the lid and the truck. It began to slide and he grunted, "Get it," at Sylvie who caught the end.

"Over the fence," he gasped. They flipped it over together.

A car rolled past. They all flinched, but it kept going. He stilled his breathing and listened for the chop-chop of a helicopter, and thought that, yes, he heard it.

"Over the fence," he said. "All of us."

Marcel opened his mouth.

"Not a word," Roscoe said. "If you say one goddamned word, you're out. Fence. Sylvie, you stay here and cover the camper bed with snow. Kick it over. As much as you can. Marcel. Drag the gear."

They entered the dark toilet single file, and once the door had closed behind them, Roscoe pulled out his flashlight and clicked it on.

"We're not going home ever again. Whatever you had in your pockets, that's all you've got. Do you understand?"

Marcel opened his mouth and Roscoe lunged for him.

"Don't speak. Just nod. I don't want to hear your voice. You've destroyed my life, climbing that tower, pulling that gun. I'm over, you understand? Just nod."

Marcel nodded. His eyes were very wide.

"Climb up on the toilet tank and pop out that ceiling tile and bring down the bag."

Marcel brought down the bag and Roscoe felt some

of the tension leak out of him. At least he had a new license plate and a change of clothes.

Sylvie had covered the bottom third of the camper bed and her gloves and boots were caked with snow.

"I don't know that it'll fool anyone who walks over here, but it should keep it hidden from the road, at least," Roscoe said. His heart had finally begun to slow down.

"Here's the plan," he said. "I'm going to swap the license plates and drive into town. Sylvie lies down on the back seat. Marcel, you're walking. Don't let anyone see you. Find somewhere to hide until tomorrow, we'll meet at the Donut House near the Rainbow Bridge, eight AM, okay?"

Marcel nodded mutely. The snow was falling harder now, clouds dimming the moonlight.

Roscoe dug out a pack of hot pads from the trash bag and thrust them at Marcel. "Go," he said. "Now."

After Marcel slunk away into the night, Roscoe helped Sylvie over the fence, then hunkered down, using a small wrench to remove the plates from the truck. Sylvie crouched beside him, holding the flashlight.

"Did you know he had a gun?" Sylvie said, as he tightened down the bolts.

"No," Roscoe said. "No guns. We don't use guns. We're fucking network engineers, not pistoleros."

"Thought so," she said, but made no further comment as he fastened the new plates in place.

Finally he stood up. "Okay, let's go," he said.

"What's the plan?" She paused, hand on door handle.

"The plan is to get away from here. Then figure out what to do next." He glanced at her sidelong, calculating. "I think you'll be all right, whatever happens. But that little idiot—" He realized his hands were shaking.

He drove slowly, starting every time he saw moving shadows. One time he passed a parked police car on the shoulder. He nearly jumped out of his skin, but managed not to put his foot down or even turn his head.

Sylvie sighed as the police car vanished in the rearview. "You're going to go the rendezvous, like you told him?" she asked.

"Got to. We're in it together."

"No."

Roscoe stared at her in the rearview.

"I don't trust him."

"What?" Roscoe shook his head then looked back at the road. "He's young, is all. Too young." They were not far from Main Street, and he began looking around for somewhere to park the truck. "We're going to have to walk a ways. You up to an hour on foot?"

"Listen, you've got to pay attention! If you go to the Donut House, they'll arrest you. You'll go down as a terrorist."

Roscoe didn't dignify her paranoia with a response. Instead he pulled over.

"There have been arrests you haven't heard about."

Roscoe opened his door and climbed out. He picked up the trash bag from the back and left the door open, keys dangling enticingly in the ignition.

Sylvie hurried to catch up. "There's a guy called Dennis Morgan, on the Texas border," she said quietly. "Don't know where he is, the feds won't say—they pulled him in on firearms charges, but all the warrants, search and seizure, went through a special FEMA courthouse. We tried FOIA notices and got denied. Dennis had no record of violent offenses. He was just an unwirer, but they charged him with attempted murder of a federal agent and stuck him in a hole so deep we can't find him."

Roscoe slowed, hearing her breath rasping.

"*Secret* trials, Roscoe, special terrorism courts. Records sealed—no defense attorneys. A woman, Caitlin Delaney in Washington State, they found a meth lab in her garage after they shot her resisting arrest, you know? They made her out to be some kind of gangster. She was fifty, Roscoe, and she had multiple sclerosis, and her backyard had line of sight to the Surrey side of the Canadian border."

Roscoe slowed even more, until he felt Sylvie walking beside him. "FCC, Roscoe, they've been making sure we know all about these dangerous terrorists. But I did some digging with my stringers. Unwirers are disappearing. Their turf gets too visibly unwired and then they vanish, leaving behind guns and drugs and kiddie porn. That's the *real* story I'm here to cover. Roscoe, if you go to that donut joint and Marcel is what I think he is, you'll . . . *vanish*."

She took his hand and stopped. His jacket felt icy-slick with freezing sweat. "What do you want?"

"I don't want you to get yourself killed," she said. Up close he could see the scar on her lip, the smudged foundation on her cheek. "Shit." She leaned against him and put her chin on his shoulder, nosing in like a small animal in search of warmth. "Come up to my room. We can discuss it there."

They ended up naked in bed together. And before anything much could happen, Roscoe was asleep, snoring quietly, dead to the world. He didn't notice: what he noticed was waking up to Sylvie's face on the next pillow, the dim red glow of the alarm clock's digits flickering toward seven o'clock.

"Hey. Wake up."

"Mm-hum." Sylvie rolled toward him for a warm moment, then her eyes opened. "We didn't?"

"Not yet." He ran one hand along her back, cupping her buttocks with a sense of gratified astonishment. *How did this happen to us?*

Her gaze traveled past him, settling on the clock. "Oh shit." She hugged him, then pulled back. "There's never enough time. Later?"

He nodded miserably.

She leaned over and kissed him hard, almost angrily. "This is so unprofessional—look, if I'm wrong about Marcel, I apologize, all right? But I think it's a sting. If I had a repeater, I could stake it out with a webcam, but—"

"A repeater?" Roscoe sat up. "There's one in my bag."

"Right." She rolled out of bed and stretched. He couldn't take his eyes away from her. "Listen, let's freshen up and get outta here." She grinned at him, friendly but far from the intimacy of a minute ago, and he had a tangible sense of lost possibilities. "Let's get the donut joint wired for video. Then we can go grab some coffee and figure out what to do next."

Roscoe glommed his last repeater onto a streetlamp above eye level. "They'll probably take it down later today," he said. "Hope it's worth it."

"It will be," she reassured him, before striding away to plant a webcam on the back of a road sign opposite the donut joint. He stared after her, a slim figure bundled in improbable layers of cold-weather gear.

Sylvie was smiling as she caught up with him and grabbed his arm. "Come on, there's a Starbucks on the next block," she said.

They shed gloves and caps as they went in past the Micronet booths and the pastry counter. Sylvie ordered a couple of large lattes. "Mezzanine open?" she asked.

"Sure." The gum-chewing barrista didn't even look up.

Upstairs, in a dark corner well back from the shop front, Sylvie produced her phone and began fiddling with it. "Let's see." She turned it so he could see the tiny color display. The front of the donut shop was recognizable.

"Seven-thirty," he said, checking his watch again. A gray minivan pulled up in front of the shop and disgorged a bunch of guys in trench coats and one very recognizable figure. His stomach lurched. "Who are those guys? That's Marcel—" He stopped.

"Party time," Sylvie said dryly.

Marcel entered the donut store. Two of the men in trench coats followed him. Most of the others moved out of frame, but one of them was just visible, hiding down the alley at the side of the store.

It was five minutes to eight. Roscoe went downstairs for another coffee, his feet dragging and his spirits sinking.

"Roscoe!"

"Coming." He hurried upstairs. "What is it?"

"Look." She pointed the phone display so he could see it. A pickup truck roughly the same color and age as Roscoe's drew up in front of the donut store.

"Hey, that's not—"

"I told you we employ stringers."

A man wearing a jacket and cap climbed out of the cab. He looked a little like Roscoe.

Trench coats boiled out from behind trash cans. They swarmed the truck and blocked the doorway and two of them covered the parking lot. There was chaos and motion, then another trench coat barreled out of the door and started yelling at them. The guns vanished. Marcel appeared in the doorway behind him, pointing. Two of the trench coats began to walk toward the camera.

"I think we've seen enough," said Sylvie, and killed the feed. Then she hit one of the speed-dial buttons on her phone. It rang twice. "Bonjour. Ou est le—"

Roscoe shook his head. He felt like a tuna might feel, a wooden deck under one flank and the cruel sun on the other, gills gasping in thin air. Sylvie was speaking to somebody in rapid-fire French while he was drowning on dry land.

She finished her call and closed her phone with a snap. She laid her hand across his: "Okay, you're all set," she said, grinning.

"Huh?"

"That was the French consulate in Toronto. I set it up in advance so they'd see the webcam. If you can get to the consulate, you've got diplomatic asylum." She reached into her pocket and pulled out a small box; it unfolded like brushed-aluminum origami, forming a keyboard for her to plug the phone into. "We're going to hit the front page of the *Journal* tomorrow. It's all documented—your background, Marcel, the gun, the stakeout, all of it. With a witness." She pointed a thumb at herself. "We've been looking for a break like this for *months*." She was almost gloating, now: "Valenti isn't going to know what's hit him. My editor." She slurped some coffee. "He got into the game because of Watergate. He's been burning for a break like this ever since."

Roscoe sat and stared at her.

"Cheer up! You're going to be famous—and they won't be able to touch you! All we have to do is get you to Montreal. There's a crossing set up at the Mohawk Reservation, and I've got a rental car. While I'm at it, can you sign these?" She thrust a bundle of papers at him and winced apologetically: "Exclusive contract with the WSJ. It covers your expenses—flight included—plus fifteen grand for your story. I tried to hold out for more, but you know how things are." She shrugged.

He stared at her, stunned into bovine silence. She pinched his cheek and shoved the papers into his hands. "Bon voyage, mon ami," she said. She kissed each cheek, then pulled out a compact and fixed the concealer on her lip.

Paris in springtime was everything it was meant to be and more. Roscoe couldn't sit down in a café without being smartmobbed by unwirer groupies who wanted him to sign their repeaters and tell them war stories about his days as a guerrilla fighter for technological freedom. They were just kids, Marcel's age or younger, and they were heartbreaking in their attempts to understand his crummy French. The girls were beautiful, the boys were handsome, and they laughed and smoked and ordered him glasses of wine until he couldn't walk. Billboard ads for Be, Inc. and Motorola, huge pictures of him scaling a building side with a Moto batarang clenched in his teeth.

Roscoe couldn't keep up. Hardly a week went by without a new business popping up, a new bit of technological gewgaggery appearing on the tables of the Algerian street vendors by the Eiffel Tower. He couldn't even make sense of half the ads on the Metro.

But life was good. He had a very nice apartment with a view and a landlady who chased away the paparazzi with a broom. He could get four bars of signal on his complimentary Be laptop from the bathroom, and ten bars from the window, and the hum of the networked city filled his days and nights.

And yet.

He was a foreigner. A curiosity. A fish, transplanted

from the sea to Marineland, swimming in a tank where the tourists could come and gawp. He slept fitfully, and in his dreams, he was caged in a cell at Leavenworth.

Roscoe woke to the sound of his phone trilling. The ring was the special one, the one that only one person had the number for. He struggled out of bed and lunged for his jacket, fumbled the phone out.

"Sylvie?"

"Roscoe! God, I know it's early, but God, I just had to tell you!"

He looked at the window. It was still dark. On his bed stand, the clock glowed 4:21.

"What? What is it?"

"God! Valenti's been called to testify at a Senate hearing on Unwiring. He's stepping down as chairman, I just put in a call to his office and into his dad's office at the MPAA. The lines were *jammed*. I'm on my way to get the Acela into DC."

"You're covering it for the *Journal*?"

"Better. I got a *book deal*! My agent ran a bidding war between Bertelsmann and Penguin until three AM last night. The whole fucking thing is coming down like a house of shit. I've had three Congressional staffers fax me discussion drafts of bills—one to fund $300 million in DARPA grants to study internetworking, one to repeal the terrorism statutes on network activity, and a compulsory license on entertainment online. God!"

"That's—amazing," Roscoe said. He pictured her in the cab on the way to Grand Central, headset screwed in, fixing her makeup in her compact, dressed in a smart spring suit, off to meet with the Hill Rats.

"It's incredible. It's better than I dreamed."

"Well . . ." he said. He didn't know what to say.

"See if you can get me a pardon, okay?" The joke sounded lame.

"What?" A blare of car horns. "Oh, crap, Roscoe. It'll work out, you'll see. Amnesty or something."

"We can talk about it next month, okay?" She'd booked the tickets the week before, and they had two weeks of touring on the continent planned.

"Oh, Roscoe, I'm sorry. I can't do it. The book's due in twelve weeks. Afterward, okay? You understand, don't you?"

He pulled back the curtains and looked out at the foreign city, looking candlelit in the night. "I understand, sweetie," he said. "This is great work. I'm proud of you."

Another blare of horns from 6,000 miles away. "Look, I've got to go. I'll call you from the Hill, okay?"

"Okay," Roscoe said. But she'd already hung up.

Six bars on his phone. Paris was lit up around him with invisible radio waves. Coverage and innovation were everywhere. They thought he was a hero, but 6,000 miles away the real unwiring was taking place.

He looked down at his slim silver phone, glowing with blue LEDs, a gift from Nokia. He tossed it from hand to hand, and then he opened the window and chucked it three stories down to the street. It made an unsatisfying clatter as it disintegrated on the pavement.

Revision Point

In 1995, Congress held a series of hearings on the "National Information Infrastructure." At that time, lobbyists for the entertainment industry petitioned the government to redesign the Internet so that copyright infringement could be detected and stopped.

This bid was wisely ignored by the Congress—after all, these were the same companies that sued to get rid of the piano roll, the radio, and the VCR! In "Unwirer," Congress had adopted regulations that defund any research into the decentralized Internet, and has created a series of criminal offenses for the use of the Internet in the commission of a crime. Consequently, America's technology boom never arrives, while abroad, Jean Louis Gassee's Be, Inc., turns France into a technology juggernaut.

C.D. and C.S.

WHEN THE MORNING STARS SANG
TOGETHER

by Isaac Szpindel

*Where were you when I laid the foundation of
the earth? Tell me, if you understand! Who decided its measurements, if you know? . . . Where
are its bases fastened? Or who laid its corner-
stone; when the morning stars sang together and
all the sons of God shouted for joy?*

—Job 38:4-7

THEY'RE coming for you now. You knew they
would.

You knew better. There are no secrets in the Broth-
erhood and your theory is dangerous, not only to you,
but to the world. It threatens 300 years of Holy Science, 300 years of history and stability. But you had
to satisfy your curiosity and some misconception of
justice and truth.

You knew better. You are a scientist, a Jesuit like
all scientists, but your faith couldn't protect you. It
won't protect you from them now that they come as
they should.

Your heart pounds through your chest and your
head. So hard to think. Destroy the evidence. Destroy
it, before they use it to destroy you. Destroy it before
it gets out and poisons minds.

They'll be here soon with their computers and their technologies. Saint Galileo had no Inquisition like this, those three centuries ago. But this is 1946, Saint Galileo's 1946, and the Church's. And now you threaten their world from your little apartment in a converted motel room in the shadow of the Holy Observatory in Tucson, Arizona.

You should have kept your ideas to yourself, you should have stayed in Rome. But you live here, too, you trained here, and from here you were called to the Vatican to be curator of the Holy Galileo Letters. How fitting that you and those very Holy Letters be the Inquisition's next victim. You can still recall the way the coarse textures of their aged pages felt through your gloved hands. You can smell their intoxicating musk even though you were allowed the experience only once, to scan them for the archives and for analysis. They were so fragile, so delicate, like the people and the ideas preserved, trapped forever, within their folds.

Most Affectionate Daughter Suor Maria Celeste,

I am warmed by your words as I am by the shirts you have so delicately and expertly mended for me. They keep the cold from this old man's bitter breast, even within this house that has become his prison.

The unexpected magnitude and progress of your illness is most unwelcome news, as it deprives me both of the works of your hand and of those of your mind. And I must confess, that without them both, I am at a loss. Vincenzo, my pupil not your brother, has arranged for one of the Sisters, a Suor Maria Joseph, to read to you my words at your bedside that they might hasten your recovery and return you, merciful God willing, from his heavenly world to ours here on earth.

By your leave, then, you will forgive and indulge me in continuing to speak to you of my work, as I have become accustomed. I have made significant improvement to my invention of the mirror telescope by suspending a secondary flattened collecting mirror at a centrally direct and perpendicular distance from the main curved reflector. This secondary mirror's diminutive size, and the four slender metal threads that suspend it above the first, block only a small fraction of the incident light from the main mirror. A trifling obstruction when compared to the large primary collecting mirror areas now possible. And so very little of the image is lost or distorted. The other Vincenzo, my pupil, has kindly supervised its construction at a local silversmith's.

It seems also that I have made the gravest error in sharing this news with Vincenzo, your brother, ever the practitioner of a failing wit. He reacted thus to a demonstration of the new device only this past evening. "I fear, Father," said he, "that your confinement, has dimmed your mind perhaps more than your ailing vision. Do you propose to gaze upon the heavens with this eyesore, or do you intend to merely collect within? It resembles more a hideously large bucket than it does a spyglass."

"My dear Vincenzo," I responded. "My vision has not entirely taken leave of me, as perhaps your wit has of you, and I daresay that with the aid of this hideous bucket, as you call it, I will be illuminating the very light of God's own truth."

As I told Vincenzo thus, I inserted the final component—a diminutive telescope no longer

than my own hand—upon a focusing track in line
with the secondary mirror's reflection. This miniature eyepiece telescope, as I call it, collects the
reflected light into a final, albeit inverted, image.
Considering that we are gazing upon the heavens, however, I scarcely feel the orientation to
be of issue. Moreover, by doing so I have added
to the distance the light must travel before pro-
ducing an image at the eyepiece telescope which
allows me to achieve celestial magnifications of
a hundredfold. And due to the much larger aper-
tures possible with mirrors rather than lenses, I
have realized a sixteenfold improvement in light-
gathering capacity over even the most sizable
spyglass.

While these abilities are impressive, I must
admit that at high magnifications I find myself
making constant minute adjustments to the telescope's position to match pace with a viewed object's celestial motion. At my age, and in my
condition, I find this quite maddening. I have
written to my colleagues in the East, the Orient
to be precise, of this problem and they have gra-
ciously offered to devise a solution.

Nevertheless, my mirror telescope remains im-
pressively functional to the extent your brother
was stricken mercifully speechless at the sight of
a highly magnified Jupiter and its moons. I must
also say that we were then both stricken by a
marvelous view of Saturn. Saturn, dear daughter,
has not eaten its children, as I had previously
speculated, it simply gathers them about itself,
enclosed in the thinnest of ribbons.

Yet, even in this moment of discovery my
thoughts are for you. I pray that the Lord judge
you mercifully to return you to health, to return

my child to me, as He has returned those of
Saturn to my sight. And added to my sight, I
long to once again hear the sound of your words
upon your voice

Your beloved lord father,

G.G.

Inquisition sirens wail diatonically in the distance. You
gather the hard copies of your offending work together: all your calculations, your speculations laid out
logically, perhaps irrefutably. The world isn't ready for
such dangerous thoughts, you know, and you shouldn't
have boasted of them. Your consumption of wine at
Brother Al-Fahudi's birthday celebration, surely the
sin that begat the greater sin of pride.

You search now for a suitable spot in which to make
a sin offering of your hard copies. Your one-room bach-
elor apartment, once a single-efficiency hotel room, of-
fers few altars save a bathtub and a small oven.

You settle on the white enameled oven, built, you
believe, to contain fire, to contain the sacrifice that is to
become of your work and your ideas. Your hands tremble, as you straighten the papers for no reason. They
will burn as easily, perhaps better, if left in disarray.

Outside, the sirens become louder and their pitch
drops from the Galileo Effect, warning you of the Inquisition, their vehicles closing in and slowing.

Your offering lies heavily in your hands as it does
on your mind. It overwhelms you for a moment, and
you hesitate. Stand and fight, hoping for later enlightenment and greater glory in the service of the Church,
like Saint Galileo, or recant now?

But you are not Saint Galileo, even though in some
small way, you wish you could be like him.

The sirens stop.

They're here.

Most Affectionate Suor Maria Celeste,

May the words of this letter reach you through the kind lips of Suor Maria Joseph to guide you home to this earth. May they also warm your cloistered bones in this cold winter season that I now suffer more without your works of kindness. And by this I mean not only the designs of your hand, but those of your wit and your counsel. A most wondrous and illuminating event has occurred, Daughter, sprung from your own advices. You have often chastised me for my complaints and encouraged me to find blessings in my ailments within the graces of the Good Lord, and so I have of late discovered in the affliction of my eyes, which I had called a curse, to be one such blessing.

One evening upon the darkness, and while observing the full moon from my courtyard in the company of my servant, Salvatore, I remarked, "Is it not odd, Salvatore, to observe a rainbow around the moon on such a dry winter's eve?"

Salvatore regarded me with alarm. "Sire, you jest with your poor servant, I see no such rainbow. . . . Are you well?"

"Salvatore," I replied, newly humbled by insight. "In your honesty, I have found inspiration." And immediately, I set the perplexed Salvatore upon a most unusual task that found us waiting at our loggia the very next morning.

As the pale light of daybreak devoured the morning stars, a horse-drawn carriage in my employ, carrying trumpeters at the horn, announced the dawn at full gallop past our position.

"Are you most certain you are well, Lord?" Salvatore begged once again as the cacophonous procession passed, "You have surely woken, and greatly angered, all our good neighbors."

"Fear not, Salvatore," I replied. "I have simply called them to enlightenment." I did not explain to poor Salvatore, who doubtless considers me truly mad now, that my experiment, as I call it, confirmed an observation made during a childhood experience involving a similar procession during a celebration. As the trumpets approached, their tones increased in pitch, as they drew away, their pitch similarly fell. Our experiment has just now confirmed this property of sound which I expect to employ in the service of light.

I have often ridiculed Lucretius' preposterous and antiquated theories that sight is produced by ethereal skins that are shed by objects to fly through the air and dance upon our eyes. My telescopes have been the victim of many a public slander from cretinous Lucretians who condemn their lenses for distorting delicate reality by interfering with these skins.

As ridiculous as this idea might be, what if simple misguided Lucretius had hit on something, nonetheless? What if light were to the eye what sound were to the ear? What if both travel as ripples, like those on a pond? And if this be the case, then could not the rainbow-like halos I had remarked upon around the moon hint that color is to light what pitch is to sound? If not for the infirmity of my eyes, I might have missed it, but perhaps with a modification to the larger, sharper eye of my new mirrored telescope I might demonstrate the implications of this discovery for all to see. Aided by the solution I await from the East—a wondrous clockwork, I am told—we might gaze long enough upon a single heavenly body to appreciate not only its shape, but the subtle rainbow of its procession as well. And, perhaps, such observations could be of further use to me, in ways I have not yet conceived.

As always, dear Daughter, I long for your insights into these matters. Vincenzo, my student, is possessed of a keen mind for ideas already fully formulated. He has not been blessed, as you have, with the gift for lucid speculation. More so, I long for the sound of your voice, the rise and fall of your notes, even once removed through another's lips. Your illness has shut upon me a lid of scholarly silence where the counsel of others grates below my wits like gravel under a worn sole.

Your beloved and beseeching lord father,

G.G.

Car doors slam, hard soles bite into gravel. They're here.

You throw your notes into the oven, then you strike a match and set the papers ablaze before closing the oven door. You flick the overhead switch for the exhaust fan, to help draw away the smoke. The alarm in the room has never worked; you worry more about your eyes.

Flames dance across your work. They curl the edges of your work and blister the surfaces brown. Even with the fan, the odor is overpowering and sinister, like a forest fire through dead wood. But this is no natural blaze—it's an inferno, a live sacrifice, a holy offering to atone for your sins. Let someone less pious pose the question that brought you here, let them propose the theory, if it be worthy. Let it be an amateur outside the Jesuit order, a layperson who has not dedicated his life to the holy union of Church and Science. Let it be someone who may more easily beg absolution.

The flames rise and upon them your words and your work, an apology to the heavens for the century of peace your ideas threaten, for the controversy they might have created, for the doubts they would create. If not for the scientific proofs of the Church's holy doctrines, the Schism could not, would not, have been healed. With doubt replacing science as an ally, a weakened Church could not have gathered the world into its holy fold, and could not have ultimately convinced the Hebrews and the Mohammedans to join in the scientifically-proved spiritual truths.

You know now that with this act you ask for forgiveness for a theory that threatens to forever separate science from Church, that might make enemies of old allies. You confess your idea which threatens the Church's most basic and Holy precept of universal centrality, the very one that returned the sainted Galileo and his Holy Sciences to the Church. Sciences you now know were likely misconceived, products of a Galilean fallibility as monumental as your discovery of them. And instead of illuminating and protecting Holy Galileo's memory and his Letters, you stand now as their accuser.

You know the Inquisition exists to protect and to preserve. If they do not find your work, if they find only you, they might accept this penitent offering you have made of your scientific hubris. They will see that you have chosen faith over science, and then, perhaps, you will be spared.

Darling Daughter Most Beloved Maria Celeste,
 I am heartened that the Lord spares your life,

even in cruel sleep. Yet, it grieves me greatly that your mind prefers that company of the heavens above, to that of the earth below. This poor sinner prays for you daily, though I fear that I am becoming weak.

My bones are made cold and wretched by the passing winter and by the chilled drafts allowed against me by hands less skilled than yours in the mending of my vestments. More than my garments, I fear that without the wisdom of your words, I am truly imprisoned, my confinement unbearable. I have sought leave, and await permission, to travel to your convent in San Matteo if only to be by your side, to hold your delicate fingers within mine, and to beseech you in my own voice to return to me.

Until then, I offer word of all that remains me, that of my experiments.

My friends in the East have been most kind in delivering to me a wondrous and elaborate clockwork upon which to mount my mirror telescope. This gargantuan clockwork, once trained on Polaris, causes the telescope to then follow the celestial body it is fixed upon across the duration of the night sky without need for further adjustment.

Moreover, in the Easterners' luminous kindness—and I believe that in His infinite wisdom, God gifts even the heathens thus—they have provided me also with a recipe for an amazing gelatin bath exquisitely more sensitive than the eye to color. These baths may be laid out in dishes, where the light emanating from my telescopic eyepieces may fall upon their surfaces. And while the gelatins are poor representatives of contour, they react precisely according to color.

Moreover, inspired by the nature of the affliction of my eyes, I have devised a method to reproduce the rainbows I had observed around the moon and to project a representation of color, rather than shape or form, from the telescope's eyepiece. This I have achieved through the simple artifice of the placement of a metal disk possessed of a fine central slit over the eyepiece, the slit approximating the narrowed gaze of my failing vision. Light emanating from the eyepiece is thus translated from shape or form into a most divine assembly of color. And thus, when the telescope is trained to follow a celestial body across the night, the object's rainbow autograph is recorded.

Most promising, is that in this apparatus that I have dubbed a Telecolorimeter, I believe I have found the means to my salvation. You will forgive me if I explain in simple terms, as I grow weary and no doubt your condition will not suffer the details. My reasoning and methods are thus: I first intend to train the device on our sun, to capture its characteristic color autograph which will serve as my universal model for all such stars. I will then train the device on a duller distant sun such as Aldebaran. (An homage to the Mohammedans for their excellent studies of the heavens and for their superb work regarding the nature of light. A crystal wedge sent to me by one of their natural philosophers was my first attempt at devising a colorimeter.) With the ability to follow a distant sun through the night, and by affixing a gelatin plate to rotate along with the clockwork mount, I hope to capture the star's color imprint. This color signature should be identical to our sun's, since they are stars just the same, but for the color perturbations according to my earlier theory likening sound to light. Owing to Aldebaran's motion, I will expect to see a change in its colors as I would expect a change in pitch with approaching or receding sound.

I suspect also that what appears to me to be distant suns may, in fact, be assemblages of stars, not unlike that which encompasses our own planet, and I will require an even larger telescope in order to better appreciate their colors. To this end I have commissioned the manufacture, and will soon take delivery, of a mirror telescope of such generous measure that it is limited in size only by the clockwork's ability to carry its weight.

If I am mistaken and the Church is correct and we find ourselves at rest at the center of a fixed celestial sphere, no color perturbations should exist, since these objects maintain a fixed distance from us. If I find this, I will humbly publish my discoveries and recant fully to the public. Should I find, however, a tapestry of varied color perturbations, it will prove that our world is engaged in an intricate dance of advancing and withdrawing celestial motions. I expect my vindication will come with shifts toward the color red on the one hand and blue on the other, these being the colors of the rainbow's edge.

I fear my reasoning may require further reflection and I pray that you recover to aid me in the refinement of this theory, so that you might also bask in the glory and holy illumination that

it will provide. With much shame, I admit likewise, that I am possessed of a more selfish desire
to see you recover to mend this old man's longing heart along with his increasingly threadbare
garments. I beseech you, darling Daughter, to
quit your Father on high and to return to me,
your humble and earthly father below. As the
Phoenix of myth is reborn from ashes and flame,
I beg you, Daughter, to return to me that we
might both truly live.
Your most beloved and affectionate father,
G.G.

The fire within the oven consumes your ideas and
transforms them to flame, ashes, and dust.

Footfalls fill the stairwells and echo through the
hallways toward your room. The sounds of doors
opening and closing, and of your Brethren emerging
from their apartments, complete the cacophony that
announces the Inquisition's arrival.

The sounds grow louder and stop at your door.

Then you remember your computer, an early-
forties' point-and-click model squatting on the metal
writing desk in the corner of your apartment not occupied by kitchen, lavatory, or bed. The computer, cra-
dled between two bookshelves overstuffed with
volumes of science and divinics, blinks innocently at
you, not realizing that it holds within it the evidence
and power to condemn you and change the world.
The computer itself, a convenience of the scientific
theocracy it threatens to tear asunder.

In a moment you are at the computer, manipulating
its mouse, dragging files to the wipe window. Backup
files, memos, animations, calculations, anything that
might incriminate you. The wipe program will read
every bit of information, will then overwrite each with

a zero and once again with a one. The evidence will be irrecoverable.

You continue to the sickening rhythm of an Inquisition ram slamming into your door. The computer screen mocks you with its Church-logo wallpaper: two reflecting telescopes arranged into the shape of a cross, a Barberini bumblebee perched proudly atop its apex.

A voice booms through the door, "Stand aside, Brother, we intend no harm." You recognize the voice, Father Julius Rosenberg, the Grand Inquisitor himself, and a fellow Jesuit. Has he come to Tucson specially for you, or was he here, like you, for his allotment at the observatory and seminary?

Maybe you believe Rosenberg, maybe you're still looking for a way out. Maybe you just need a little more time to gather and wipe the necessary files. You can't let them distract you from the computer and the files. "Go ahead, break the door down, I'm safe and I'm not—"

The door splinters through your apartment before you can finish the sentence. Rosenberg fills the doorway, tall and gaunt and moving mechanically like an animated corpse. The others remain out of sight, likely standing at the ready. Julius steps across the threshold, the fluorescent lights of your apartment scattering through the dark tangled edges of his wild hair like a halo.

You stand, your hand hovering at the ready over the mouse button, one click away from activating the wipe, a warning and a threat. One press, no evidence, no doubt, no threat. But you know it's also the evidence Rosenberg wants most. It's your only bargaining chip.

"Brother," says Rosenberg, in a low growl. "You are making a terrible mistake." He stares at your hand, and you wonder what he'd do if faced with the same horrible secret, the same horrible decision you have before you. Then you notice that his eyes are twitching, or maybe it's just another trick of the light.

Most Venerable and Beloved Daughter Suor Maria Celeste

I have received word that you have begun to stir and that my letters have caused on at least one occasion a most gentle fluttering of your eyelids. Though I feel the Lord has forsaken me in many endeavors, I thank Him for such small gifts.

Vincenzo, your brother, happened upon me yesterday morn as I examined the color autographs from the distant suns that I had been following. Since my last letter, I have trained my clockwork mirror telescope on many stars, whether bright or faded, whether seemingly orange, or seemingly blue. The many gelatinous plates, upon which star autographs have been preserved with a fixative, now extend through my poor garden like rays from my old stone sundial like the pagan goddess Shiva's many arms. They obliterate what little grass remains not overgrown with weed. Fortunately, the hedgerow hides this from my already angered neighbors who have taken to complaining of the clockwork's unsightly appearance. It appears that I had indeed offended them with my experiment of the trumpets, as Salvatore so rightly feared.

"Father, you are distressed," Vincenzo remarked in concern from his perch on the dial. "Not our Sister-Sister?" He has named you thus out of love and a poor sense of pun.

"I am distressed always over your sister," I

replied, "but currently I am consumed by my inexplicable failure in this experiment."

Vincenzo approached the plate closest to him and examined it. "An excellent rainbow," he declared, "albeit, overly crimson. Beautiful, nonetheless."

"They are all tainted crimson," I confessed. "My other Vincenzo has checked and rechecked the baths, and our apparatus, and after several correspondences with the East he swears no error or failure in apparatus or in method exists."

"Would that I could assist you."

"No. I am lost without your sister's ear and her counsel. Only two explanations remain in this matter. For if one is correct, then my very sciences have failed me; and if the other, I have failed my God."

Vincenzo then raised himself from the dial. "Father, I have thought much lately of your former pupil, Delmedigo the Spaniard. He is an excellent physician who is said to heal within the graces of God even though he be a Hebrew. Perhaps he might be of assistance?"

An excellent suggestion, I thought, even for your brother. And so, with the disposal of my humble invitation, my onetime student, José Solomon Delmedigo, has now graced your side. I understand that, with great skill and attention, he has been hastening your healing some time now. I have received word, that with his good work nearly completed, he promises to visit with me on his return to Spain.

I continue to pray for you. Your progress has renewed in my purpose, even though my results fail me. My heart leaps to share more with you, my daughter, but the hour is late and my bones

have become as fragile and as quarrelsome as
my spirit.

Your most affectionate and beloved father,

G.G.

"Don't fail us now, Brother." The words escape like
steam from Rosenberg's mouth. He doesn't call you
by name, won't meet your eyes.

"The contents of this computer are too dangerous,
Julius. Not just to me."

Rosenberg takes a step forward and you stop him
with your thumb against the mouse's button. "This is
a test, Brother," he says.

"Is that why you're here?"

"Indeed," Rosenberg half whispers, meeting your
eyes for the first time, not looking away, not blinking.

"The Church, our world, is predicated on Saint Galileo's science, and my theory could prove him wrong,"
I tell him what he must already dread. "Were there
others who stumbled across this same discovery in the
past? Were they silenced, or have we all simply been
led away from this discovery through the scientific
control of the Church?" My voice rises. "Is what
might have been discovered years ago without the
Church, only being discovered by me for the first
time now?"

"Had others made the same discovery, Brother, the
world would already be a different place. It may yet
be, thanks to theories such as yours," Rosenberg answers without emotion.

"What kind of place would it be," you ask, "without
Church and science uniting us under one theology?
War and dissent would replace progress. How backward would the world be, how backward would we
become?"

"The world would be different, that is all. Whether

better or worse, depends only on us. We move backward, we become backward, when we hide the truth."

"And if that truth reveals a mistake made by an old man overjoyed by the recovery of his daughter and of his faith, a misstep so powerful that it has affected the course of history for hundreds of years?"

Dearest Darling Holy Daughter Suor Marie Celeste,

Joy is the kingdom of the Lord and all his wonders, greatest of which is the news of your convalescence. I have news that your eyes have opened, and I expect you have made an even greater recovery in the time it has taken these words to travel to you. Your recuperation has renewed my faith in the Lord and in His Church, and with my work I will honor all.

Your physician, Delmedigo, as I spoke of last, has visited with me and remains the strange and marvelous fellow I once knew as my pupil. It seems that since he has left my tutelage, he has become recognized as a great biblical scholar, mathematician, encyclopedist, and scientist (I borrow the term from your brother, as I have taken a liking to it). Moreover, I have discovered Delmedigo to be a fellow Copernican. After some pleasantries, both usual and unusual, and while surrounded by the gelatinous oddity of my garden, I put forth the problem of my failed colorimeter experiments to him.

"Most troubling," he pondered, while standing over the sundial as your brother had not long before. "The baths in each plate favor the red, whether on hot days or on cold, on clear nights or cloudy, under moonlight or in darkness. Yet your reasoning that color and light are like sound, ripples in a pond, rings true."

"Indeed," I responded, marveling at Delmedigo's play on words, and wondering if it was play also with me. Still, I know Delmedigo well, and he is not one for idle games.

"It occurs to me," Delmedigo continued, "that dragging a stick toward oneself in a pond, pushes the closest ripples together, and rarifies those that trail. To sound, this becomes the changes in pitch you have described. To light, as you have surmised, it is color. In a rainbow, the color blue is closest to earth, red the farthest away and possibly most rarified. If your methods and apparatus are true and there is no error, then all these bodies you observe, they move away from this earth? If I am mistaken, then they must all move toward us, no? In any event we can conclude that they move with respect to us in altogether the same way."

"But the Copernican view describes celestial movements that should display themselves as color shifts in many directions."

"Then perhaps our interpretation, or our understanding, of Copernican theory is flawed, rather than your apparatus."

"But this is vexing. My observation of the tides proves that we ourselves must also be in motion."

Delmedigo pondered a moment. "Yes, but not to our own senses. Perhaps to understand this problem, another perspective must be adopted?" Delmedigo offered this suggestion, as if it were nothing more than a daily tea, then took his leave of me as humbly and as respectfully as he had arrived.

I have much to think on, Sister-Daughter: your recovery, and the awful truth only now becoming apparent to me borne on the wings of Delmedigo's words. You have taken a long journey in your illness, as have I in my experiments and in my faith. Now we must both return. And it strikes me odd that we have been aided, both of us, by pagans, Mohammedans, and a Hebrew. It seems almost silly, not unlike one of your brother's humorous tales.

Mend well, my most beloved intricate and perfect creation. In illness and in health, it seems you provide me more with solution than with problem.

Your most humbled and affectionate lord father,
G.G.

"Truth can be a problem, indeed," says Rosenberg, staring you down. "A test of faith, in the least."

"Not if you prevent my poisonous ideas from spreading," you say. "Not if my theory disappears along with me. It's the reason you're here, isn't it?"

"There will be others with similar ideas—you've said so yourself. Perhaps there have been others already, but their fear of the Church or the scientific limits of the time prevented them from coming as far as you have."

"Or maybe their faith was stronger, their hubris weaker?"

"Word has spread about you, wild stories that your theory involves parlor tricks, balloons even, according to some."

Rosenberg's words terrify you because they are true. If your Brethren know about this, then others might easily discover what you have. They will. So why does Rosenberg toy now with you?

"No tricks," you're almost lying, "it's all about mistakes. Saint Galileo was wrong about the tides, and he was wrong about this, too. Had he come to the proper conclusion about universal centrality, it would have divided the Church and set both it and science back hundreds of years."

Rosenberg rubs his eyes unsteadily. "Saint Galileo's mistake, Brother, may well have been something else entirely, as may yours."

Most Blessed and Beloved Sister-Daughter,

To have your few words reach my failing eyes, even in your unsteady hand has, if I am not mistaken, been my greatest pleasure in this miserable life. Autumn is upon the land once again, stealing from nature its color and from me what remains of my disposition. Within the grace of your words, however, there is summer and sunshine, so my mind does not protest even as my bones do. In exchange for this, your gift, I return to you another, in your service, in that of the Lord, and in that of our beloved Church.

I have deciphered Delmedigo's cryptic observations and I realize now that I did not fail. Vincenzo, my student, and I have captured the colors of countless more heavenly suns since my last letter. They, too, are red and our methods remain sound, but the merciful Lord in his kindness has allowed me to only now see the meaning in all this. Please forgive me, once again as I summarize and simplify.

The redness of the night's stars can mean only that they move altogether away from us (or failing that, toward us, altogether, nonetheless). If our world inhabits a universe of constant motion, then this can only be true if one condition is met:

that our world finds its place at the very center of that celestial movement. The Church has been correct all this time, but in a way heretofore unimaginable. Our earth constantly rotates and revolves around the sun, I still believe that, but by adopting a different observation point as Delmedigo suggested, from outside that of our planetary sphere, one may find a position, perhaps one that rotates, from where one is able to appreciate this most intricate dance that places our earth at rest at its center.

I have reviewed my conclusions with the Pope and he has accepted both them and my humble self back to the fold. I have been bestowed with the title of Astronomer Holy of the Vatican, and with a position at the right hand of the Pope, a man who once again calls me friend. In this honor, a pamphlet describing my conclusions will be published in unheard of numbers by the Church itself. And furthermore, it has been agreed that my methodologies and my sciences, as we are now calling them, are to be administered through the Jesuit order and the holy offices of the Church.

I can only give thanks to the Lord for returning you to me, and by making of me a more perfect instrument by which to illuminate his heavens. With the proofs of science at our disposal, the Pope and I are confident we can heal the schism that has developed lately within the Church. We believe also that we have finally found a common language, or even a proving grounds, with which to win over the Hebrews, the Mohammedans, and scores of nonbelievers.

Glory to God and all his creations, foremost amongst them my most gifted daughter, Marie

Celeste. Peace and understanding to us all.
Amen.
Your most illustrious lord father,
G.G.

"Understanding may well reside within those computer files you threaten now, Brother. They may be of help to us, rather than harm," says Rosenberg in cool, measured tones.

You don't know if you can believe Rosenberg, if you should trust him, or his Inquisition. They've been a benign arm of the Church for centuries, but their history is that of ruthlessness beforehand. It doesn't matter now, though. You've made up your mind with Saint Galileo as your example. You have purified yourself with fire, and with the click of a mouse you will repent. You choose the Church as Saint Galileo did, that is the test, and you will wait for divine inspiration to show you the correct way, as it did Saint Galileo, even if it be flawed.

Your thumb depresses the mouse button.

Click.

Rosenberg watches the computer screen flicker to life, watches the progress bar which indicates the data being wiped forever from the magnetic surface of its hard drive. You have made your choice, passed your test. Why then does Rosenberg seem so sad? Didn't you choose correctly?

"It's better, safer, this way," you say.

"We should not have entrusted you with the Holy Galileo letters," he answers. "As their curator, you have fallen victim to Saint Galileo's same mistake."

"No, I haven't. I've forsaken my pride in favor of the Church. I have no intention of pursuing my theories or proving them, not as Saint Galileo attempted."

"And that is your mistake. The Inquisition is as its

name states, an office of inquiry. Scientific or spiritual, they are the same. The Inquisition's objective is to enlighten, to discover and disseminate the truth. By abandoning your hypothesis, one possible truth, you do a disservice to us all. Saint Galileo's error was in his inability to accept possibilities, in his insistence that his was the one and only truth. The Church fell victim to this same error, in its own way, until its truth finally agreed with Galileo's at the time of his ultimate discovery. The same truth you feel you now threaten. But the Church has since learned from this episode, as it appears you have not."

"I don't understand," you say honestly.

"God is infallible, but man's interpretation of God is not. Only once this is accepted can the scientific search for understanding share a common goal with religion."

"But you know the Scripture. Doesn't the Book of Job warn us specifically against just this kind of arrogant attempt at understanding God's creation?"

"That is one interpretation. The one the Church prefers, the one that has united the world, is that Job invites us to attempt to understand that which we may never fully grasp. Job invites us to learn, to fail, and to succeed. Your theories may well do so in someone else's hands, if not your own."

Rosenberg motions at the doorway. An acolyte in tech robes, a battery pack belt attached to the parabolic antenna in his hand, slides into view. You realize they have it all now. Your computer's magnetic hard drive reads and writes information using Modified Frequency Modulation techniques just like any FM broadcast and, given the proper equipment, is detectable just like any other radio signal. They have your work, every bit of your data; they read it on the first pass of the wipe. Rosenberg knew he'd get it one way or another, even without you. It was a test of your faith all along, a test of your faith in the Church and its offices.

"I failed," you say, embarrassed and ashamed.

"Your faith is weak," says Rosenberg in a formal tone, about to give sentence. "Do you accept the penance I now charge you with through the office of this Holy Inquisition?"

"I do."

"You are to continue to illuminate this, your hypothesis, without fail. And as you progress, you are to report regularly to this Holy Office. This, in addition to the penances demanded of you by our Holy Father at your next audience."

"Yes."

"Tell me, Brother," Rosenberg's tone and posture soften. "Many of us seek divine enlightenment our entire lives, with little success. I myself have never been so blessed. Please share with me one thing now. What was your inspiration? What are these stories of balloons?"

You consider explaining, but instead you reach into your pocket, the better to show him. Rosenberg watches you remove the deflated balloon, the one you had decorated with polka-dots for Brother Al-Fahudi's party. He watches you put the balloon to your mouth, and he watches you inflate it slowly. Through the distorted membrane of the balloon's yellow skin you see Rosenberg's expression turn from puzzlement to wide-eyed realization. The balloon expands, the dots on its surface move apart, all moving away from each other, all at once across its expanding surface, with none at its center.

Rosenberg takes it in for what seems an eternity, nods to you in acknowledgment, then departs without a word. The sounds of footfalls follow him.

You are alone again, the door to your apartment shattered, your notes burned, your computer's memory, like you, empty. All that remains now is your regret and your overwhelming fear of the task before you. What of the consequences of your sciences? What world will they invent? What world will they destroy?

And you hang your head in your hands and you weep.

Revision Point

Galileo Galilei is famous for many scientific innovations, including the astronomical application of the telescope and his experiments with gravity. He is perhaps most famous, however, for his feud with the Catholic Church over the heliocentric theory of the universe. This conflict ultimately led to Galileo's appearance before the Holy Inquisition, and his sentencing to house arrest for the crime of heresy, under which he served the remaining years of his life. Galileo, nevertheless, remained a devout follower of the Church.

Much of what we know of Galileo, the man, comes from the correspondences of his daughter, Maria Celeste, a cloistered nun. Of Galileo's three children, she appears to have been the most scientifically gifted and is suggested by some historians to have been his sometime intellectual collaborator. Galileo's letters to his daughter, on the other hand, remain lost; only his professional publications have survived. They reveal a brilliant, albeit flawed, scientific and artistic mind capable of great feats of reason that often led to correct conclusions through erroneous means. For instance, Galileo argued that the ocean tides were a result, and proof, of the Earth's rotation, rather than properly attributing them to the moon's gravitational pull. And although his conclusion that the Earth did indeed rotate was correct, the means by which that conclusion was reached remained cogently and elaborately spurious. Even in his support of the Copernican heliocentric theory of the universe, Galileo maintained that planetary orbits were perfectly circular, rather than accepting Kepler's elliptical theory.

A common misconception is that Galileo invented the telescope. Rather, he innovated its use for military and astronomical applications. Given enough time and proper inspiration, and had he not been deprived of the collaboration of his daughter by her untimely death, he might well have gone on to further discovery, invention, innovation, and conclusion. These would likely have remained elaborately conceived and crafted, brilliantly insightful, and, at times, fraught with error.

I.S.

HERD MENTALITY

by Jay Caselberg

I SAW another Einstein today. Just pedaling down Sycamore Avenue on a bicycle. As if we didn't have enough, and here was another one, large as life. I knew for sure it was another one, because ours doesn't ride a bike—he gets around in a chauffeured limo. Not that he comes around our town much, anyway, except for big corporate dos. I stood there, watching the Einstein whirr and clank past in no particular hurry, and I felt that sinking feeling grow inside me. I waited, hefting my rucksack on one shoulder, chewing at my bottom lip and I watched his old-guy form disappear into the distance. What on earth he was doing in our neck of the woods, I didn't know, but I could speculate. There had to be an opportunity there somewhere. Wherever there was opportunity, you'd find an Einstein. Briefly, I wondered what he might be looking for in our little town, but there was no way I could even really guess. Usually, we had some warning if another one was going to turn up. Still, we'd find out soon enough, Mary and me.

We just wanted to get on with our lives. We didn't need another Einstein. They were everywhere you looked anyway, without adding another one to the mix. It was hard enough for us common folk to make a mark as it was.

I made my way home and as I dumped my laptop on to the kitchen table, told Mary about what I'd seen.

She wiped her hands on the front of her apron, waiting for me to say something else. Behind her pots were steaming and clanking on the stove, and the smell of cooking vegetables filled the kitchen. One strand of hair was hanging down over her cheek and she brushed it away, blinking at the annoyance.

"Well?" she said.

"Well what?" I didn't know what she wanted me to say.

"How do you know? It's so hard to tell them apart. Why they all have to try and look the same beats me."

"Well, they're Einsteins, aren't they? Some sort of genetic predisposition to looking the same. They sure as hell do the same sorts of things. How do I know? I'm no expert."

But *he* certainly was. All of them. Every single one of the Einsteins seemed to make a success of whatever they turned their hands to, and their influence dominated everything we did. I even worked for Compu-Soft, another subdivision of a particular Einstein Enterprise, but then, the whole town survived because of the CompuSoft tech park. It gave us employment and lives and homes and a whole industry that kept the local region alive. When I'd first discovered the job opportunity, I leaped at the prospect and Mary and I had packed up and moved to Chaplin, lock, stock, and barrel. Quality of life, a nice professional community, one of the more advanced Einstein companies, it was the chance of a lifetime.

We ate dinner together in silence, and then settled in to watch television for the rest of the evening.

There was a half-decent movie I wanted to see on the Einstein-Warner channel. We snuggled in on the couch together, my arm around Mary's shoulders. I gave a wry smile and a snort as the old guy's head appeared above the corporate logo in the opening credits.

"What is it?" said Mary.

"Oh, nothing. Just something I remembered from work. Let's watch the film, okay?"

Einstein was getting old now. All of them. Not so old that he was past it, but you had to wonder. When our troops liberated the Spemann Lab complex in 1945, the Einsteins had been just five years old. The government had done the humanitarian thing and brought them back home. Eventually, someone had leaked the information and slowly, slowly, public pressure and outrage had grown. The big hush-hush operation our government had mounted was shut down and the Einsteins were released—or rather, they were integrated into society in a humanitarian manner. That was the wording the government press releases used. Two hundred and fifty is a lot of Einsteins.

We never called them Albert, or Al, or Bert, or anything else. They were always just the Einsteins. I don't know whether they were searching for identity, or a sense of where they came from, but they all grew the mustache and wore the crazy hair, just like the original back in Germany. They never did find him— the original—but he sure as hell lives on, or at least his legacy does. You have to wonder what would have happened if he'd had the opportunities that our Einsteins had, the original one. I guess we'll never know. There was a lot of speculation about what might have happened to him, but from the bits and pieces from our Einsteins' lives, we knew at least part of the story.

I kept thinking about it. Two hundred and fifty is still a lot of Einsteins, and we just didn't need another one. Not here. That a new one had cropped up unexpectedly was worrying me. It gave me an unsettled feeling deep in the pit of my stomach.

The next day at work, I asked around discreetly to see if anyone had heard anything. The guys in Technical Support where I worked didn't seem to know anything, or at least they were keeping quiet about it. About thirty of us worked in the section, our pods stretched out across bright, glassed space, the soothing blue carpet adding a clean uniformity to our working environment.

As often happens, the coffee machine became my source.

Bill joined me as I was waiting for the machine to finish its program.

"You know what you were talking about before?" he said.

I glanced at him and looked back at the machine, reaching down to retrieve the small plastic cup as it whirred to the end of the cycle. The coffee was pretty ordinary, but it was free. Just one of the things CompuSoft did for us, along with our ordered corporate community. All mod cons, everything on hand.

"Yeah, what about it?"

"I saw another one yesterday."

I lifted my coffee and sipped, looking at Bill over the rim, the hot synthetic aroma washing up into my face. "Oh, yeah?"

"Yeah, came in by cab. Came here. He wasn't ours. The clothes weren't right."

"Hmm," I said.

Bill stood in front of the machine, pretending to make a selection, peering through his smudged, geeky glasses. We didn't really like talking about the Einsteins too much. They were just too much an ever-present part of life in general.

"What about yours?" asked Bill.

I took another sip of the coffee before answering. "Kind of casual. He was on a bicycle."

"You don't say," said Bill. "Well, that's three. I wonder what's going on."

"I haven't heard anything."

"No, me neither," said Bill. "But you wouldn't, would you?"

"How do you mean?" I asked him.

"Well, they own so much of the media that they could probably shut it down if they wanted. I mean if a lot of them wanted to do something. Just one or two, they wouldn't bother."

"Hmm," I said again. He was right, and it didn't make me feel any more comfortable about it.

"Thanks, Bill," I said. "I'll let you know if I hear anything." And that was the end of the conversation. I returned to my pod, carrying what remained of my coffee with me.

It was a day like any other: support calls, incompetent users and questions that should have provided their own answers had they taken a few minutes to look. There was one legitimate hardware failure in the lot. The only thing different was the nagging sense of unease lurking in the back of my head.

As I was walking back from the callout through the long glass corridor that looked out over the parking lot, I saw another one. He'd just pulled up in his nice new top-of-the-range silver-gray Lexus. This one was different again—all slick and corporate in a neatly cut gray suit. How many Einsteins were we going to get? I stopped in mid-step, watching him as he headed toward the double glass doors. That made four.

Later that afternoon, Bill came and hung over the side of my pod.

"Just got a call," he said.

I glanced up from my screen. He was grinning. "Yeah, what is it?"

"Big meeting tomorrow in the auditorium. They need tech support. Screen projection, audio, that sort of thing. Upstairs said there's going to be a couple of hundred. We need a couple of side rooms with e-mail link and everything else. Now what do you think that's for?"

Technically, Bill was my superior, but we ran a pretty flat structure in CompuSoft. He was a whiz with software apps and with his shapeless sweater, perpetually smudged glasses and boyish face, you'd never really think of him of being in charge of anything, but he was good at what he did. I was good on the hardware side of things and we recognized our separate strengths. He was waiting for me to say something.

"Gee, I don't know." I wasn't going to give him the pleasure, but his grin stayed all the same.

"Listen, you want to do the setup and everything, you can take it if you like. It shouldn't need more than one of us. You seem all fired up about whatever's going on, so let's put your curiosity to bed. What do you say?"

I smiled back. "Thanks," I said. "Appreciate it."

"No problem. Just let me know what you come up with."

He disappeared, back to his own pod. I got up, headed for the stores and then to security for the keys to the auditorium. The place was only really used for large sales presentations to impress big external clients, or the major annual meetings, but it helped the company image. It was wired for sound and vision with the state of the art, and at CompuSoft we had the state of the art, so there wouldn't really be that much setup involved. I was eager to get started though; it would get me one step closer to finding out what was going on.

Though we didn't really need it, I decided I'd set up an auxiliary video feed in the room itself. That way I'd have a legitimate excuse to be inside the auditorium when whatever was going to take place happened, and then I'd know for sure. If they were really up to something, they might not like my being there, but I knew from experience that tech support guys were pretty much invisible to anyone who mattered.

I wheeled the equipment in, set up the table and the leads and everything, looked over my handiwork, then stood there at the front of the room, looking at all the empty seats. With a satisfied nod, I killed the lights and locked up for the night. I still didn't know what was going on, but I sure as hell would.

Later that night, I discussed my suspicions with Mary. Whatever might draw them all together, it couldn't be good. It couldn't be good for us, the little people.

It took me a long time to get to sleep, and when I did, it wasn't easy.

I was there early enough, everything unlocked and the hardware and feeds kicked into life to see the first Einsteins arrive. It was peculiar watching them trickle in and take up their positions around the auditorium. Close together, you could see the subtle differences— this one was more tanned; that one was skinnier than the one next to him. Apart, with nothing else to compare them to but memory, it was harder, but there were other signs. The clothes, the manner, the way of carrying themselves.

I sat behind my desk, pretending to make minor adjustments to the equipment, surreptitiously watching them over the top of my screen. A few were in conversation, and there was a quiet buzz around the auditorium that grew as the numbers swelled. Our Einstein came in, dressed in a crisp blue suit, paused in front of the desk where I sat. He stood there, looking slightly troubled.

"Everything set up?" he said.

"Yes, Mr. Einstein," I replied, barely meeting his eyes.

"No trouble?"

"No. Not at all."

He lingered for a moment, seemingly about to say something else, then he headed for the stage and the central podium. He waited for a couple of minutes as the last few Einsteins came through the doors and found their places. There were so many of them. I kept glancing from the screen to the auditorium. Rows and rows of Einsteins sat looking at the stage, like some bizarre picture. For a couple of seconds, I wondered if maybe I was just dreaming it.

The Einstein on the stage cleared his throat and a hush settled over the room.

"Welcome, and thank you all for coming. As we all know, we are fewer this time. There have been accidents, a couple of us have drifted, but these things happen. We still number above two hundred. I am honored that we have chosen my facility this time."

So they did this often. I diligently watched the screen as the Einstein on stage continued.

"We have made great headway over the last couple of years, but as you all know, our time is getting short. Way back then, back in the place of our birth, Professor Hans Spemann solved the telomere problem, but much of his work was lost. We are close to finding the solution to that problem, thanks to the work of one of our brothers." He lifted a hand indicating an Einstein in one of the central rows and inclined his head slightly. A couple of other Einsteins turned to look in that direction.

All attention turned back to the Einstein on the stage. I still had no idea where this was going, what they were doing here.

"We've also made great progress in accumulating the needed resources to do what we must. The break-out sessions we will split into shortly will follow the course of what we need to do over the next few years. The material and your assignments are all set out in your agenda packs."

A couple of the Einsteins reached down and started shuffling through their papers.

"Please," said the Einstein from the stage. "I cannot stress enough the importance of what we are doing here today. You all understand the resistance and the fear. We have each and every one of us worked against those pressures in each of our chosen fields. World government is not an easy thing to achieve."

I'd heard the words, but my mind just registered disbelief. I swallowed, trying not to show any reaction. I couldn't afford to make myself suddenly visible. World government? They couldn't be serious. At that moment, I was really glad to be sitting there, if this was what they were really planning.

"Our own government, as you know, has been resistant to our plans, and time is running out." He leaned forward on the podium. "We scare them and they don't really know why. That's why they passed that anti-cloning legislation in the first place, not for any ethical consideration. The antitrust actions we've had to face have been another mark." There were mutters of assent. He held up a hand. "But we will start dying soon. One by one, we will disappear." There were nods and low grumbles from the audience. "So, we have choices to make, here, today, that will impact the future and what happens."

He paused for maximum effect, then stood tall. "We have a lot of work to do today. If you would now follow your agendas and head to your assigned break-out rooms, we will reconvene here in three hours."

One by one, the Einsteins stood and filed out through the side doors into the cluster of meeting rooms.

I was kept pretty busy over the next three hours, checking connections, walking various Einsteins through the e-mail connect procedures and generally troubleshooting what they needed. Inside, I was still reeling from what I'd heard, trying to come to terms with it, trying to believe it and understand. I had a responsibility now, to find out what they planned and to let people know. Well, that's what I thought.

The three hours finally passed and I headed back into the auditorium to take up my place at the side table, watching and waiting. Our Einstein headed back to the central microphone, waiting for the last of the other Einsteins to take their seats.

"I am pleased to say we've made good progress. From the information we've collated today, it's clear that we are farther along in the program than we thought. We are now in a position to commence our next generation, our successors. We may not have the time to finish what we've started. You, me, every one of us will die some time in the next few years, but we should have enough time to prepare those who will follow us—the next generation of Einstein—and we will have put enough in place for them to succeed where we have not yet succeeded. One world government guided by those who with their collective imagination can do more for the world than petty nations and politics and geographical boundaries and ideologies. This is what we must do. We, together and our next generation, our successors, and after them, their successors, however long it takes."

The Einstein at the podium waited, looking out over the heads of his assembled brethren. The sea of old guy faces looked back. Slowly, slowly, he removed his finely tailored dark blue jacket, stepped back and draped it over the back of a chair. The others watched in silence. The way they all held themselves was almost reverent. I frowned, and watched, not really understanding what was about to happen. Just as slowly, he returned to the podium, then unbuttoned and rolled up his right sleeve. He held the arm aloft, his hand closed into a fist, turned out toward the audience.

"We cannot forget," he said. "We cannot let this happen again."

I glanced up at the big screen, then down at the small screen from where the video was being fed and leaned closer. There was something on the outside of the Einstein's forearm, faded blue and etched deep into the pale and aging flesh. Whatever it was had blurred with time, but it looked sort of like a row of numbers running at a slight angle. A couple of the Einsteins sitting in the front row gently gripped their own forearms, lightly squeezing. There was a ripple of motion through the entire auditorium.

"We mustn't forget," said the Einstein at the podium again. "We *will* be the last."

One or two of the shaggy heads nodded. Others closed their eyes. As I thought about it, I realized I'd never seen any of the Einsteins in anything other than long sleeves.

I looked back from the auditorium down at the

small screen. The Einstein at the podium slowly lowered his arm and rebuttoned his sleeve. He scanned
the assembled faces. Slowly, slowly, there came a
spark of understanding. I started to comprehend what
was going on here. A deep chill rose inside me. If that
mark really meant what I thought it did . . .

I swallowed and looked back up at the podium.

"I think we all know what we need to do. Each one
of us will communicate with our appropriate counter-
parts to put the plans in motion over the next few
weeks. The minutes from the breakout sessions will
help guide us as a first step. They will be transmitted
through our secure network as always."

He gripped the sides of the pedestal with the CompuSoft logo etched clearly on the front and then nodded once more.

"Thank you all for coming."

Slowly, then gently swelling around the auditorium,
applause broke out, then died away. One by one, the
Einsteins got to their feet, in their shirts and their
suits and their sports jackets. One by one, they filed
out of the auditorium in their trousers, their jeans,
their chinos, their loafers, or smart business shoes in
groups and singly, a sea of old shaggy heads and mus-
taches, washing out of the room, carrying their collective wisdom and perception and their vast imagination
with them.

The Einstein at the podium waited for the others
to leave, then stepped down from the stage and
walked over to the table with my equipment and the
wires and leads. This was our Einstein, CompuSoft's
Einstein. He stood in front of the table for a few moments watching me as I shut down the equipment and
busied myself with unplugging leads and putting
things away.

"The session went well, I thought," he said.

"Yes, it seemed to," I responded without meeting his eyes. The hollow chill was still nestled inside me and my mouth was dry. I swallowed. It was hard to meet the enormity of my realization face-to-face.

"Ray—it is Ray, isn't it?" he asked.

"Yes, Mr. Einstein," I said, stopping what I was doing and looking up into his speculative gaze.

What had they been through? What had they seen? They'd just been kids.

He waited for a few seconds, watching my face with those deep, puppy-dog eyes. "Ray, I want to thank you for your help today."

"No," I said. "Thank you, Mr. Einstein."

"We value our employees at CompuSoft. We value all of our people. It's a good company. We're doing good things. You do understand that, don't you, Ray? We're doing good things."

I waited.

The Einstein cleared his throat. "You know we've put together resources. You know we have our means. It's something I try and spell out in the company vision. They're important things, vision and trust, particularly trust. I hope I can trust you to . . ."

"You've no need to say anything, Mr. Einstein," I said.

He nodded once more. "Thanks again, Ray," he said. He cleared his throat one more time, then turned and walked from the auditorium, disappearing out the side door. I stood there for some time, watching the door, then let out a long slow breath, turning back to pack away the last of the gear. Maybe he thought that those few words were enough. I was just one of the little guys, after all. It didn't matter. But I kept remembering what I'd seen.

Once I was done, I headed out to find a trolley to load the equipment, thinking all the while. As I left the vast room, I looked at all those empty seats, my hand hovering above the red light switches on their stainless steel panel. A sea of Einsteins. I shook my head, killed the lights, and shut the door behind me.

There were questions, of course, from the other guys. I sidestepped most of them. Oh, you know, standard corporate stuff, rah, rah, all pretty boring really.

So do they meet like that often?

I simply shrugged and said I guessed so. Wouldn't you? They're sort of family, aren't they?

It seemed to satisfy them. There was a bit more discussion during the rest of the afternoon, but I tried to stay out of it as much as I could. I was still thinking of the pictures that lingered in my head, what they really meant. I thought about what our Einstein had started to say. I packed up as soon as I could and left, making my way through our clean, well-maintained, suburban streets to home.

Mary was waiting for me eagerly when I got home, barely able to restrain the questions.

"So . . . ?"

"Let me get in at least, hon," I said to her. I wasn't really sure how much I was going to end up telling her.

She hovered about while I dumped my things and got rid of the jacket.

I stood where I was, my hands resting on the back of a chair, composing my thoughts.

"So, come on."

"Okay, okay. I'm thinking."

I didn't know how much I should tell her. Our very own Einstein's unspoken request was still hanging with me. But Mary was my wife, my partner, she had a right to know as much as I knew. I figured it couldn't do any harm.

"You'd better sit down," I told her.

She pulled out a chair and sat, a frown on her face. "What is it, Ray? This sounds serious."

"Okay, well they had a meeting. All of them. All the Einsteins. They were all there. It was really weird."

"Wow," she said. "All of them?"

"Yeah." I shook my head, still only half believing it myself. "It was the strangest thing to look at. You get used to seeing them all the time, but all at once, all together . . ."

"How many?"

"I think he said there were two hundred and twelve left, or something like that."

"Wow." The word was long and drawn out. "So, what did they talk about? You said you thought they were up to something. Were they?"

I looked at her long and hard. "Yeah, in a way. They reckon they're going to make more of them. More Einsteins."

She looked at me blankly. "How can they do that?"

I shrugged. "They're Einsteins. They'll find a way."

"But that can't be right. How can they? Isn't it illegal? I seem to remember something about them banning it. I'm right, aren't I? They already have too much power. You've got to tell someone, Ray."

I reached across the table and took her hand. I placed my other hand gently over the top of it. "I don't think so, hon," I told her. "I think they know what they're doing. Remember, they're Einsteins. They're a lot smarter than us."

She didn't look convinced.

I patted her hand gently. "Trust me, Mary. It'll be all right. I spoke to our Einstein today. I actually spoke to Mr. Einstein himself. They do know what they're doing. They really do. Come on. Let's go and watch TV for a while, then we can think about dinner.

It's been a pretty full day. I just want to relax for a while and not really have to think about anything else, okay?"

She nodded, slowly.

After all, I knew, there was someone else to do the thinking about the really big stuff. There really was.

Mary seemed satisfied for the time being and if it came up again I knew I'd be able to reassure her. I was confident about that much, at least.

We headed into the living room and took our place on the couch. As the Einstein-Warner logo came up on the screen, I caught myself in the middle of a half-formed smile.

Revision Point

Hans Spemann, a German embryologist, is one of the original pioneers of modern embryology, and one of only two embryologists to ever be awarded the Nobel Prize. His studies focused upon the differentiation of embryo cells during an organism's development.

In the late 1920s Spemann performed work with salamanders. He transferred the nucleus of a sixteen-cell embryo to a single salamander embryo cell with no nucleus. The cell took up the nucleus and developed into a normal salamander.

With this process, Spemann completed one of the first cloning experiments using the nuclear transfer method. In the 1938 publication of his results, entitled "Embryonic Development and Induction," Spemann proposed the "fantastical experiment" of cloning an organism from differentiated or even adult cells using the nuclear transfer method.

Between 1921 and 1923 Albert Einstein traveled, among others, to the US, Britain, France, Japan, and Palestine. From that time he began commenting on political issues more and more frequently, based on a pacifist point of view. In 1922, Einstein became a member of the League of Nations' International Committee on Intellectual Cooperation. Opposed to any kind of violence, Einstein supported pacifist movements whenever he had the chance. He spoke up for the Hebrew University to be founded in Jerusalem to which he later also bequeathed his entire written legacy. In November 1952, Einstein even received the offer to become President of Israel, which, however, he turned down.

When Einstein and his wife left Caputh in December 1932 to hold a series of lectures in the US, the political situation in Germany had drastically changed. In the 1932 elections the Nazis had become the strongest political party and, in January 1933, Hitler seized power. Einstein never again set foot on German soil. In March 1933, he resigned from the Prussian Academy of Sciences and cut off all contacts with any German institution with which he ever had dealt.

J.C.

ABOUT THE AUTHORS

Geoffrey A. Landis is a scientist and a science fiction writer. As a scientist, he is a physicist who works for the NASA John Glenn Research Center. He was a member of the rover team on the Mars Pathfinder mission, and is currently a member of the science team for the exciting Mars Exploration rovers mission. He holds four patents, and is the author of approximately 250 scientific papers on subjects. As a writer, he has won two Hugo Awards, the most recent in 2003 for his story "Falling Onto Mars." He won the Nebula Award in 1990 for "Ripples in the Dirac Sea." His novel *Mars Crossing* won the Locus award for best first novel in 2001. His most recent book, the short story collection *Impact Parameter (and Other Quantum Realities)* was published in November 2001. It was named as a notable book of 2001 by *Publishers Weekly*. His many science fiction stories have been translated into nineteen languages, ranging from Chinese through Turkish. He lives in Berea, Ohio, with his wife, writer Mary A. Turzillo, and two cats.

Julie E. Czerneda, a former biologist, has been writing and editing science texts for almost two decades. A regular presenter on issues in science and science in society, she's also an internationally best-selling and award-winning science fiction author and editor, with eight novels published by DAW Books (including two series: the *Trade Pact Universe* and the *Webshifters*) and her latest, the hard SF trilogy, *Species Imperative*. Her editorial debut for DAW was *Space Inc.* Her short fiction and novels have been nominated for several awards, including being a finalist for the John W. Campbell Award for Best New Writer, the Philip K. Dick Award for Distinguished Science Fiction, and winning two Prix Aurora Awards, as well as being on the preliminary Nebula Ballot. A proponent of the use of science fiction in classrooms, Julie is series editor for *Tales from the Wonder Zone* (winner of the 2002 Golden Duck Special Award for Excellence in Science and Technology), *Realms of Wonder,* and author of such acclaimed teacher resources as *No Limits: Developing Scientific Literacy Using Science Fiction.* She currently serves as science fiction consultant to *Science News*.

Laura Anne Gilman made her first sale in 1997, to *Amazing Stories*. Since then, she has published over twenty-four short stories, written three nonfiction books for teenagers, and edited two anthologies (*OtherWere* and *Treachery and Treason*). In August 2004 her first original novel, *Staying Dead*, was released. She is also a professional editor and copywriter. She can be found on-line at *http://www.sff.net/people/lauraanne.gilman*

Kage Baker is best known for her stories and novels of Dr. Zeus Incorporated (AKA The Company) whose immortal servants plunder the past for future profit. Her first novel, *In the Garden of Iden*, has been translated into German, French, Italian, Spanish and Hebrew. Her most recent work, *The Anvil of the World*, is a fantasy in the style of Fritz Leiber and Jack Vance. *The Life of the World to Come*, the next Company novel, is a 2004 release. Ms. Baker lives in Pismo Beach, California.

After obtaining a degree in wildlife illustration and environmental education, Doranna Durgin spent a number of years deep in the Appalachian mountains, riding the trails and writing SF and fantasy books. She's moved on to the Northern Arizona mountains, where she still writes—more eclectically than ever— and rides, focusing on classical dressage. There's a Lipizzan in her backyard, a mountain looming outside her office window, a pack of dogs romping in the house, and a laptop sitting on her desk—and that's just the way she likes it. You can find a complete list of books (*Dun Lady's Jess, Wolverine's Daughter, A Feral Darkness* . . .) and tie-ins (*Angel, Mage Knight*) at *http://www.doranna.net/*, along with scoops about new projects, silly photos, and a link to her newsgroup. She's never been to Zion National Park—the setting for "A Call from the Wild"—but writing this story will probably change that.

James Alan Gardner was born in Bradford, Ontario, and currently resides in Waterloo. His work has appeared in *Amazing Stories*, *The Magazine of Fantasy and Science Fiction*, *Asimov's Science Fiction Magazine*, *On Spec*, and the *Tesseracts* anthologies. His short story "The Children Of Crèche," won the Grand Prize in the Writers of the Future contest in 1989. His short story "Muffin Explains Teleology to the World at Large" won an Aurora Award in 1991 and his short story "Three Hearings on the Existence of Snakes in the Human Bloodstream" was an Aurora Award winner and a Hugo and Nebula Award finalist. He has seven published novels. His novel, *Commitment Hour*, made the preliminary Nebula Award list in 1998 and *Vigilant* was on the 1999 preliminary ballot. *Hunted* and *Vigilant* are sequels to his first novel *Expendable*. Look for James' newest in the series, *Radiant*.

Robin Wayne Bailey is the author of numerous novels, including *Talisman*, *Dragonkin*, *Night's Angel*, and *Shadowdance*. His short fiction has appeared most recently in *2001: The Best Science Fiction of the Year*, *Future Wars*, *Thieves' World: Turning Points*, and *Re-Visions*. He's also edited *Architects of Dreams: The SFWA Author Emeritus Anthology* and *Through My Glasses Darkly: Five Stories By Frank M. Robinson*. He's the current chairman of the Science Fiction and Fantasy Hall of Fame, an avid book collector, and student of Ryobu-kai Karate. He lives in North Kansas City, Missouri.

John G. McDaid is a media ecologist from Brooklyn, NY. Born the year NASA was created, he grew up reading science fiction: Robert Heinlein and Andre Norton were his other parents (as he grew up, they morphed into James Tiptree, Jr. and Thomas Pynchon.) He attended Syracuse University, did graduate work at the New School University, and is a doctoral candidate in Media Ecology at NYU. He attended the Clarion workshop in 1993, and sold his first short story, the Sturgeon Award–winning "Jigoku no mokushiroku" to *Asimov*'s in 1995. A novelette, "Keyboard Practice," is scheduled to appear in *F&SF* in late 2004. He wrote one of the first hypertext novels,

Uncle Buddy's Phantom Funhouse, a *New Media* Invision Award finalist, in 1993, and has spoken on digital narrative at dozens of colleges and conferences. He lives in Rhode Island, where he is webmaster for a management consulting firm.

Peter Watts (*http://www.rifters.com*) is a reformed marine biologist whose first novel, *Starfish*, netted a "Notable Book of the Year" nod from *The New York Times*, an honorable mention for the John W. Campbell Memorial Award, and rejections from both German and Russian publishers because it was "too dark." (Too dark for the *Russians*—think upon that and tremble.) The sequel, *Maelstrom*, was starred by Booklist and may mark the first time that *The New York Times* used the terms "exhilarating" and "deeply paranoid" to describe the same novel. *Behemoth*, the concluding volume of what (inevitably) turned out to be a trilogy, is a 2004 release. Dr. Watts' short fiction has been collected in *Ten Monkeys, Ten Minutes*: earlier works appearing in the *Journal of Theoretical Biology*, the *Canadian Journal of Zoology*, and *Marine Mammal Science* are, when you get right down to it, no less fictitious.

Jihane Noskateb lives with a black cat on a thirteenth floor in Paris, France. Fascinated by ancient history, science fiction, and fantasy, she's currently and hectically engaged with a PhD and one or two novels. That bigamous situation between past and future leads her to view the present as an overrated thing, whose existence is dubious. Don't tell her she's presently published for the very first time. She might well think it's not real.

Kay Kenyon is the author of a dozen science fiction short stories and novels. Her 2003 novel, *The Braided World*, like several other of her novels, deals with an alien culture and the dilemmas of cross-cultural contact. Her novel *Maximum Ice* was nominated for the 2002 Phillip K. Dick Award, and has been translated into French. It is the tale of a ship of gypsies who return to Earth to find it altered, both wonderfully and dreadfully. Kay lives in Wenatchee, Washington, with her husband Thomas and a large, orange tabby named Sumo.

Mike Resnick is the author of more than forty science fiction novels, ten collections, and 150 stories, and has edited more than thirty-five anthologies. He has won four Hugos (and been nominated for twenty-three as a writer and two as an editor), a Nebula (with ten nominations), and awards from all over the globe, including the Prix Tour Eiffel (France), the Hayakawa SF Award (Japan), the Futura Award (Croatia), the Prix Ozone (France), the Fantastyka Award (Poland), the Ignotus Award (Spain), and the Sfinks Award (Poland).

Susan R. Matthews has several novels in print—many concerning the life and hard times of Andrej Koscuisko, who is not a nice man—but has only recently ventured into shorter fiction. She believes that nothing can withstand the awesome power of compassion except, perhaps, people who read Faulkner voluntarily. She and Maggie Nowakowska, her spousal equivalent of nearly twenty-five years, live in Seattle with two young Pomeranians whose worldview as regards potty training is staunchly situational. You can find her website with news, gossip, pictures, and Scenes from the Cutting Room Floor at *http://www.sff.net/people/Susan.scribens*.

Cory Doctorow (*http://www.craphound.com*) is the Campbell Award-winning author of the novels *Down and Out in the Magic Kingdom* and *Eastern Standard Tribe*, and the short story collection *A Place So Foreign and Eight More*. He is the coeditor of the popular weblog Boing Boing (*http://boingboing.net*) and works for a civil rights group in San Francisco called the Electronic Frontier Foundation (*http://www.eff.org*).

Born in 1964, Charles Stross lives in Edinburgh, Scotland, where he works as a freelance journalist and author; before switching to writing full time he pursued careers as a pharmacist and computer programmer. His most recent novel is *Singularity Sky*.

Dr. Isaac Szpindel is an award-winning screenwriter, author, producer, electrical engineer, and medical doctor/neurologist. Some of his recently published SF short stories include "Porter's Progress" in the DAW anthology *Space Inc.* and the Prix Aurora Award finalist "By Its Cover" in *Tales from the Wonder Zone: Explorer*. Isaac's screenwriting credits include the Prix Aurora Award-winning "Underwater Nightmare" and Aurora finalist "Bat's Life," both for the hit Warner Bros. TV series *Rescue Heroes*. He is the story editor and a screenwriter for the television series *The Boy*, and is cocreator and writer for a TV series currently in development with a national Canadian broadcaster and an Emmy Award-winning production house. Other screenwriting projects include an SF/fantasy feature film and episodic television for a company based in France. Isaac was executive producer of the award-winning short *Hoverboy*, lectures often at various educational levels, and is a frequent on-air guest for Canadian Talk Television. For more, visit *http:/www.geocities.com/canadian_sf/szpindel*

Jay Caselberg is an Australian writer based in London. His short fiction and poetry has appeared in many places around the world, including The Mammoth Book of Future Cops, Interzone, The Third Alternative and others. His novel Wyrmhole, from Roc Books, came out in 2003 and the followup, Metal Sky, is due in 2004. Growing up in Australia, he traveled the world extensively, then moved to London in 1991. His work for major consultancies took him to many countries around the world, and to date he has worked in about fifty-five different countries. He is constantly working on new material and usually has one or two novels in progress at any one time. He also writes as James A. Hartley. You can visit his website at http://www.sff.net/people/jaycaselberg